HILLS OF MOAB

Hills of Moab

Copyright © 2024 by Elizabeth Faye

All rights reserved.

ISBN: 9798876479617

No portion of this book may be reproduced in any form without written permission from the publisher or author.

ELIZABETH FAYE

Hills Of
MOAB

To the friends who gave me courage

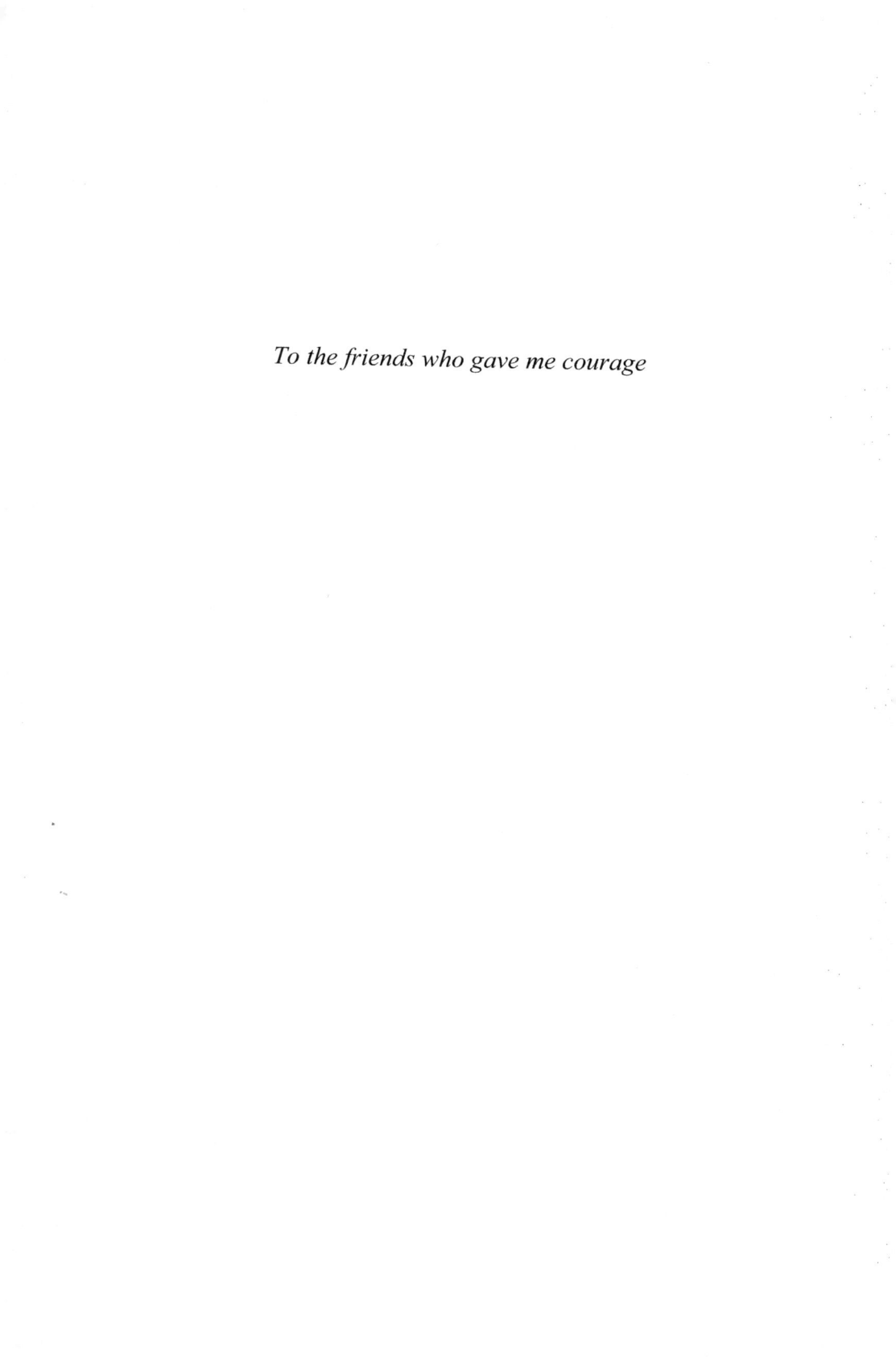

A note to the reader

This book is a work of fiction, based on the biblical story of Ruth. It explores certain themes including domestic violence, human sacrifice, PTSD trauma and suicidal ideation, which may be difficult for some readers.

HILLS OF MOAB

RUTH

MOAB - 1195 BC

"Haven't you seen enough?" Orpah asked. "What you *think* you see, and what this *is,* are two different things."

Ruth shrugged off her friend's whine. "Orpah," she replied, her eyes scanning the crowd before them. "You're ruining it for me."

The glow of the moon hadn't arrived, but darkness struggled to dominate the night.

A large bonfire threw light over the village, licking the underbelly of the clouds and surrounding land. It pulled tired inhabitants from their homes. Unable to resist, they moved towards the glow like disorientated insects. The urge to join the dance overcame their will to sleep.

Ruth rushed through the unguarded village gates towards the rising blaze, pulling Orpah behind her.

A thin layer of smoke wafted through the cool air; light and breathable. Certain aromas were unfamiliar, but Ruth recognised the scent of charcoaled timber. A smile formed on her lips.

People filled the streets as they filed out through the gates towards the grove. A swelling of chanted incantations echoed off the walls. Loud beats of goat skin darbuka drums drove the emotions and tensions of the crowd.

Ruth dragged Orpah, ignoring the resistance. Too giddy with excitement to notice the depth of Orpah's reluctance.

The unfettered freedom blocked out every thought in Ruth's mind. For the first time, she was able to join with her people in worship of Chemosh, Moab's heavenly provider and protector. A ceremony which was, as her parents reminded her, only for the villagers. A ceremony her parents had never let her attend, whilst refusing to give her an explanation as to why. But now she was here, without their knowledge, soaking it all in.

Ruth shivered as a hot, sour breath caressed the nape of her neck. She turned to see a middle-aged woman's face, inches from her own.

Large hoop earrings of yellow gold dangled from the woman's ears, reflecting the fire's light. They swung from side to side on her lobes as the woman fought to keep her balance. Her garments hung loosely around her, barely preserving her modesty and only saved from falling to the dusty ground by a single cord wrapped diagonally around her midsection. Her bare shoulders glistened with droplets of sweat as she clutched her hands together tightly, golden bracelets clinking against each other on her thin wrists.

A wide smile spread across her full lips, revealing teeth stained with wine.

"Come, young one," the woman said, pushing waves of black hair away from her bloodshot eyes with the back of her hand. She reached out for Ruth's arm. "Join us." Her voice honeylike; enticing and smooth.

The woman glanced at Orpah with a raised eyebrow. "Leave this one behind," she said with an accusing finger. "Your companion isn't a believer."

Ruth snatched her hand from the woman's grasp.

The woman shrugged, then smiled again as she danced off, giggling hysterically. The mass of bodies surrounding them swallowed her from view.

Orpah grabbed Ruth's arm and motioned back towards the village. "We should leave," she said, her voice faltering. "I only brought you because you promised we wouldn't go further than the gate."

Ruth shook her head. "We've only just arrived!" Her words were lost as the screams and drumbeats of the villagers intensified.

"Can we at least stop here?" Orpah called out. "Stay behind the people?"

Ruth frowned. "We travelled all this way," she said, moving forward. "I want to go in further."

They continued to slide through the sweat-soaked dancers towards the fire. The mob grew thicker and tighter. They moved as though joined at the hip, a mass of people yet one.

Ruth's eyes widened in fascination; her pupils enlarging with excitement. A part of her she didn't recognise had been unlocked.

They pushed through the last dancers and fell onto the earth surrounding the towering blaze. No longer shielded by the bodies that blocked the fire, Ruth's skin stung under the oppressive heat. She climbed to her feet, brushing the dirt and sand from her hands as she backed up to the edge of the dancers.

To the left of the fire, a brass altar towered above them. At its base a handful of worshippers crouched, holding darbuka drums between their thighs, striking the stretched skins with open palms in a continuous rhythm. Only their quick moving hands were exposed to the fire. Black cloaks covered their bodies; their faces hidden by the large fishlike hoods covering their heads.

Orpah squeezed Ruth's hand as the drumbeats increased in speed, triggering a trance-like frenzy in the mob.

A scream erupted beside Ruth.

The man beside her held a small dagger in one hand as he repeatedly opened and clenched the other, flexing the muscles under the slash on his lower arm. A line of scarlet trickled down his wrist and off the edge of his fingers, forming irregular patterns of red spots on the sand.

His gaze reached Ruth's. His pupils had enlarged; black pebbles pushing the whites of his eyes to the outer edges. His eyes stayed on Ruth as he tossed the dagger skilfully between his hands, before slicing the other arm. He ground his teeth in agony, then a moan of delirious ecstasy left his lips.

Ruth watched as the man lay the dagger flat on his open palm and held it out to her. He nodded towards it, inviting her to join him.

Take it. Take it.

It was only a small voice inside her mind, but the sensation of momentarily losing control of her senses shocked Ruth to the core. She shook her head and stepped back, bumping into Orpah.

"We need to leave," Orpah yelled. "We need to go right now."

Sweat trickled down Ruth's back. She rubbed against it, wondering how the dancers continued their fervent exertion in this temperature.

"No," she replied, wishing she'd come on her own. "You can go, but I'm staying."

"But the priest is here!" Orpah continued.

Ruth turned away, overlooking the tears which had formed in her friend's eyes.

It was in this moment that a new sound reached Ruth's ears, a sound so out of place in this atmosphere of hedonistic pleasure and self-release.

Over the incessant thud of the drums, the stomping of feet, and chanting wails of the singers, a small but clear cry of a newborn was heard.

Confusion pushed through Ruth's mind, replacing the sensation of freedom that had liberated her minutes earlier. The intense aura of the crowd was sensual and self-gratifying. This cry of a baby didn't make sense. Ruth had heard the sound many times with her ima delivering babies; there was no mistaking it.

Orpah whimpered beside her and reached out for Ruth's hand.

Ruth was too focused on the sound, too busy scanning the crowd to notice.

It was as a tall man pushed through the mass of bodies and approached the brass altar that the hairs on the back of Ruth's neck rose. Something inside her cowered, begging her to run.

"The priest," Orpah choked.

The man was clothed similarly to the drummers, in a flowing black cloak and a fish mouth-like hood over his head. Unlike the drummers, his cloak had the addition of gold and scarlet lacing around the bottom hem and hood. Although he was tall, his physique was not lean and muscular, but round, and his gait lethargic. An abundance of rich foods available to those who held his office.

A bundle of white linen lay in his arms.

One bare foot after the other, the priest ascended the altar steps with deliberate drama. At the top step, he moved towards the fire. The fabric of his long garment scraped against the flat surface of the altar with each stride. He paused and surveyed the villagers, then raised his left hand into the sky, signalling for the drummers to stop.

The crowd waited in silence, their chests rising and falling with exertion. They stared as the priest reached into the bundle that lay in his arm and pulled out a newborn child.

A lump formed in the back of Ruth's throat as she watched the priest raise the baby above his head with both hands. The white linen flapped against his arm in the breeze, before sliding off, floating down through the night air. It caught on the edge of the altar.

With his arms still raised, the priest bellowed ten words at the night sky in an unfamiliar tongue, then stopped.

The naked baby cried out, yearning for its ima's warmth; a voice of innocence echoing forcefully over the waiting villagers.

For a moment, the priest stood stiffly, frozen in time.

Ruth glanced around, to see if someone, anyone, would do something.

Then, with no warning, the priest let the newborn slide from his hands and plunge into the flames.

The villagers roared, no longer able to hold themselves back. Screams of praise to Chemosh filled the air, demanding blessings in return for their sacrifice. The drummers joined in, and the feet of the villagers once again pummelled the earth, stirring up dust. They pushed and shoved against Ruth; their thrill too great to notice their surroundings.

Ruth stiffened.

It's not true. Chemosh is a god who cares for his people. He would not ask this.

Pain shot through her skull as the surrounding sounds became muffled and distant; her mind's grip on reality slipping.

Fingers wrapped around her hand roughly, and pulled her through the writhing mob, away from the grove and towards the village gates. Ruth stumbled over her feet, obediently following the hand that yanked her along.

The unfamiliar aroma she had noticed at their arrival wafted through the air again. Ruth turned back towards the bonfire. Now she understood. Newborns.

When the black tunnel appeared before her, Ruth welcomed it. She did not resist as the dark pit engulfed her.

....

A groan of discomfort escaped Ruth's lips as she rolled onto her back amongst the tall stalks of wheat. Broken shafts clawed at the fabric of her robe, but she didn't mind. It was the only way to capture the warmth and energy of the earth against her back.

Two months had passed since she visited the village grove, but the memories had stayed. Those moments in time, those detestable few minutes, which were seared onto the eternal landscape of her mind, now refused to be ignored. She shook her head in frustration, refusing to be sucked into the evil abyss of that night.

Orpah had not wanted to go further than the gates.

Ruth knew she should have listened.

The scent of trampled wheat soothed her heart. It was an aroma of comfort and familiarity, flour and baking.

A happier memory surfaced.

In her mind's eye she watched as her ima's nose crinkled at the flour particles drifting through the sunlit room.

"That is not the way of kneading," Cajsa had said, slapping Ruth's hands away from the sticky ball of dough that lay on the flour covered table. "How will you ever wed if you can't achieve this, the simplest of tasks?"

Ruth had laughed. "I don't need a husband, Ima," she said, resisting the temptation to grasp Cajsa's face with her dough covered fingers. She watched as her ima's skilled hands worked the dough into a smooth, relaxed ball on the wooden table.

The memory faded.

Ruth wriggled on her back as her eyes surveyed the never-ending blue above her. A single white cloud caught her attention, hovering in the open space. It was hard to tell if it was moving or not. Ruth pinched a blade from a nearby stalk and held it up between her eyes and the oblivious cloud.

Screams of torment pushed into her mind, accompanied by a hot sickly stench.

"Leave me!" Ruth demanded. The thoughts recoiled into the background as she forced herself to focus on the cloud. It appeared to be moving, but at a pace slower than a snail.

Another thought toppled into Ruth's consciousness. A nagging sensation she had promised her abba something that afternoon. *Or was that tomorrow?*

Ruth sat up and flicked the blade into the air, watching the breeze catch it and carry it away.

Small goosebumps appeared over her slender arms and legs as the sun dropped, signalling time to return home.

She climbed to her feet, groaning. Her bones had stiffened and her body ached, but the scent of earth filled her nostrils. A smile formed on her lips as she closed her eyes and raised her open hands towards the skies above, inhaling fresh air until her lungs were full.

This was her special place, in the field of wild wheat, a forgotten crop of years ago. High on the side of the mountain. The whole world visible.

Ruth let the air leave her lungs and lowered her arms as she scanned the hillside below. She imagined herself dashing down an invisible track amongst the rocky outcrops, down the rugged hills of Moab, and into the valley flats by the shores of the Dead Sea.

"I don't want you going up to the hill on your own," Malak, her abba, had said. "It's not safe."

But Ruth sensed a connection up here. To what, she wasn't sure, or how it was even possible, but here, the mountain spoke to the essence of who she was. A haven of peace.

No interference from humans here, merely the secrets of the breeze, as they played along the tops of the tall grass and untamed wheat. Shivers and whispers.

Yes, Malak hated her coming here, but she came often, obeying the unknown pull on her soul.

Ruth smirked, remembering how soft he was. No matter what he demanded of her, he would buckle. So different to her ima, who wanted Ruth married. Having already seen eighteen summers, the pressure for Ruth to find a husband was increasing.

Ruth didn't care. She was happy. Whether she bathed in sunlight, or helped Cajsa bring new lives into the world, for her, every day was fresh and new, washing over her as a wave of renewing energy. There was no need to add to her life.

Besides, she didn't know much in the way of her family's history, something potential husbands would want to know. Malak and Cajsa refused to speak of their imas and abbas, or siblings. They'd also never had any other children besides Ruth, another fact that hadn't gone unnoticed by her.

A loud snort exploded behind Ruth. She turned to see her dusty brown fuzz ball of a mountain mule, Harnepher. Not quite a donkey, or a horse, but the perfect combination of both. The snort continued down into the valley, bouncing off the rocks and crevices.

Ruth smiled, shielding her deep teal eyes against the glare of the setting sun with her hand.

"You scared me, friend."

Loose chaff irritated his soft nostrils. Harnepher tossed his head and snorted again, before disappearing into the tall wheat, nuzzling the ground for more sweet wisps of goodness.

Ruth's mind drifted to Orpah, her closest friend, whose soul had knit tightly with her own from the moment they'd met in childhood.

As the first born of twelve children, Orpah had been dealt a harder life. Her abba worked some distance away, and as her ima's abdomen expanded with a thirteenth baby, raising the children had been placed on Orpah.

Ruth's stomach turned over with guilt, realising her insistence to go to the village may have weakened their tight bond. Something had changed. She could sense it.

The fine hairs on her soft brown skin rose as the temperature dipped. The mountains of Israel loomed on the opposite side of the Dead Sea, casting a shadow over Moab and bathing Ruth in an unnerving chill.

She knew little of the Israelites. Only scraps of conversations she'd overheard as a child. But it was enough for her to know that Israelis were a dangerous people; a threat to surrounding lands.

As the sun sank further behind the mountains, the horizon became a splash of blue and violet. There was also a hint of a crimson red in the sky; the same colour as Ruth's long, loose curls that framed her face and rolled off her shoulders.

Ruth twirled a red wave around her slender finger.

"You must marry," she said, mimicking her ima's voice.

She knew it wasn't only her noticing the pressure to wed. Orpah had seen seventeen summers. The problem lay in the shortage of men around their area of Moab. The men who weren't married were either wispy-white elders or babies.

Babies.

Nausea welled in Ruth's stomach. An odd sensation tickled in the back of her throat. As her stomach threatening to spasm, she stumbled forward and fell onto her hands. Tears formed in her eyes, blurring her vision.

Orpah, why didn't you tell me? You knew I'd never been to the village before! Ruth knew the answer. She remembered the horror that had crossed

Orpah's face when she realised Ruth hadn't known the purpose of the ceremonies. Human sacrifice, Orpah had explained, and especially that of a child, was seen as the highest form of worship to gain favour from the gods. Hidden away in the hills, Ruth's parents had kept her sheltered, and Orpah, too disturbed by the practices of her people, had been thankful it never came up in conversation.

Harnepher, oblivious to Ruth's turmoil, ripped at the foliage on the ground. Rhythmic and violent.

No! Stop!

Ruth groaned as she sat back on her knees and rubbed her eyes, smearing tears and dirt across her face. She closed her eyes and exhaled, releasing the thoughts that plagued her. As she opened them, she noticed her hooded cloak still lay on the flattened wheat where she had been lying. She climbed to her feet with unsteady legs and snatched up her cloak, shaking it before pulling it around her shoulders.

The breeze picked up, caressing her face with cool relief.

Harnepher snorted.

Ruth pulled the hood over her head, struggling with the volumes of hair that refused to be tamed into the small space. She would chop it all off in a heartbeat, but Cajsa refused to let her.

The ground crunched under foot as she pushed through the tall stalks towards Harnepher. He moved away, turning his furry rear in her direction.

"Don't be rude," Ruth said.

He turned his head towards Ruth, his big brown eyes watching for her next move.

She pulled a pomegranate from her bag. "One step ahead of you," she said.

His grey lips wriggled, and his nostrils flared as he blew hot air into the breeze.

It was too much for him. He turned and plodded in defeat towards Ruth. Any ounce of resistance overwhelmed by the desperate need to fill his furry gut with more food.

....

"Ruth!"

A voice boomed from the threshing floor. Malak stood in the middle of the harvested wheat, gripping the bridle of his donkey.

His servants stopped winnowing the wheat to watch as the daughter on her fat mule received a scolding from the master.

"Where have you been?" Malak asked, wiping his forehead.

Ruth sensed frustration in his voice.

He glared at her, with a creased brow, and pointed to the east. "Why are the goats still on the hill?"

Ruth groaned inwardly. There it was. That thing that had nagged at her. *Bring the goats in.*

"It's not too late," she said, tightening her legs around Harnepher's middle. "I'll go now."

Malak scratched his bushy beard with a weathered hand and sighed. He passed his donkey's bridle to the servant standing closest.

"Keep working," Malak instructed them. "There isn't much light left. When you're finished, clean up and come into the house for supper."

He stepped over the scattered mix of wheat and chaff towards Ruth.

"I'll come with you to the stable," Malak said as he walked past her. "I haven't checked to see if Efrat's kids are still nursing well this evening."

"Efrat has kidded?" Ruth asked. Efrat wasn't due for another week. She squeezed her legs against Harnepher's round middle again, and he reluctantly stepped forward to follow Malak.

....

The goats arrived at the empty feed trough before Ruth reached it, their strident bleats heralding to the world what a failure she was.

"Calm down," Ruth laughed as they pushed against her legs.

A smaller kid climbed onto her back as she bent down to find the ladle in the vessel of grain, before bouncing off sideways.

"Ruth!"

Ruth stood and turned. Wet lips nibbled at her fingers, impatiently seeking the grain that had been promised. She squinted in the faint light.

It was Malak.

"What is it?" Ruth asked as he reached her.

Malak slowed to a stop, holding his hand to his chest, struggling to swallow, his throat dry. "Go and wash up," he said, his voice raspy. "Ima needs you at Jabez's house … Rivka's baby. There's trouble."

....

Her sandals were new and rubbed uncomfortably against her toes as the soles crunched against the chalky road. Jabez's house wasn't far, but Ruth hurried. She held a lamp to light the path, a soft glow in the black night.

It had been a few months since Cajsa began instructing Ruth in the ways of midwifery, insisting Ruth become skilled to provide for herself. Cajsa was certain all unmarried women over the age of seventeen would become beggars on the street or women of the night, unless they learnt a skill.

Their last visit to Rivka had indicated no problems.

In her usual skilful way, Cajsa had moved her hands gently around Rivka's stomach and finally smiled.

"Your baby has aligned, Rivka," Cajsa said. "It is ready to birth."

Rivka had grinned at her round belly, caressing it with her hands. "I'll see you soon, little one," she said. "You'll be my beautiful boy, or beautiful girl and you'll only know love." She held out a hand to her ima, Jabez, who took it in her own, squeezing it tightly.

Jabez had supported her daughter when the abba of the unborn child had not. He had left Rivka soon after discovering he'd created a life inside her out of marriage. At sixteen years, Rivka couldn't do this on her own.

In the distance, a pin prick of light became visible. The house was close.

Unease slid into Ruth's heart.

Rivka will be fine. Cajsa performs miracles.

A faint cry broke through Ruth's thoughts. Distant, but she'd heard that anguish enough times to know it was a woman in labour.

Another howl of agony echoed up the road, louder this time. Ruth's heartbeat quickened as her steps increased in pace, her sandals hitting the uneven ground with loud thuds.

Inside the house, members of Jabez's family squashed together as tightly as seeds in a pomegranate, swaying in prayer to Chemosh. Watching and waiting for the new arrival.

Ruth squeezed through the bodies, following the sound of shallow moaning to a small, dimly lit room.

Moist, putrid air engulfed her as she entered.

Inside, Rivka lay on the floor on her back, her naked body wet with sweat.

Cajsa knelt on the floor beside Rivka, her hands prodding the glistening bulge. Jabez sat opposite, stroking Rivka's arm.

A quiet whimper escaped Rivka's quivering lips and her eyes rolled back, showing bloodshot whites.

"Shhh, shhh," Jabez comforted, pushing her daughter's black, sweat-soaked hair from her forehead.

Cajsa sat back on her heels. "Your baby needs to come out, Rivka," she said. "You've been in labour too long."

Rivka shook her head. "No," she said, attempting to sit up. "It is enough. I can't do this. Make it stop."

"We can't stop it now," Cajsa said. "You'll soon have your baby in your arms, and you'll forget all this."

Rivka held onto her ima's hand. "I don't know if I can do it." She let out a sigh and closed her eyes.

Cajsa glanced up and noticed Ruth in the doorway. She climbed to her feet and seized Ruth by the elbow. They pushed past the thick body of family members and through the front door.

Outside, the fresh night air provided relief and a promise of hope.

Cajsa glanced over her shoulder. "I don't know what to do, Ruth," she said, blinking back tears.

Ruth watched the light of the lantern flicker on her ima's wet hands.

"The newborn is twisted," Cajsa said. "I've tried turning it from the outside and turning it from the inside. I can't get it out." Her jaw clenched as she stared into the distance. "And did you smell it?" she asked. "That odour filled the room when her waters broke."

Her arms dropped to her sides as she clenched and unclenched her fists. "Something is wrong inside Rivka," Cajsa said. "I don't know what it is, or what to do." She broke into sobs and buried her aging face into her hands.

Ruth wrapped her arms around Cajsa. "Oh, Ima," she said.

"I've never lost a baby before," Cajsa said, her voice muffled in Ruth's arms. "I'm going to lose Rivka as well. Oh, Chemosh help us!"

Chemosh?

The events of the village had been suppressed in Ruth's mind, but at the mention of Chemosh, they swiftly returned. A seed of hate formed in her heart towards Chemosh.

She peered into her ima's eyes. Dark circles lined the underside on both sides.

"How long have you been here?" Ruth asked. "How long since Rivka's contractions began?"

Cajsa pulled away from her daughter, wiping her forehead with the back of her wrist. Her face had changed. Determination. "We will keep trying," she said, ignoring Ruth's questions. "I'll need you to hold

Rivka."

The foul odour hit Ruth again as they re-entered the room, and her stomach turned when Cajsa closed the door behind them.

"Ruth!" Cajsa waved her hands frantically at her rigid daughter. She ordered Ruth to take hold of Rivka's leg from the outside, bent at the knee, and Jabez to do the same on Rivka's other side.

Ruth kneeled on the floor beside the exhausted girl and did as Cajsa commanded. She didn't want to be there. Didn't want to be a part of whatever this was going to be. She glanced up at Cajsa out of the corner of her eye.

Cajsa shuffled forward on her knees, sitting between Rivka's legs.

Rivka sucked air in through her mouth, slow and shallow. Her eyes were closed and limbs loose. There was no resistance from Rivka as Ruth adjusted her hold on the exhausted girl's thigh.

Ruth stared at the rug on the floor. A braided rug, made from scraps of fabric, all different colours. A chant formed in her mind, as she attempted to trance herself out of the room by focusing on the different shades of the rug. *Ochre, sienna, umber, olive, ochre, sienna, umber, olive, ochre, sienna, umb—*

A tortured scream ripped through the room.

Ruth was thrown backwards as Rivka pulled her leg from Ruth's grip, no longer a lifeless body, but a woman with the strength of ten men.

"Hold her!" Cajsa demanded, struggling, her arm deep inside Rivka as she attempted to turn the baby.

"What are you doing?" Jabez screamed as she lunged at Cajsa, sending her sprawling backwards onto the floor. "You'll kill her!"

"She's already dying, Jabez," Cajsa yelled, tears welling up in her eyes. She swallowed, rubbing away the pain in her elbow.

Ruth glanced at Rivka. Once again, the rising and fall of her chest was the only sign of life.

"She *might* die if I do this, Jabez," Cajsa said. "But she *will* die if I don't."

Jabez's breast heaved, and her face contorted with grief.

"Let me try to save them," Cajsa said, placing her trembling hand on Jabez's arm.

Jabez nodded, tears falling as she took hold of her daughter's thigh again.

Ruth adjusted herself and held on tight.

As the screams echoed somewhere in the back of Ruth's consciousness, a new memory formed in her mind. Textures, colours, odours, and wails of a woman consumed by pain.

Rivka's fingers ripped at Ruth's arms, her ragged nails piercing the skin, but Ruth held on. For Cajsa. For Rivka. For the baby. She continued to focus on the braided mat, continuing the chant of colours. The muscles in her slender arms stung under the strain.

Rivka's youthful and beautiful countenance had become red and blotchy, as wave after wave of unearthly howls left her throat. She pulled at Ruth's hair in desperation.

Hot tears spilt from Ruth's eyes, but not for her own pain. She squeezed her eyes shut and gasped for air as the room swirled around her.

She opened her eyes again to see Cajsa's cheek pressed hard against the inside of Rivka's thigh.

A linen cloth, which lay beneath Rivka's pelvis, suddenly darkened, as scarlet liquid spread rapidly, consuming the cloth within seconds.

"Ima?" Ruth choked.

Silence filled the room and Rivka's leg relaxed. Her pale hand slid onto the braided mat with a soft thud.

Ruth reached out and gripped it in her own, desiring to reassure Rivka that all would be well, but a sorrowful wail startled her.

Jabez leant over Rivka, moaning as she held her daughter's face in her hands. She pulled their foreheads together and rocked back and forth, her wails becoming louder.

"Ima?" Ruth asked. Her hands shook as shock spread through her entire being.

A second rush of fluids flooded the floor, and Cajsa groaned as she pulled a baby out from between Rivka's limp thighs. She lay the tiny creature on a fresh sheet of linen beside her, wrapping the folds carefully around its small arms.

It was a boy. A beautiful, pale little boy. But no cry. No first inhale.

Cajsa's shoulders slumped as she lifted the wrapped baby up to her chest. She placed a light kiss on its forehead as tears ran down her cheeks.

Ruth dropped Rivka's leg as her stomach contracted. She turned away as liquid spewed from her mouth in violent surges. When there was nothing left to give, she collapsed backwards and wiped the tears from her eyes. Her body shivered uncontrollably.

Jabez cradled the head of her daughter in her arms, stroking the white cheeks with quivering fingers. Rivka was at peace, her struggle over.

The room spun as the floor rushed upwards to meet Ruth.

....

"What is happening?" Ruth asked, her voice strange. An echo.

A touch, soft and warm, stroked her cheek.

"We're home." It was Cajsa.

Ruth blinked. She didn't recognise the room.

Cajsa sat on the bed beside her. "I had the servants carry you back," she said, squeezing Ruth's hand.

"What?" Ruth asked. She glanced across the room. Malak hunched over the table, running his hands through his hair.

Ruth pushed herself up on her elbows, as the burning in her stomach returned.

"Don't sit up," Cajsa said. She stood, pushing Ruth's shoulders down onto the bed. "I'll fetch you some water."

Ruth's throat contracted and tears stung her eyes as pain emerged from the depth of her soul. "Chemosh did this," she whispered.

"Do not ... blaspheme the gods," Cajsa said, her voice faltering. She held out a cup of water to Ruth. "Anger the gods and it won't end well for us."

"Is that what Rivka did?" Ruth asked, taking the cup. "Anger the gods?" Her face flushed. "Chemosh is no different from any of the other gods in this world."

"He provides," Malak said.

"He demands the blood of the living," Ruth replied. She raised the cup to her lips and observed her parents. *Did they know? Had they been to a sacrifice?*

The cool water flowed easily down her throat, but she could tell Cajsa had added something to it.

"Tread carefully, Ruth," Malak said.

Ruth lay back on her bed, pulling the prickly blanket up around her chin. She cursed every god under the sun. All the ones she knew of. She named them all and cursed them all.

But what if there are *no gods?*

Ruth stared at the timber which braced the ceiling, wondering why she hadn't thought of that before. What if there were no gods? At all? What if they were stories? Made up. Why prayers were never answered. Why every nation had a different one. Why there was no *one* single god.

Gods weren't real. Humanity was on their own. They were born, they grew old, and they died. It was all random, void of planning.

There never was – or ever would be – gods.

Ruth rolled onto her side, thumping her pillow to flatten the lumps, satisfied with this conclusion. But this new perspective didn't remove the pain from her heart.

NAOMI

ISRAEL – 1195 BC

Dry heat pushed through the house, searching for moisture. After rising to the second floor and finding none, it left through an open window, leaving the house a few degrees hotter.

Naomi slouched by the window; shoulders hunched with the years she carried. Her hazel eyes scanned the horizon as she blew loose strands of grey hair out of her face.

She prayed today was the day. The day, that somewhere in the heavens, rain would form. Deep down she knew that just as yesterday had been, and all the yesterdays before, there would be no rain.

Outside, the sky remained blue and the soil barren. No green on the hillside or the valley below.

El Shaddai, my God, where are you?

Naomi massaged her aching neck with weathered hands. Too old. Too sore.

It had been years since their last crop died. Now the cypress and oak trees, which held on to life whilst the rest of the landscape disappeared, were showing signs of giving up as well.

As their supplies ran low, her husband, Elimelech, sent the servants away. Life now a vague shadow of what it had been.

Naomi had never experienced a famine such as this. When she was young, her parents spoke of 'the bad ones.' It wasn't until this famine struck, that Naomi truly understood the enormity of what it meant for her people Israel.

She lived in her beloved Beit-Lechem — the house of bread. But since the heavens had refused to let down their water, Beit-Lechem had become a house of dust.

Families starved. Children begged on the streets.

Naomi's heart broke, wanting to feed every hungry soul she saw. But Elimelech wouldn't allow it.

"*Our* grain is for *our* family," he had said. "We don't have enough to share!" His face reddened with each word.

"You forget Yosef," Naomi replied, ignoring his changing countenance. "El Shaddai our God used Yosef to secure Egypt in the time of famine."

"I am no Yosef," Elimelech replied, slamming his hand on the table. "And that was a long time ago." He rubbed his hand, refusing to back down, then pointed an accusing finger at Naomi. "El Shaddai doesn't do things like that anymore."

Naomi couldn't believe what she was hearing. "You would place limits on El Shaddai?"

Elimelech's eyebrows came together. "He doesn't expect us to give our hard-earned food to those who were too lazy to ration their grain, so that they survive, as we die. You can't solve the problem, Naomi. Poor people will always be here; it's not our job to fix it. El Shaddai will feed them if he wants them to eat."

Naomi's sighed as the memory disappeared from her mind.

How does Elimelech think El Shaddai will feed the poor, if not through others like us? And how can I expect El Shaddai to keep my family safe, in His loving arms, if we ignore the cry of His children?

"Naomi," Elimelech called from downstairs. "Did we use all that grain I put in the large holding vessel last week? It's full again."

A quiet groan escaped Naomi's lips as she headed for the stairs, aware her husband's reaction would not be pleasant when he found out.

She ran her open palm along the wall of bricks and mortar as she steadied herself down the stairs, her fingers lined with the small crevices of age.

Flying down the stairs, two steps at a time, remained a memory from the past.

"Can you hear me, Naomi?" Elimelech asked, his voice louder than before.

"I'm right behind you El," Naomi said, moving off the bottom step to join him. "No need to yell."

"Why is the grain vessel full again?" he asked, tugging his ear. "I filled it six days ago. It should be at least half empty by now."

"It was getting low," Naomi replied. "I asked Mahlon to refill it." She moved closer, placing her hands around Elimelech's broad shoulders and nestled her face in the comfort of his untameable white beard.

When they met as young people, Elimelech had been tall, muscular and handsome, unlike the other wiry boys of their childhood. The moment Naomi had met the gaze of his big brown eyes, she knew he would be hers.

Even now he was handsome, but he'd aged, the same as Naomi. The famine encouraged the aging process, creating new strands of white hair on their heads every day.

"Are you even listening?" Elimelech asked. "If we've already filled the vessel again, we're going through our supplies faster than I originally estimated."

Naomi shrugged "Everyone makes mistakes El," she said.

Elimelech glared at her, then his eyes widened. "You've been giving it away!" He threw his head back, cursing under his breath.

Naomi watched the muscles along his jaw tighten.

"You don't understand what you've done," Elimelech said.

What have I done? Naomi thought. *Given ourselves something more to worry about?*

"It means we can't stay in Israel, Naomi," Elimelech said.

His words stung Naomi more harshly than if he'd hit her.

"What do you mean we can't stay?" she asked, taking a step back. "Where would we go?"

"Lord, give me strength!" Elimelech whispered, rubbing his forehead as he groaned in frustration. "We've discussed this! We go where the famine is not. We are going to Moab."

"Moab?" Naomi replied. "We can't leave Israel to go *there*!"

Elimelech cursed again.

"I know we talked about moving," Naomi said. "But you never said anything about Moab. A land full of lustful pagan worship and sexual immorality! You're comfortable exposing *your* sons to those types?"

"You would *prefer* starvation and the certain death of our sons over exposure to a few pagans?" Elimelech asked. "The two of us would starve to death shortly after. Would that please you more? Would that be more tolerable for you?"

Naomi accepted that difficulties were part of their existence; like festering wounds in their side, forcing them to rely on El Shaddai through life. There were highs and lows. Life danced precariously between the two.

She would never forget the brokenness of her heart after each miscarriage she endured. But after giving up, El Shaddai had blessed them with twin boys. Mahlon and Chilion. Twenty summers had passed since their birth, but Naomi still remembered the joy that had filled her heart.

Mahlon and Chilion both appeared healthy at birth, and life was full of babbles and giggles, but as time passed Naomi realised something wasn't right. Each illness that spread through Judah would take hold of them, lingering in their small bodies weeks after other children had recovered. Even now, twenty summers later, Naomi would isolate them inside the home at the first sign of a sickness spreading through Beit-Lechem. She had taken them to numerous healers during their lives, but nobody could tell her what was wrong.

"We can ask your cousin Boaz for help," Naomi said. "He has more than enough to share."

"I'm not asking for help," Elimelech replied, shaking his head. "I can provide for my own family."

"Has he even offered to help," Naomi asked.

Elimelech ignored her.

"But Moab?" Naomi knew she kept repeating herself, but Elimelech clearly wasn't listening. "Moab is where they practice sorcery. Where they enjoy the pleasures reserved for marriage with their brothers, uncles, sisters, parents, children –"

"– enough!" Elimelech shouted, slamming his fist against the wall.

He winced in pain.

Naomi knew she'd angered him, but he had made her angry too.

Elimelech flexed the knuckles of his hand and glared at his wife. "We are going to Moab," he said. "We will live in the isolation of the hill country. Away from the cities, and the pagans, and worship."

Naomi's chest tightened. "Please, El," she said. "Please don't take us there. Think of what it will do to our sons. What if they are seduced away? What if we lose them to the Moabites?"

"You usually place so much trust in El Shaddai, Naomi," he said, leaning down to pick up his hat from the back of a nearby chair. "Maybe you should show more faith in Him now, at this time, to watch over our boys. Because there is an abundance of food across the Jordan, and that's where we're going."

Naomi watched Elimelech's back as he pushed through the door and disappeared outside. She wondered if he was right. He might be. But what if he wasn't? She walked across to the door and stepped out to survey the sky. Not a cloud in all that blue. Once more she prayed for rain, begging El Shaddai to keep them out of Moab.

....

A pink sky hugged the mountain line, preparing for sunrise.

Naomi leant against the side of the house and yawned, pulling her thick cloak around her light linen tunic. She watched her boys load their possessions into two timber carts. The last of their livestock, two grey mules, waited patiently in their harnesses.

Today they were leaving. Leaving Naomi's beloved Beit-Lechem.

Leaving the Promised Land of Israel to travel to a country – as far as she knew – El Shaddai had warned them to reject.

Elimelech promised the journey would be a mere five days, but Naomi prepared her mind for longer. She knew the road was steep and rocky. Travelling through wilderness, then across Jordan River would not be easy.

Chilion threw the last bag of grain into the second cart with a thud, startling the mule. It took several steps forward, before Chilion rushed forward to grab its bridle.

"Woah," he said, stroking the animal's long nose. "You're ok."

Naomi sighed, pulling her cloak tighter around her arms. The air smelt of freshly crushed wheat on a threshing floor, tormenting her soul by the memories they would leave behind.

She had not ceased in her prayers for rain, but none had come.

I know you are present … Why don't you answer?

Their two carts were full of as many belongings as they could fit after the grain had been loaded. Most of their possessions would stay, locked inside a house Naomi knew would be overrun by thieves starved of food as soon as their departure became known. She forgave them in advance. It was desperation that drove her people to such acts.

A smile spread across her face as she remembered the small bags of grain she'd left hidden in the house for the hungry to find.

Her eyes drifted over to Mahlon and Chilion as they helped Elimelech finish securing the carts with ropes. Her boys who had become men quicker than she had liked. Their excitement to travel to Moab hadn't escaped her attention, and it bothered her. Both had strong friendships with the lads in Beit-Lechem. Naomi had hoped they would resist Elimelech's idea. The loss of her own friends — knowing she might never see them again — caused a sharp pain in her chest.

Perhaps they've heard that Moabite damsels are free and easy.

Naomi's lips tightened, and her stomach churned. She rubbed the creases of her forehead, knowing if these thoughts continued, her head would ache. An ache that could turn into something much worse, afflicting her for the rest of the day.

Elimelech squeezed Naomi's shoulder as he passed her on his way into the house. Naomi made a mental note to take the concerns of her sons to him when they reached Moab. *He will instruct them on marriage in the way that El Shaddai designed. To Israelite damsels.*

Elimelech stepped through the front door. "Is my family ready to leave?" he asked. He pulled the door shut behind him, tugging on the handle to snap the lock into place. A long exhale left his lips as he stood in front of Naomi. "That's it, I guess," he said. "You ready?"

Naomi raised her arms around his neck and pulled him close. The cool of the morning snuck under her cloak.

"Are you sure you want to do this?" she whispered into his neck. "The lads worry me."

"Why?" Elimelech asked, wrapping his arms around her waist.

"They're too excited," Naomi replied. "And my thoughts have gone through all the possible scenarios of why."

Elimelech laughed as he let her go. "Oh Naomi," he said. "Your mind is impossible."

"I'm not joking," Naomi said. Heat rose in her face as she followed Elimelech to the cart. It infuriated her when he mocked her fears.

Elimelech took her hand as she secured her footing on the cart step.

He glanced behind to wink at their sons who were watching, before turning his smile to Naomi as he pulled himself up beside her.

"My dove," he said, vigorously grabbing her around the waist and pulling her close. "You worry too much." His lips brushed against her forehead. "I swear on my life I will keep them safe."

Naomi's heart melted at his touch. She could almost forgive him.

Elimelech slapped the reins on the back of the mule and the cart pulled forward with an uneasy jolt.

Chilion's laughter echoed from behind. "What are you two arguing about?" he probed.

"Ask your abba!" Naomi snapped, refusing to explain.

Her neck ached. She reached up to massage the tense muscles that had twisted together in a tight knot. *If Elimelech isn't worried, he can be the one searching every harlot house in Moab when the boys go missing.*

Mahlon muttered something, sending Chilion into a fit of laughter.

Elimelech glanced at Naomi with a grin. She rolled her eyes and glanced away.

Chilion's laugh morphed into a course, gagging cough, as he struggled to inhale.

A deathly cold spread through Naomi's bones as she turned to the cart behind them. "Mahlon, help him!" she demanded.

Mahlon shrugged his shoulders, with a smirk on his face. As Naomi's glare intensified, he handed Chilion a sheepskin of water.

After a moment Chilion recovered, but the tension in Naomi's mind remained. This cough was new. Possibly the onset of the sickness his friend had a month ago.

El Shaddai forbid.

"Stop worrying," Elimelech said, as he moved Naomi's hand off her neck and pressed his fingers deeply into her muscles.

Naomi closed her eyes, sighing inwardly as the pain alleviated. She couldn't work out how he did it, but he possessed a power over pain. She opened one eye a crack to see Elimelech watching her with a boyish grin on his face. Naomi squeezed her eyes shut, refusing to acknowledge his charm. But she had lost the battle. Her lips broke into a smile.

They moved further down the hill, the cart rocking gently from side to side, as their farm grew smaller and smaller till it was nothing more than a speck.

....

The mountains of Moab loomed in the distance, dark and unwelcoming.

Naomi shivered, pushing the anxiety aside as she passed bread around. Not the usual comfort meal of home, but the crunch as it cracked open, and the aroma that escaped with the steam, calmed her.

They had passed through the Jordan with little trouble, despite Naomi envisioning a disastrous crossing. Heart palpitations had become her close companions as they had drawn near. But it hadn't been perilous at all. Narrow, and shallow enough for the carts to easily pass through. Another year of dry skies had stopped the annual flooding from arriving.

They weren't the only ones escaping the drought in Israel. On the other side of the Jordan were another Hebrew family. A young husband and wife had set up camp with their five small children.

They ate together with Naomi and Elimelech, sharing a meal around the campfire.

"Sit, Naomi," Elimelech said, tugging at her arm.

The colour rose in Naomi's cheeks, realising she'd disappeared into her thoughts. Pain shot through her aging knees as she sat on the stiff folded blanket beside her husband. After rubbing them briefly the pain subsided.

Elimelech closed his eyes, turning his palms to the sky.

"Blessed are you, Lord our God, king of the universe, who brings forth bread from the earth. We thank you for the family we share this meal with, and the protection you give us on our journey."

Before Elimelech had finished praying, the children devoured their bread.

A squeal of anger echoed across the valley.

"She kicked me," one of the small boys said, pointing a plump finger at his sister.

"I did not," she protested.

The boy continued to bellow and pulled off his sandal to inspect his injured toes.

Naomi glanced around. There were lions in this area.

"Keep them quiet," the young husband growled at his wife. "Do you want the armies of Ammon to find us here?"

The wife pulled her son into her lap, gently consoling him until he settled.

Naomi chewed on her bread and examined the wife. The woman was only young, but dark circles lined the underneath of her eyes and her dangerously frail frame alarmed Naomi.

"Why did you and your husband decide to leave Israel?" Naomi asked. "Why now?"

The woman's face dropped. She shot a cautious glance at her husband.

The husband turned his attention to Elimelech. "We were running out of food." His words were muffled, his mouth too full of bread. He gagged, then covered his mouth with his hand to cough.

Naomi pulled apart some of her bread. It *was* dry now that the heat had left it.

"I need water," the young husband demanded. His wife climbed to her feet and left their small gathering.

Naomi shot a glance at Elimelech, who ignored her gaze.

"We were running out of grain too," Naomi told the young husband. "I didn't want to leave, but Elimelech decided we were going," she laughed. "Whether I agreed to it or not."

"He doesn't need your approval," the husband replied, avoiding Naomi's gaze. He turned to Elimelech. "A husband is lord and master of his wife." He continued to chew on his food, slowly, reminding Naomi of a cow in a mindless daze.

His young wife returned with a vessel of water. The husband snatched the cup from her trembling hands and emptied the contents at her feet, sending water through the cracks of her brown sandals, muddying her toes.

A soft whimper escaped her lips.

"This vessel is empty," the husband said, throwing it at her face. "I said I want water."

As the wife left, hot anger burned in the pit of Naomi's stomach. She elbowed Elimelech.

Tell that man that his woman has been provided by El Shaddai to be his companion, not slave!

Elimelech ignored Naomi, choosing to chew on his meal in quiet. As the wife approached, he turned the conversation to the stars, which had taken their allocated places in the sky.

Naomi watched the wife, who kept her eyes focused on the ground. Naomi yearned to reach out to her, to hold her hand, to give her the love and attention she lacked. But she resisted, aware that any gesture of affection or empathy for her situation could bring swift punishment from the husband. A lord and god in his own mind.

Unable to endure the tension and injustice, Naomi politely bade them shalom and retired to the makeshift bed under the linen tarp hanging from their cart.

....

They travelled further into the west of Moab, and the heavy darkness that plagued Naomi's mind, dissipated. The landscape brought back memories of Israel, from years ago. Isolated hills, and lush green farmlands. No harlots or idols.

Each night they set up a makeshift home, and by early morning, campfire embers were the only proof they'd been there.

One night had been different.

"Did you hear that?" Elimelech asked, tapping Naomi. He sprung from his bed and rushed from their shelter into the open field with bare feet.

Naomi peered outside, eyes wide, struggling to focus in the dark. Mahlon and Chilion stood beside Elimelech.

In the distance, along the horizon, a flash of light streaked across the black sky. Seconds later a low rumble moved across the land towards them.

Naomi laughed, as the cold breeze swirled around her.

How long had it been?

"Come here Naomi," Elimelech called out. His beard barely hid the broad smile underneath.

As the storm moved closer, the lightening intensified, and within minutes the gentle wind whipped around on itself, sucking back into the tempest heading their way. The linen tents flapped angrily, wanting to be free of restraints.

The scent of rain hit first, before the wall of water moved across them.

As it unleashed the life-giving liquid of the sky, Naomi watched in euphoria, raising her open hands towards the clouds.

"What do we call this strange wetness?" Chilion laughed, pulling his soaked tunic away from his skin. "It's been a long time."

Elimelech laughed as Mahlon ploughed into Chilion, sending him sprawling on the soaked earth.

Naomi skipped through the mud with the hysterics of a crazed child. Tears of happiness ran down her cheeks. Her bones ached with the movement, but she ignored the pain, her joy too immense.

Maybe Elimelech had been right to leave Israel.

As the rain continued to fall around them, Naomi wondered if they would still have the covering of El Shaddai's protection, now they had left Israel. A sensation of guilt, deep in the pit of her stomach, hungered for home.

They were not guaranteed the security of the land promised to their forefathers, Avraham, Yitz'chak and Ya'akov.

....

Naomi stared out the window of their new home, as she stretched her arms out to release the ache in her wrists.

It had all been too easy. Nothing fell into place this effortlessly. The obvious answer would be the divine hand, but Naomi struggled to accept this new life as El Shaddai's plan.

Why does He want us here?

After travelling into the hills to avoid the cities on the plains, Elimelech had met a farmer named Malak. In return for work on his farm, Malak gave them a small house to live in. Despite Naomi's questioning, Elimelech hadn't given her much information about this man from Moab. She only knew that Malak lived with his wife and daughter. Naomi prayed they would stay away from her family, but now her sons had found work on nearby farms and were also vague in their responses to her questions. She didn't understand why everyone was being secretive.

The house Malak had given them was a third the size of their Beit-Lechem home, but a welcome relief from the makeshift residence they'd been living in.

The bottom floor of the house was divided into two areas, separated by a wall. On one side of the wall there was room enough for a small table and chairs, with a fire beside the window. A stable graced the other side of the wall, small and compact, but it was all they needed.

A thick wooden ladder led to the upper second floor, where they slept together in one room. Never had they shared a room as a family before, and even after a month living in these new conditions, they still struggled to adjust.

Outside, several meters from the new home, stood a great oak tree. From there, was a view of the shimmering Dead Sea below them. Past the sea were the mountains of Israel.

Under the shade of the oak's strong branches, Naomi would sit in the cool of the afternoon. She'd watch heavy grey clouds drop low over Moab, releasing their water as they travelled towards the Dead Sea, only to dissipate before they reached Israel.

A polite tap on the door pulled Naomi from her thoughts. Blood drained from her face as she stepped towards the door. It was too early for the men to be back from the farms.

Outside stood a woman. She was clothed in layers of purple fabric which shimmered under the rays of the sun.

Naomi knew this fabric would not have been easy to find or affordable. She glanced down at her own beige tunic, realising she hadn't noticed the many signs of wear until now.

Dark umber hair framed the woman's face, blending into the tone of her skin, with white hairs sprouting along her hairline.

A weak smile formed on Naomi's lips. "Shalom," she said. Her stomach churned.

A pagan on my doorstep. Where are you Elimelech? This isn't supposed to happen.

The woman smiled in return and bowed. Without waiting for Naomi's invitation, she slid past Naomi and into the house, surveying the room with a critical eye.

Naomi clenched her jaw.

The presumptuousness.

Another woman appeared in the doorway. This one much younger, with wild, fiery red hair. The young woman surveyed Naomi with suspicion. Her skin was a darker shade than the first woman's, but her eyes had Naomi mesmerised. The colour of them as teal as the piece of fabric which draped over her shoulders, and a stark contrast to the golden ring in her nose.

A chain hung loosely over the young woman's earthy orange skirt. Naomi's eyes moved from the chain to the soft skin of her exposed waist, then over the white linen that covered her breasts.

The young woman lowered her eyes and followed the path of the first woman, also entering the house without invitation.

Naomi turned, watching as the women surveyed the room. She knew it was her family who lived here, yet now, she felt as though she was the one intruding.

Oh, give me the strength to ask them to leave!

"I am Cajsa," the older woman said. Her dialect familiar yet different. "I am the wife of Malak. This is my daughter Ruth."

Naomi swallowed, thanking El Shaddai she had kept her mouth shut. "Peace to you and your family," she replied, finding her voice despite the dry desert forming in her throat. "My men are at work, farming." She wrung her hands, unsure what to say under their intense gaze. "We are Ephraimites from Beit-Lechem, Judah, in Israel."

Cajsa nodded, running her hand over her hair. "Yes, I know where you are from," she said.

Ruth's eyes narrowed but flickered with curiosity. "Your words are strange," she said. "I thought it was Ishril, across the river Jordan, but you say it Is-ray-el."

"Yes, Is-ray-el," Naomi replied. She watched Ruth as she took it all in. "Who are you the wife of?"

Cajsa groaned and muttered something under her breath.

Ruth raised her eyebrows and smirked. "I am not wed."

"Well, you have made this little house a home," Cajsa said, gesturing around the room. "It hasn't been used in years and I did wonder if it would even be liveable when Malak told me your family had moved in."

"We have been blessed to have settled this fast," Naomi said, as her nerves settled. "Our journey here has been smoother than I ever imagined."

"Ah, yes," Cajsa replied. "You will find Chemosh blesses all newcomers of Moab. And to continue his blessings I have brought you a gift."

Cajsa rummaged around through the bag that hung loosely over her shoulder and pulled out a small wooden carving. She held it out for Naomi to admire. Half man, half cow; an ugly combination of creation that didn't make sense.

Naomi's eyes widened in fear. "Oh," she said. "That's an idol. When I said blessed, what I meant was ... well ... I ..." She envisaged Elimelech returning after work to find them homeless, over rejecting a lifeless piece of wood. Not knowing what else to do, she reached out, hoping they wouldn't notice the tremble in her hand, and took the idol from Cajsa.

Forgive me, El Shaddai.

Ruth laughed. "Ignore my ima," she said, aware of Naomi's discomfort. She waved her arms around in the air like a sorcerer, mockery clear in her actions. "Ima believes we are watched and protected by celestial beings!"

Cajsa shot Ruth a glance.

Ruth paid no attention. "I can see *you* know differently, Naomi," she said, her eyes lighting up. "It is refreshing to meet someone else who doesn't believe in the 'gods'!"

"Well, that's not entirely accurate," Naomi replied, rubbing the back of her neck. "I *do* believe in a god." *Tread carefully, Naomi.* "It's not the *same* god as your ima. My god is El Shaddai."

Ruth glanced between Naomi and her own mother, then shrugged her shoulders.

Naomi pointed to a vessel on the small wooden table beside them. "Are either of you thirsty? I have water."

Cajsa raised her hand and smiled. "We have work to do but thank you for your kindness. This was a short visit on our way through to the next diseased. I'm a healer and midwife … if you ever need assistance please send word."

Naomi laughed out loud at the thought of needing a midwife at her old age. She noticed the offence on Cajsa's face and cleared her throat. "I may require that offer of healing one day soon," she said. "My son, Chilion, has had the cough since we left Israel, and it's becoming concerning."

Cajsa nodded and smiled again. "Let me know when he is home and I will come," she said, before turning to follow Ruth out the door and into the sunshine.

As they moved out of eyesight, Naomi collapsed onto a chair, exhausted from the interaction. Replaying the conversation over in her head, didn't help, as she changed what she wished she'd said differently and added what she'd forgotten to say.

She had hoped to avoid mingling with the Moabite pagans altogether, but now they had met her, she knew this wouldn't be the last time they'd visit.

"I didn't even share my faith," she muttered under her breath as she rocked the little man-cow idol on its edge along the table.

El Shaddai isn't any *god. He is the* only *God.*

....

With age came pain, and the daily process of making bread had taken its toll on Naomi's hands. Her fingers and wrists ached, as did her back, but she persevered, knowing her boys were working the farms.

The sticky dough told her it needed more flour, and she listened, scooping another fistful from the clay pot, dusting it over the top. She continued to press in, folding and pressing, ignoring the sharp sting in her knuckles.

The months had passed by swiftly, as if the seasons couldn't wait their turn. For Naomi, life in Moab had become normal, no longer a foreign land but home.

Mahlon and Chilion were content, Elimelech was thriving, and as much as she hated to admit it, Naomi had found peace.

She had managed to destroy the idol Cajsa had gifted her with. Burnt to ashes in the fire the same night.

Elimelech had laughed when she told him what had happened. "I wish I'd seen your face," he said, grabbing her by the waist and planting a kiss on her cheek.

"What if she wants it back?" Naomi asked.

"Don't worry," Elimelech said. "Cajsa won't ask for it back. Their house is littered with them."

But Naomi *was* worried.

A tap sounded on the door as Ruth pushed it open and entered, letting the sunlight stream through the room.

"Knock and wait," Naomi muttered, but smiled as Ruth approached.

"I have your grain," Ruth said. "Abba said to bring it over. Do you want me to bring it in here or leave it outside?"

Naomi dusted her hands on her apron and shuffled towards Ruth. "Don't worry yourself," she said. "Chilion is home today. He can unload the grain and bring the mule back to your abba afterwards."

Ruth hesitated, tucking a curl of hair behind her ear. "I don't mind waiting," she said. "There will only be work waiting for me at home." She ducked out of sight.

Naomi suspected there was more to Ruth's excuse than farm work, but she pushed the thought out of her mind. She refused to entertain the idea that Ruth wanted to wait for Chilion to appear.

Outside in the warm sunshine, Naomi spied the sacks of grain sagging over the back of a furry mule, with Ruth standing beside.

Naomi sighed, realising the stubborn girl wasn't going to leave. She cupped her hands around her mouth and called out to Chilion, her voice not unlike the screech of a crow. She'd always been envious of other imas who could call their children in from miles.

Ruth leant down to whisper in the mule's ear, rubbing its fluffy forehead affectionately.

Strange girl, Naomi thought.

"You know, Ruth," she said, before realising what she was doing. "There *is* a real and living God. His name is El Shaddai."

Ruth turned her face away, but not quickly enough.

Naomi had seen the smirk. The temperature rose in her face as she clenched her fists by her side. "You think all gods are the tales of men," she said. "And all the gods you *have* heard about *are* tales. But not my god. The God of Israel. He is as real as you and I."

Ruth rubbed the neck of her mule. "I *have* heard of this El Shaddai," she said, turning her face to Naomi. "But your god will be no different to the others. The designs of man, made for one purpose, control others through the demands of blood lust and other evils."

"El Shaddi is different," Naomi replied. "He is too beautiful, just and glorious for a mortal to have dreamed up."

Ruth shrugged her shoulders.

"Oh, the stories I could tell you," Naomi continued. "Of all that He's done for His people Israel; they would make your heart sing in wonder."

"And *there's* the catch," Ruth said, her bangles clanging together as she scratched her forehead. "He cares only for Israel. Do you see what I mean? With limitations such as this, it proves he's obviously a manmade myth."

A sudden shattering behind Naomi sent her heart racing. She turned in time to see a second stack of clay pots topple over, throwing dust into the air.

Chilion climbed to his feet, patting his legs down as he mouthed the word 'sorry' to his ima. A boyish grin spread across his face, under the fair stubble that lined his jaw. Thick blond curls covered his head. He was unusually fair; neither Naomi nor Elimelech were fair, and neither were their parents before them.

Naomi smiled at Chilion. She would forgive his clumsiness. She always did.

The smiled dropped into a frown as she glanced back to see Ruth's wide eyes focused on Chilion.

Admiration or embarrassment?

Naomi hoped it was the latter. "I need you to bring those sacks of wheat into the house for me, Chilion," she said, hoping this interaction would finish quickly. "Don't just stand there," she added, agitation rising as the muscles in her legs tired. "Ruth needs to get this mule back home."

"Pfft," Ruth said, shaking her head. "I'm not in a hurry." She stepped back as Chilion walked towards her and reached over the mule to untie the rope.

He lifted a sack off the mule with ease, his young twenty-year-old muscular body barely straining under the weight. He threw it onto his left shoulder and made his way to the house.

Naomi kept her eyes on Ruth as a spark of uncertainty formed in her chest. This pagan woman showed far too much interest in her son. Even now, a smile of appreciation had formed on her young face, her eyes twinkling and her skin glowing under the light of the morning sun. Naomi shivered as the spark of fear inside her grew wings and soared. If *she* knew this woman was attractive, then Chilion had noticed her.

The approving smile dropped from Ruth's lips; her face turning a shade paler.

A low groan escaped Chilion's mouth. Naomi turned as he doubled over, and a violent cough ripped through his lungs. He fell to his knees beside the house. The sack of grain slid from his shoulder and hit the ground, bursting on impact. Grain exploded in every direction.

"Chilion!" Naomi rushed to his side. The coughing continued. Forceful and hard. He ripped at his throat with his hands, the colour draining from his face.

"Breathe, Chilion," Naomi demanded.

Lord, give him air!

Ruth called out, something about her ima, but Naomi's mind was a blur, focused solely on her son.

As the coughing subsided, Chilion relaxed onto his back against the dust, his chest rising and falling in a steady rhythm. He smiled at Naomi. "Don't look at me like that," he wheezed. "I'm fine."

His teeth, and the creases of his gums, were covered in a red tinge.

Naomi choked back a sob.

Chilion's grin disappeared, as he licked his teeth, sensing the new taste in his mouth. He sat up and spat on the dirt. A small splatter of blood. His eyes searched Naomi's face, fear visible in his wide eyes.

Naomi refused to let him see her own terror. "Come inside," she said, controlling her voice. "Come and lie down."

Grabbing his arm in her own, Naomi led him past the spilt grain and into the house.

"What's wrong with me?" Chilion asked, with childlike panic.

Naomi ran her wrinkled hand over his forehead, pushing the thick blond hair from his face. "You have a bad cough, that's all," she replied.

"Ruth disappeared so I suspect she left to fetch her ima. Cajsa'll know what you need."

"It's bad then?" Chilion asked. His eyebrows came together in a frown. "To send for a healer?"

Pain shot through Naomi's chest. She bit her lip and turned her face away, hot tears threatening to emerge. "Who knows the plans El Shaddai has for us," she said, her voice faltering. "But whatever plans they are, they will be for the best."

"But you know it's true," Chilion replied, placing a hand on Naomi's. "You've known it since I was a small child, haven't you?" He closed his eyes. "Even I know I won't live to see thirty summers."

Pigeons fluttered about under the roof of the house as Naomi stroked Chilion's forehead. His eyelids fluttered as he fell into a restful sleep. His breath deep, slow and quiet.

Shortly after Cajsa rushed through the door with a bag full of herbs and dropped to Chilion's side.

ORPAH

MOAB – 1194 BC

A small girl cried out in pain. Her hand hovered above her knee, resisting the urge to touch the fresh graze. Her tunic, which had been removed and thrown to the side, absorbed moisture from the mud surrounding her, but the child was too distracted to notice. Small dots of blood had appeared in the shallow cuts of her skin.

"What happened Ishat?" Orpah asked, kneeling beside her young sister.

Realising her fall had been noticed, Ishat resumed her howl.

"Come, it's not that bad," Orpah said, scooping the little girl into her arms. "We'll get you cleaned up and your clothes back on, you silly thing."

Ishat's muddied thumb found its way into her mouth, and the cries died down. With her free hand she twirled a finger around a loose strand of Orpah's straight brown hair.

"There's no bread," a voice called out from inside the house. "Why isn't there any bread?"

"She knows exactly why there isn't bread," Orpah whispered to Ishat, bopping her on the nose as they continued to the house.

There had been no time to mill, knead or cook bread. Arising from bed before dawn, Orpah had been busy with other household chores her ima, Izevel, demanded be done.

As she passed through the doorway, a sharp slap clipped Orpah across the back of her head, and her grip on Ishat faltered, sending the small child toppling to the ground.

New howls commenced.

"Answer me when I ask you a question," Izevel shouted, readying her hand for another strike, her large arm swaying from the motion. An insatiable appetite and lack of motivation to venture further than the front door, had created an overweight and angry woman. Her big frame imposed a force of authority over Orpah she couldn't withstand.

"I've been washing, drying and cleaning all day, Ima," Orpah replied, as she held the back of her head. "I'm going to start on the bread once I've cleaned the cooking pans."

Izevel scowled and moved around Orpah on thick, swollen legs, searching for a weakness in her daughter.

Orpah's mind reverted to its usual torment. *You won't have to look hard. She knows she's useless.*

Orpah winced, pressing her hand against her forehead, straining to suppress the thoughts that plagued her.

"I've got my hands full with these children," Izevel said, "and a growing baby in my stomach. Do you hear me making excuses or complaining?"

Don't answer. You're not worth listening to.

"Hurry up and finish what you're doing," Izevel said, wobbling a chubby finger around the room. "And make twice as many loaves today so we don't starve tomorrow!"

Orpah watched Izevel waddle back to her sleeping quarters and pull the curtain shut behind her.

Ishat, realising she'd milked as much sympathy as she was going to get, slipped past her sister and out the door, happy to stay free of the restrictions of clothing.

Orpah bit at a jagged fingernail and sighed. She wished her abba knew what was going on, and the work she did. But he left early in the morning and returned late, entering the house with a stride that signalled sore bones. Orpah didn't want to burden him with her problems. Besides, if she complained, there was a chance her ima would turn her abba against her, with lies of how lazy his daughter was.

"Orpah!"

A mess of red hair appeared in the open window across from her.

Orpah's shoulders dropped. Things hadn't been the same between them since Ruth insisted on going to the village. Orpah had tried to explain what was going to happen, but she was sure Ruth blamed her for not speaking up.

Orpah shook her head at Ruth, the sting of Izevel's slap still throbbing the back of her head. "Keep your voice down."

"You must come with me," Ruth said. "We have Hebrews staying in the old house. Ephraimites from Beit-Lechem."

"What?" Orpah asked, moving to the window.

Ruth reached in and grabbed Orpah's hand, as a large grin stretched across her face. "Yes, Hebrews. Can you believe it? They've been here for about six months now."

Orpah's eyebrows rose. "Why haven't you told me this before?"

"… and one of their sons fell sick, and almost died," Ruth said. "But Ima, as usual, worked her magic and saved him."

Orpah watched Ruth blankly. It was usual for her friend not to listen; to talk over her.

It's what you deserve. Just as Ima says, you're a waste of air.

Three of her brothers yelled at each other in the distance. Orpah scrunched up her nose, wondering if she should check.

"Stop glaring at me like that," Ruth said. "I want you to come with Ima and I this afternoon when we visit the Hebrews. Strictly as healers, obviously. This man, he is not the same as a Moabite man. Neither is his brother."

"Are you listening to yourself?" Orpah asked, pulling her hand free. "Look at me. I can't come. I need to clean the kitchen, then make two days' worth of bread, which I'll be lucky to finish before the sun goes down!"

Oh, I see what you're doing ... trying to act tough. In control. Why bother. You are utterly useless.

Ruth's smile grew larger on her face. "I'll help you clean when we get back. And give you some of our loaves."

Orpah rubbed the back of her neck. "I don't know."

"Come on!" Ruth whined, leaning back on the windowsill. "You never get a break."

Orpah observed Ruth's gleeful eyes, realising saying no wasn't an option.

"Your ima works you too hard," Ruth said.

Orpah shrugged. "Ok but swear to me that we won't be long."

Typical ... no backbone.

Ruth's smile dropped as she held her hands together in a solemn prayer stance. "I swear."

Orpah smiled weakly and threw her apron on the kitchen hook. Before leaving the house, she peered into her ima's room through the soft curtains. There was a mound on the bed snoring softly. Ishat had snuck back in the house and now lay sprawled over the dirt floor beside Izevel, deep in sleep.

"Listen," Orpah said to Ruth, once she was outside. "I know you might be sick of me repeating this, but I *am* sorry I took you to the village."

"Orpah, that was almost a year ago," Ruth shrugged. "At first I wished you *had* told me, but I'm actually glad you didn't," she said. "Now that I witnessed it, I know gods aren't real."

Confusion surfaced in Orpah's mind, but the relief her friend didn't hold a grudge soon removed Ruth's strange comment from her thoughts.

....

As they approached the house of the Hebrew's, sweat formed on Orpah's palms. The ground moved uneasily beneath her feet as she walked forwards.

You're an imposter, not a healer.

Orpah watched as a woman hobbled out of the house. Her face appeared old and weathered by life, but her smile was youthful and warm.

"Cajsa and Ruth," the woman cried. "So happy to see you both."

"This is my friend," Ruth said, wrapping her arm around Orpah. "She came along for the walk."

"I am Naomi," the woman said, holding her arms out to Orpah.

Pent-up breath left through Orpah's lips. She inhaled deeply as relief washed though her body. "I am Orpah."

The connection was brief, but Orpah sensed a calmness overtake her.

"Any friend of Ruth's is welcome in our home," Naomi said, releasing Orpah from her grasp. "You must have heard how Cajsa and Ruth nursed Chilion back to health. He is still quite weak but improving every day."

Cajsa placed a hand on Naomi's shoulder. "I thought I might check Chilion one last time," she said. "And remind you to give him the herb mix every day."

Naomi nodded, clasping her hands together.

As they turned to enter the house, Orpah positioned herself behind the others. The sensation that she shouldn't be there resurfaced.

You're a bother, a nuisance. It may look like they're being kind to you, but it's a cover for their distaste of your presence.

Inside, the women blocked her view, until Naomi moved slightly, and a man came into sight. He was shirtless, sitting on a makeshift bed beside the wooden kitchen table.

Orpah's heart fluttered. Ruth had been right. There were no men around Moab like him. His skin was a beautiful olive brown, his hair and stubble thick and blond. He didn't appear to be sick at all.

Cajsa sat beside him and put her ear to his hairy chest, her eyes roaming the room as she listened.

As Orpah continued to stare, Chilion raised his eyes and met her own. Heat rose in her cheeks.

"Shalom," he said, his voice low and beautiful. "Are you another healer in training? What's your name?"

Orpah realised he was talking to her. He'd asked for her name, but she couldn't remember what it was. Or how to speak. Or how to breathe.

"She isn't a healer," Ruth answered, pulling Orpah through to the front "This is my friend, Orpah."

Chilion smiled. "I'm glad they asked you to come."

"Leave us, damsels," Cajsa ordered, "I need to check him over fully."

Convinced her face was on fire, Orpah hurried out of the room.

"What did I tell you," Ruth giggled as they left, nudging Orpah in the ribs with an elbow. "He is something isn't he?"

"Yes, you were certainly right," Orpah replied, finding her voice at last. She didn't want to talk of the experience again. "You also told me you'd give me some loaves and help clean the house."

However, cleaning and loaves of bread were the furthest thing from her mind.

....

Orpah stepped through the front door and noticed Izevel had risen from bed.

"It's all done, Ima," she said, wringing her hands together. "As you requested."

There was a pause.

"It's not all done Orpah," Izevel moaned. "Balak needs bathing. He stinks. Why can't I rely on you for anything?" She waddled back to her room. "Why do I even bother?"

Orpah's heart sank.

She's right and you know it. You'll never be good enough. There's obviously something wrong with you.

Orpah's bottom lip quivered as she held back tears. She walked outside to find Balak, hoping after the bath Ima would finally be pleased.

Would she though?

From a small child, Orpah had faced continual threats from Izevel. She didn't know if it was because she was the firstborn, as her siblings were spared the hate that spewed forth from her ima's mouth. She remembered clearly the worst threat as if it were yesterday. A threat to her three-year-old self that she would partake in the sacrificial ritual to the gods if she didn't do as Izevel had commanded. Seeing the fear in Orpah's small grey eyes had only brought laughter to Izevel's lips, as she reminded Orpah that the gods wouldn't accept such a pathetic offering.

Izevel didn't believe in gods. She'd shown her children from birth that she reigned supreme. Gods were a distraction from the attention and worship Izevel believed she deserved.

Orpah knew this was the reason she and her siblings had been spared from the fire. They were born into the reign of their ima's kingdom. Power was her addiction, and children provided her with helpless servants. She would live the life she craved whilst her slaves bowed to her every demand.

Orpah's abba, however, believed in the divine. She had witnessed him praying to Molech, the small wooden statue in his room. Some nights, under the warm flicker of a candle, he would cut the inside of his arm with a small dagger, wincing in pain as the blood dripped onto the calf head statue. The whispered chant that proceeded from his mouth was incomprehensible to Orpah. But she knew her abba believed Molech would give him the world in return for obedience.

It was also Orpah's desire to worship Molech one day. When Abba showed her how. More than anything she wanted to be rid this life of slavery and knew the gods were the answer to providing her with everything she wanted.

She didn't fully understand why Molech and Chemosh demanded children as sacrifice, but she knew there must be a reason why something so terrible was necessary. Her abba would know. He was smart and smart men wouldn't cut themselves for an idol if there wasn't a good reason.

"There you are," Orpah said, chasing after Balak who zig zagged out of her reach. "Come here before we both get into more trouble."

....

Chilion became a constant visitor in Orpah's thoughts. Three weeks had passed since their awkward encounter, but for Orpah it was if three months had.

She groaned, pulling a basket of wet clothes up the bank of a cold stream. Exposed tree roots grabbed at the weaving, threatening to send the clean clothes back into the water.

Chilion had lingered in her mind, blocking out the pain in her arms as she scrubbed the clothes against the rocks; the memory of his smile making her life more tolerable.

A surge of jealousy consumed her, as she thought of Ruth, who was able to see the olive-skinned boy whenever she wanted.

She cursed, realising she wasn't even sure if Ruth *had* been visiting the Hebrews since Cajsa had finished her treatment.

So quick to judge. You are a weeping sore in the earth.

There had been no mention of attraction, but it was clear to Orpah that Ruth was intrigued by him.

Of course she's attracted to him! They'll be married soon. You never had a chance.

Dry leaves crunched under Orpah's sandals as she walked over to the eshel pines that lined the road. Their branches spread out horizontally, as if grown to provide room for wet clothing to dry.

Izevel disliked Orpah leaving clothes on these low-lying branches; fearful they would be stolen from the road. There had been no thefts, Orpah had informed her, and a family as poor as theirs had no desirable clothes to steal.

"Don't talk back to me," Izevel had said. "Just do what I say."

As Izevel's words echoed in her mind, Orpah concentrated on her work, rhythmically flopping the wet clothing over the branches. Her fingers ached as the cold afternoon breeze blew against the wet linen, chilling it in her hands.

The echo of laboured footsteps carried up through the breeze. Orpah stood and scanned the road. Travelling men. Too distant to recognise. She pulled herself up into the branches and spied from her new vantage point.

As they grew closer, her stomach turned. She didn't recognise the man with the dark brown head of hair and beard, but his companion was undoubtably Chilion.

Orpah glanced down at herself as they approached, realising her dusty brown tunic held the unrelenting memories of her day so far. The stains retold the battle of retrieving Balak from the mud. The repulsive odour of dry milk, acquired during an altercation with a defiant goat, proved she'd fed Ishat. And more recent, the needles of the eshel tree, which clung to her tunic, told of her boisterous climb.

She raised her hands to her head in despair, her fingers catching a knot in her hair.

Orpah refused to let the men see her in this state. She knew she couldn't escape the slavery her ima imposed on her, but for it to be known would be humiliating. She sat still, clinging to the rough trunk of the tree, praying Molech would make her invisible.

"Why are you stopping?" Orpah heard an unfamiliar voice ask. "I need to get back."

"Wait," Chilion said. "Orpah, is that you?"

Orpah froze, unable to believe he'd remembered her name. She wanted to reply, something eloquent and witty, but her mind had turned to stone.

"What *are* you doing?" Chilion asked, moving off the road towards her.

Orpah struggled to swallow the knot in her throat, as she descended through the tree, sliding to the ground once she'd reached the bottom branch. She wrestled with her tunic, adjusting the twist that formed during her climb.

"Peace be with you."

It was all she could manage, and barely a whisper, as she tried to brush the bark and pine needles off herself.

Chilion grinned, pointing at the tree. "You like to climb?" he asked. His eyebrows came together. "*Or,* were you trying to hide?"

The man beside Chilion laughed and nudged him in the chest. "Leave the poor soul alone," he said.

Orpah winced under his words.

That's all you are, a poor creature to be pitied. Nothing else.

"Orpah, this is my brother," Chilion said, wrapping his arm around the other man's shoulder. "This is Mahlon. And Mahlon, this is Orpah," he said, holding an open palm in Orpah's direction.

She smiled weakly.

"I've been walking to work up my strength again," Chilion said. "And Mahlon here has been brotherly enough to join me."

Mahlon laughed again, deep and throaty. He grabbed Chilion around the neck and used his other hand to scruff Chilion's hair. "Ima has ordered me to," Mahlon said. "Worried you'll collapse to the ground with nobody around."

As they laughed, Orpah watched Chilion, and warmth filled her heart. His health had improved compared to the last time she'd seen him. Stronger. More colour in his complexion. His brother Mahlon was the bigger of the two men, but he wasn't as stunning as Chilion.

"Would your family share a meal with us?" Orpah asked, surprising herself.

The smiles drop from the men's faces.

Idiot.

"Sorry, I shouldn't have …" Orpah said, lowering her gaze.

Stupid. Stupid.

Chilion shook his head, raising a hand in reassurance. "No, no, don't be sorry," he said. "It's our ima … well she doesn't … she hasn't quite settled into this new life yet and –"

" … she doesn't want to mix with you Moabites," Mahlon finished for him.

"What are you doing?" Chilion hissed between his teeth.

"What?" Mahlon replied. "It's true. She hates Moabites. You've heard her, she never stops."

Orpah's heart raced.

"Just stop," Chilion said. He turned to Orpah. "He doesn't know what he's talking about. Our ima has practically adopted Ruth and Cajsa."

"That's different," Mahlon replied, stretching his arms above his head. "Cajsa saved you, so Ima makes allowances for them."

A donkey brayed loudly in the distance.

Orpah tried to smile, but her lips refused to move, stuck in a straight line. "It's fine," she said. "I shouldn't have asked."

Deep down she was relieved Chilion would never meet her family. But the pain of knowing she would never be accepted into their family, or even as a human, stung her more than she knew was possible.

Don't act surprised. You've known it for years. Worthless.

"Orpah," a voice screamed from somewhere behind her. "Where

are you!?"

Orpah's shoulders slumped as she watched the Hebrews scan over her head, searching for the owner of the voice.

The voice bellowed again.

Mahlon kicked at the dust on the road. "I think someone wants you," he said.

"Yes," Orpah replied, swinging clenched fists by her sides. "I'll have to go and see what they want."

The men said their shaloms, but Orpah barely noticed. Nor the smile which Chilion shot her before he turned to leave.

Worthless. Worthless. Worthless.

Tears ran down her cheeks, leaving lines in the dust on her face, as she trudged back towards the house. She wiped them off with her sleeves, cursing. Ima would not be allowed to revel in the pain she inflicted.

As for Naomi, she was a prejudiced old woman.

Orpah decided she'd be happy if she never saw any of the Hebrews again.

BOAZ

ISRAEL - 1194 BC

"Now you've done it!" Devorah called out.

Boaz raised his head. His calm, steel-blue eyes searched the field.

Devorah stormed into view – an accusing frown creating lines on her forehead.

"What have I done now, Devorah?" Boaz asked as he leant against a large well. He smoothed down the stiff hair of his trimmed beard. Cool stones pressed against his legs as he loosened his grip on the rope in his hand, sending a clay vessel down into the abyss. A splash echoed up the stone sides.

He swept his shoulder length hair off his bare back, tying it on itself in a messy knot. Grey-white hairs peppered through the thick brown hair of his head and beard. A few years ago, only a small number of white strands had been present. When the heavens stopped giving rain, the white hairs arrived in droves.

The famine refused to let go of its grip on Beit-Lechem. Crops withered; livestock faded. Thirsty winds pressed in against forgotten fields. Men became mad, seeing hope where there was none, as people deceived by the lure of a desert mirage.

Devorah approached and pulled herself onto the well. She adjusted her robe under the large shadow of her cousin. The bangles on her wrists clinked together as she pushed frizzy black hair from her face.

"I hear you've laid off half your workers, old cousin," she said.

"What?" Boaz asked. "I would never do such a thing."

The flow and dance of Devorah's purple robe against the still harsh grey of the weathered stones caught his eye. The fabric flapped against the well, collecting dust in its folds. *Opposing forces. Untamed and unseen energies, revealing mysteries for those with ears to hear and eyes to see.*

"I don't provide you with fine linen to wallow in the dirt." Boaz said, scratching his head.

Devorah shrugged. "This robe is a year old," she said. "I have three more being made at present."

Boaz inhaled deeply. He wondered if Devorah could smell the stench coming from his armpits. Work in the fields had been unrelenting.

"I haven't put anyone off," he said, dipping a ripped cloth into the bucket of muddied water beside them. "Not that it's any of your concern, young cousin."

He squeezed the wet cloth over the back of his tight neck and shoulders. Tiny rivers of straw-coloured water ran down his muscular arms as the day's filth washed away. His workers had left the fields, and he had hoped to bathe in the peace and quiet of the afternoon.

"That's not what I heard," Devorah said. "Yamin and Lemuel both came to me, wanting to know if I could help feed their families because you'd fired them."

Boaz leant down to rinse the cloth in the bucket. "I don't know anything about it," he replied. Mud swirled slowly through the water.

"Are we running out of money?" Devorah asked, her voice rising. "Is that why you're laying off labourers?"

Boaz laughed as he sat up. "And there it is," he said. "The true reason you're worried about my men."

"Of course," Devorah said. She slid off the well, using her slim arms for support, then flattened out the creases of her flowing robe with her hands. Jewellery around her neck caught the rays of the afternoon sun.

As Boaz bent over to rinse the cloth again, a sharp pain pierced through the lower section of his spine. A gasp escaped his lips. He waited a moment, then straightened his back gradually.

These little reminders, these pokes and prods of age, had become more frequent of late. Boaz refused to accept that his time might be coming to an end. He'd passed fifty-three summers and yet he continued to out-work the youngest labourers in his fields. A boast he would often remind them as they battled the heat of the day together.

"I am anxious when my lifestyle is under threat," Devorah said, studying Boaz's face. "*Are* we running out of money? You could always stop feeding those beggars at the gate each day."

Boaz sighed. "It would do you some good to find time in your busy schedule to venture into the city," he said. "You'll see what lifestyle is considered normal for most people and appreciate what you have."

Devorah groaned and rolled her eyes. "No thank you."

Boaz wiped the soaked cloth across the hairs of his chest and caught Devorah's glare of disgust.

"I'm trying to take a bath," he said, staring at her. "So, unless you stop harassing me and leave now, you'll end up seeing a lot more of me than you want."

"Ugh!" Devorah flinched and turned aside. "Are you sure we have enough money?"

"Please leave, Devorah," Boaz replied. "Before I throw this cloth at you." He raised the wet fabric above his head, poised to send it hurtling towards her.

"You wouldn't dare," Devorah replied, shielding her face with her hands. "Fine, I'm leaving."

Boaz laughed. "You can go back and live with your parents in Shechem if it's too hard for you here," he called out after her.

Devorah kept her back to him as she walked away, raising her hand to wave him off as if he were a bothersome fly.

"Entitled child," Boaz muttered.

Devorah's message unsettled him. He had kept all his labourers in work since the famine began, as well as employing extra men who were too proud to accept his charity without reason.

His overseer, Enosh, had disagreed with this decision. For Enosh, more field hands with fewer working fields equalled little to no profit. It made no business sense.

For Boaz, it made perfect sense. Families would survive. He would never remove any of his labourers during this time of hardship.

Enosh will know what Devorah is raving about.

Not everyone had accepted Boaz's charity. His own cousin, Elimelech, refused his help. A frown crossed Boaz's face as he recalled the pride and stubbornness of his cousin's reply when he'd offered.

The last time Boaz had seen his cousin had been the night before Elimelech left Israel. Boaz once again implored him to stay, work on his farm. But Elimelech had already decided, determined to take his wife Naomi and their sons into the unpredictable land of Moab, where he hoped to save his family from ruin.

No news of Elimelech or his family had reached Boaz since that night. By his estimation, that was ten months ago. He prayed they were safe.

A sudden thought occurred to him as he continued to wash off the sweat and dust. Devorah's parents would be arriving later in the evening. How he had forgotten he didn't know. Even Devorah hadn't reminded him.

Aunt Dalia had sent word weeks ago, expressing her desire to visit her nephew and sister. Uncle Gad planned to accompany her as usual, but Dalia mentioned a young woman would also be in their travelling party, and 'could she perhaps stay a few nights?'.

Boaz's shoulders slumped as he let out an exasperated sigh. He threw the dirty cloth into the bucket.

It was not the first time Dalia had attempted to pair him with a wife, and she would continue to do so until she won. Her heart was full of pure intentions; Boaz couldn't fault her. But it never worked.

He finished bathing and emptied the grey water over the sandy soil. It disappeared, drawn down into the thirsty earth. He drew more water from the well and raised it above his head, letting the water flow freely over his body.

Pairing with a woman had never been easy, even though opportunities had been ample. In earlier years, women encircled him like scavengers, sniffing his wealth from afar. Even his rough and rugged appearance hadn't been enough to deter them.

It was the telling of his closely held past, when the time was right to reveal it, that ended all their affections in their tracks.

....

Boaz kissed his ima's forehead.

Lines of age laced her once beautiful skin. Her closed eyes sunk deep in their sockets.

"Ima, it's me," Boaz said.

White eyebrows flinched at his voice, but Rahab didn't wake. Her frail frame, dissolved of all fat and muscle, lay on a large soft bed in the middle of the room. Blankets made of the finest scarlet and sapphire linen covered her.

Oil lamps flickered in the breeze, dimly lighting the room as they sent dancing shadows across the richly painted walls. White linen curtains hung above the open window, moving aside as the night air circulated, bringing in the scent of dry fields.

Outside, the moon shone brightly, coating the house and courtyard in a bath of light.

"Have you risen today?" Boaz asked.

Rahab said nothing as he sat on the edge of the bed. He took her pale hand in his.

A shadow of the woman she once was. Nobody would recognise this as the woman, the pagan from Jericho, who had once helped two spies of Israel escape the clutches of the Jerichoan authorities. This was *the* Rahab, whom most of Israel had heard about, who now deteriorated, day by day, in the house of her son.

She was not born in Israel to Hebrew parents, like most people in these parts, but grew up in a poor family in the midst of Canaan. As soon as she was able, she sold her body to hungry men to make an income. Over years of managing and investing her earnings wisely, she brought her family out of poverty and into the big city of Jericho, purchasing a residence on the wall with a view overlooking the rocky hills.

Boaz scratched his chin, watching her breathe.

"Your baby sister Dalia is here, Ima," Boaz said. "She's downstairs unpacking. Can you hear her?"

Rahab moved her head to the side, releasing a sigh through her nostrils.

"She'll be happy to see you," Boaz said, stroking her hand. "And have a load of gossip for you, no doubt."

He wondered if she could hear him or if she'd left her mind. Her chest rose and fell silently. Somewhere deep inside, she was determined to keep going.

"Do you remember when I was a boy?" Boaz asked. "And you caught me sneaking goat milk for that lion cub I found?" He paused. "You said I couldn't keep the cub because it needed its ima. You said I had to find its ima, or it wouldn't survive. I didn't want to listen to you. I wanted to keep it. But it kept crying for its ima, so you helped me find her."

Sorrow gripped his heart as he gazed at the fine strands of silver white hair which surrounded her weak face. "I need to find you, Ima."

A commotion erupted on the floor below.

"Where's that wine skin we brought?" Dalia asked, her voice echoing up the stairs.

"How should I know?" Gad replied. "You had the servants pack the cart."

Boaz placed his ima's hand on the bed with care. "I'm going to see what's going on," he said. "Rest, Ima."

Downstairs, Boaz found his aunt and uncle's cart had been unloaded into messy piles over the moonlit courtyard.

Gad stood beside the cart, watching his servant continue to search desperately for the missing wine skin. He showed no intention of helping. Short in stature, with a large midsection, the only hair on Gad's head was the curly grey beard which hid his lips from view.

Dalia searched through the baggage. An older version of Devorah – frizzy black hair and slim figure.

"Shalom, my family," Boaz said as he walked over to Gad. He laid an arm over his uncle's shoulder. "I have more than enough wine to share. You needn't unpack anything."

"*I* wouldn't have bothered," Gad replied. He pointed an accusing finger at his wife. "She's the wine bibber."

Dalia's face dropped into a deep shade of scarlet. "You!"

Across the courtyard, a servant motioned to Boaz.

"Supper has been served," he said as Dalia lunged for Gad.

....

They reclined outside on colourful Egyptian cushions, around a low wooden table full of food and flickering candles. Surrounding them, polished brass oil lamps stood tall. Their flames licked at the air.

Boaz choked on his wine as Dalia's travelling companion appeared with Devorah. She was much younger than he expected, possibly only seventeen. He shot a glance of disapproval at his aunt.

"This is Shoshanna," Dalia said, ignoring his rebuke. "She came with us to visit Devorah."

"Shalom," Boaz said, nodding in Shoshanna's direction. He set his wine on the table.

What on earth were you thinking, Aunt?

Shoshanna's straight brown hair flowed easily around her waist as she sat on a cushion between Devorah and Boaz. Her grey eyes widened as they absorbed the wealth before her.

Boaz cursed under his breath, knowing it was the size of the house and the plenty he had that impressed her. In his opinion, women were always the same. They saw prestige, wealth, and hard-earned work. What better man to pair with.

"Shalom Boaz," Shoshanna replied, peering up at him through her black eyelashes. "You have an impressive home. I can't imagine the joy of living here."

"Thank you," Boaz replied, before taking another sip of wine. "I do love living on the outskirts."

"Where do you get all this food?" Shoshanna asked, leaning forward to help herself to some crusty bread. "I have not seen this abundance in Israel for some years."

"Some of it I have imported," Boaz replied, setting his cup down. "Some preserved from before the famine. My sheep continue to breed and provide us with meat."

Gad reached out and snatched a handful of dried dates from a clay bowl. "How *is* the farm going?" he asked Boaz.

"The wells are our lifeline," Boaz replied, flicking a small insect from his arm. "We're down to a quarter of capacity."

"Yes," Gad replied. "Thank El Shaddai."

"He's put off half his labourers," Devorah said, chewing a mouthful of juicy lamb. "Which means things are going downhill."

"Don't talk whilst you're eating," Dalia said, slapping her daughter's wrist. "Is it that bad Boaz?"

"It's actually not true," Boaz said, shaking his head. His brows drew together in a frown. "I think I would know if I told my workers to leave."

"You need to ask your grumpy overseer," Devorah replied. "What's his name?"

"Enosh?" Boaz replied.

Devorah nodded. "Apparently, he's the one who carried out your orders." She leant forward and picked some olives off a plate.

Boaz thought on what Devorah had revealed. Enosh had never failed him before. The best overseer he'd ever employed. Investigating would have to wait till morning.

"I've also been trading with the countries across our borders," Boaz told Gad.

"Yes, I heard that," Gad replied. "There's a lot of Hebrews who think you've forsaken El Shaddai, trading with our enemies to increase your own riches."

"And they are entirely correct in their assumptions," Boaz said, tearing a loaf of bread apart. "But if it wasn't for the increase from my so-called *ungodly* trading, I wouldn't be able to feed those under my protection, or the poor."

Gad burst out laughing. "It's a nice gesture, Boaz," he said. "But El Shaddai would be far happier with you if you ceased your trading with the heathens. If you must spend your money, keep it in Israel at least."

"Do you *really* think El Shaddai would prefer I stopped trading with other nations?" Boaz said, attempting to remain calm. "Do you think El Shaddai would prefer I let the hungry starve?"

Gad shrugged and glanced at his plate.

Dalia scoffed. "Enough of business," she said, waving her hand around in annoyance. "It's too beautiful a night to be worrying about mundane issues. How did you find the journey, Shoshanna?"

Shoshanna leant in front of Boaz, letting her long hair fall onto his lap.

He shifted uncomfortably.

"I didn't mind it for the most part." Shoshanna said. She straightened and flicked the long hair back over her shoulders. "Did you see that beggar who was following us? It's distressing when they do that."

"Distressing to watch someone in need?" Boaz asked.

Shoshanna wrinkled her nose. "Of course not," she replied. "Distressing for us to worry about having our necks sliced when we stop."

Boaz held up a piece of bread. "Perhaps all he wanted was a small piece of this?"

"I doubt it," Shoshanna replied. "They're always so dirty … and the stench … I thought I would be sick."

Boaz glanced at Dalia, sending her the falsest smile he could muster. *Again, why on earth would you bring her here?*

Shoshanna nudged Boaz with her elbow. "I guess *you* wouldn't have to worry about the haggling beggars," she said. "You must have tens of servants who watch your cart at night whilst you're travelling."

Boaz watched discomfort rise in Dalia's face. He knew she understood his view on these matters. He could see the wheels of her mind turning, knowing if she let the conversation continue this trajectory, Boaz would retire to bed.

"Tell everyone what your abba does for work, Shoshanna." Dalia insisted.

Devorah rolled her eyes. "Let her eat her supper, Ima."

Shoshanna's laugh echoed around the courtyard. "I don't mind," she said. "I enjoy talking."

Boaz raised his eyebrows and scratched the back of his head. How easily Gad had escaped the conversation. Sitting in silence, chewing on his supper, Gad simply ignored the women as they spoke.

"My abba is a priest." Shoshanna said, sitting up straight. "He works in the tabernacle of El Shaddai."

"Ah, you're a Levite," Boaz said, with a slow nod. "Your abba doesn't live in Shechem with your family?"

"Our home is in Shechem," Shoshanna replied. "But Abba makes the journey to Shiloh to fulfill his duties."

Dalia wiped food from her lips with a cloth. "Shoshanna was thinking she might stay on in Beit-Lechem instead of returning home with us," she said. "Devorah could look after her, show her around the city. Meet new people. Make new friends."

Boaz sighed. "Shoshanna, did Dalia tell you what *my* abba did for work?"

Shoshanna shook her head.

"His name was Salmon," Boaz said. "He was an elite in the army of Israel. One of the official spies who risked their lives to slip into the enemy city of Jericho, before Israel invaded, to survey what defences were in place. You've heard this story, yes?"

Shoshanna's jaw fell. She glanced at Devorah, who rolled her eyes.

"That's perfectly glorious," Shoshanna said. She sat forward on her cushion and placed her hand on Boaz's forearm. "I have heard this story a million times before but have never met someone this close to those involved. And your abba was one of the spies! I recall that a Jerichoan harlot seduced her way into the heart of a man in the army of Israel. Did your abba know anything about that? I think her name was Rahab. You must share all you know with me!"

Dalia winced. "We don't need to speak of rumours and gossip."

Boaz scratched his beard. "Do you have a problem with women from Jericho, Shoshanna?" he asked. "My own abba fell in love with a woman from Jericho."

Shoshanna laughed as she shuffled her long tunic closer around her legs. "I'm not a judgemental person," she said. "But I wouldn't share that piece of your abba's history if I were you. There are many critical Hebrews who would be quick to jump to the conclusion that your abba indulged himself with filthy gentile harlots."

Boaz glanced at Dalia.

She glared back, knives in her eyes. Her eyebrows rose as she shook her head.

"The thing is, Shoshanna," Boaz said, his eyes still on Dalia. "My ima's name is Rahab, and she is the whore from Jericho you've heard all about. The same woman who seduced a man of the Israelian army. A man called Salmon. My abba."

Dalia cursed and threw a fig at Boaz's face. He ducked as it sped past and split against the stone wall behind.

"The woman who sold her body to many men in Jericho is my ima," Boaz said. "She's upstairs right now, if you don't believe me."

Shoshanna giggled. "You are too funny." She glanced around the wooden table, the smile on her lips fading as she looked from one serious face to the other. "Wait, that's not true, is it?"

"Would it matter if it was, Shoshanna?" Boaz asked, reaching for his wine.

"Of course it would," Shoshanna replied, crinkling her nose. "This is scandalous."

"Don't fear," Boaz said. "The blood of my abba flows strong within me. I have no desire to sell my body for a few coins like my ima did." He picked a bunch of black grapes from the table. "Of course, I can't be sure about my offspring. The harlot blood might pass onto them. I do worry that an uncontrollable desire to make a living from their bodies might be a problem as they reach adulthood."

Boaz watched as Shoshanna squirmed on her cushion, appearing unable to find a comfortable way to cross her legs. Guilt overcame his frustration. She was young, and unprepared to navigate life discussions that relied on wisdom gained from experience.

But he also knew her kind. Those Levites. Selected to work in the tabernacle had made them think highly of themselves. They would glare down the nose at other tribes as though they were as low as the gentiles surrounding them. Levite offspring received this perception from birth, discovering their glorious standing in Israel before they reached the age of five. By Shoshanna's age, prejudice was a constant essence that flowed freely through their blood.

Shoshanna's face flushed. "I don't feel well," she said, standing, losing her balance as the cushion caught her foot. She turned to Dalia and her eyes widened. "Wait … that means … you're … you're a *pagan*?"

Dalia sighed and nodded.

Shoshanna bowed to Boaz. "I'm going to retire," she said. "Shalom. Thank you for supper." Her hurried footsteps crunched against the ground, echoing around the silent courtyard, as she rushed towards the stairs.

"You have ruined this, Boaz," Dalia said, slamming her fist on the table. "You think I enjoy hearing you drag my sister through the mud like this?"

Gad laid his hand on Dalia's. "He didn't mean what he said."

Boaz sighed. "I'm sorry aunt."

"*You* weren't there, Boaz," Dalia said as she struggled to hold back tears. "You have no idea what life has been like since Israel invaded Jericho."

"I *do* know aunty," Boaz replied, his voice soft. He walked around the table and knelt beside Dalia, cradling her in his arms. He laid his head against her back. "I watched my ima battle it every day. Which is why I will not cave into the discrimination and cowardice of patronising Hebrews to win their approval."

"Precious Boaz," Dalia said, her lips trembling. "*You* don't need to fight them. Unlike your ima and I, you *are* one of them. You are a Hebrew."

Boaz released her from his grip and peered into her moist eyes.

"You forget," he said, shaking his head. "I am both Hebrew *and* Jerichoan."

……………….

The moon sat high in the night sky when Boaz staggered back to his room.

He'd drunk wine. A lot. But not enough to numb his mind against the oppressive thoughts that determined to torment him.

Through the open window, he saw a multitude of stars scattered across the black heavens. Envy filled his heart. All that was required of them was to flicker with light. There were no humans to contend with up there.

He sat at the table beside his bed with a groan. Regret that he'd hurt his aunt. Regret that he'd aired his ima's reputation to save himself from an unsavoury marriage.

At the young age of six, he had learnt of his ima's past. Until then, he had assumed his family were the same as all those on his street.

His abba, Salmon, had been away, fighting for Israel, leaving Boaz and Rahab on their own. One night, a man who should have been at war, pushed against the door of their house.

Boaz still remembered the terror in Rahab's eyes as she pressed her back against the wooden door, her feet slipping against the dirt as the man pushed his way in. He remembered the smell of dust stirring up, and her scream for him to leave through the back, as the door opened further, and her strength failed.

His heart had pounded against his ribs as he fled the house, taking refuge in the dark. A tiny child unsure of what was taking place, but the words the man had called his ima rang in his ears.

He found Rahab slumped on the bed when he returned. Seeing him enter, she had smiled, wincing as she pulled him into her arms. Boaz didn't understand why her cheeks were wet with tears, or why a bruise covered her swollen eye. He wanted to know what the man called her. Why had he hurt her? She refused to tell him.

He found out a few days later, when bravery overcame his fear to ask the neighbours. They had been more than happy to share with him who and what his ima was. Their voices played over in his young mind for months afterwards. They told him his ima was foreign and would never be accepted as one of their own. That she was a wicked woman who spread herself amongst many men, not just his abba. That he, Boaz, was a half breed, neither Jerichoan, nor Hebrew. That El Shaddai, the God of Israel, would only accept those with the full blood of Israel's ancestors, not half breeds.

Boaz sighed, his eyes resting on the pile of papyrus on his table. Some of the writings were records of what had happened that night in Jericho before Israel invaded. His ima had fed him bits and pieces of information over the years. She'd seen Salmon outside the tavern that night. She had known at first glance that he and his companion were not Canaanites, despite the clever Jerichoan disguises they wore. Like the rest of Jericho, she knew the army of Israel lay somewhere outside the city, a darkening storm on the horizon. They all knew Israel didn't keep survivors. As Rahab watched Salmon, a plan formed in her mind. In Salmon, she saw the key to her salvation from certain death.

What she hadn't expected was to fall in love.

"Love does not originate from earth but the spiritual realm," Rahab told Boaz shortly after Salmon had been killed in battle. "Today my heart is breaking, and I feel as though I may never recover. I know you are feeling this too, my little man. But I realise now that loving another and having that love returned is a divine gift. It is only ours to hold for a time, to experience, to learn from, then let go, as painful as that is. But we will recover."

Boaz remembered the confusion that had filled his head. "But why do we have to let it go?" he had asked. "Why can't we keep it?"

Rahab's face had softened as a gentle smile formed on her lips. "Sometimes we don't have a choice," she told him. "But this is why love is offered only to those brave enough to embrace it," she said, pulling him onto her lap. "Because after experiencing love, the agony of its absence is so much more painful than if we had not loved at all."

"I don't want to feel agony, Ima," Boaz had told her, tears filling his young eyes. "I don't want love."

"You will one day, Boaz," Rahab replied, hugging him tightly. "Because *you* are one of the brave ones. Just remember, where there is love, there you will find God."

Boaz hadn't understood her final comment, but years later, he discovered the meaning behind her words. Time alone, in the secluded beauty of the mountains, away from the distractions of life, he had found love, like a still small voice inside him. His desire to live from the presence of love, the spirit of God, became an insatiable craving he couldn't remove.

"Some people won't understand," Rahab had told him. "But be patient with them. Acceptance of love also requires you to share it with others, no matter who they are. Love others, and they will come to find God."

"How could Israelites not know about this?" Boaz had asked her. "Everything we do, every law we follow, is supposedly centred around El Shaddai, yet I can't see the love in it?"

"We are taught everything *about* God," Rahab had replied. "But knowing *about* and knowing *intimately* are two very different things."

Boaz flipped the pages of papyrus rhythmically in his fingers. Underneath the numerous words from his ima's life were pages of his own thoughts. Words poured from his heart. The darkest periods of his life, to the most beautiful.

He leant back on the stool and raised his arms, knotting his fingers together against the back of his head. The pain in his knee had returned. Some nights were better than others. But tonight, it throbbed relentlessly.

He would seek out a healer in the morning.

NAOMI

MOAB – 1194 BC

"Passover is a month away," Elimelech said. His eyes followed Naomi as she handed him a bowl of hot lentil stew. "Why the rush?"

"There is no rush," Naomi replied, wiping perspiration from her forehead. "I want to be organised." She walked back to a large pot that hung over the fire and ladled stew into another bowl. "Have you seen any sheep on the nearby farms, because I haven't. Only flea-bitten goats."

"It won't take a month to find a lamb," Elimelech said, taking the next bowl from Naomi and passing it to Mahlon.

Naomi observed her son's face as she filled another bowl. Mahlon sat motionless, staring at the supper in front of him. Steam rose from the thick liquid as he poked at it with a spoon.

"You don't want my stew?" Naomi asked.

Mahlon raised his head, a blank stare on his face.

Elimelech blew across the food on his spoon. "Answer your Ima," he said, before shoving the food into his mouth. He cried out and cursed, spitting the food onto the table. "You should have served this up an hour ago, Naomi! It's too hot."

Naomi ignored him, worry swirling in her heart as she watched Mahlon. It was unusual for him to be so quiet. *Maybe he isn't well. I'll get Cajsa tomorrow. What if he's caught what Chilion had? Where is Chilion?*

"Where's Chilion?" Naomi asked.

Elimelech removed a moth from the surface of his stew. "I'd say he is still working on the farm."

"He's late for supper again," Naomi said. She placed the pot of stew on the dirt beside the fire. "Those farmers are working him too hard."

"He'll be fine," Elimelech said. "Stop worrying." He reached behind her back and pinched her rear.

Naomi jumped around and held the lentil covered ladle above her head, ready to strike.

Elimelech laughed. "No, don't you dare!" he said. He reached up and took hold of her arm before wrapping his other around her waist, pulling her onto his lap. His bearded chin tickled the aged skin of her neck as he nuzzled his way in.

Mahlon rolled his eyes. "You are both too old for that," he said. "Beyond too old."

A broad smiled stretched across Elimelech's face as he helped Naomi off his lap. "Never too old son." His eyes followed Naomi, spanking her as she stepped away.

Outside, the shadows of night fell over Moab, and the barks of golden jackals echoed in the distance.

"Are you sure Chilion is still at the farm?" Naomi asked, wiping her hands with a cloth that hung over the fire. "Mahlon, why do the farmers let you leave work early, but not Chilion? They know he's been sick."

Mahlon glanced at Elimelech.

"What is it?" Naomi asked, her eyebrows narrowing.

"I ... uh," Mahlon started.

"Tell me!"

Elimelech sighed, tapping his fingers against the wooden table. "Chilion has taken to the young damsel down the road," he said. He reached out and took hold of Naomi's hand. "He spends his afternoons with her. That's where he is now."

Images of Chilion skipping around the countryside with Ruth, up to all sorts of ungodly activities, filled Naomi's mind. Nausea formed in the pit of her stomach. She pulled her hand from Elimelech's.

"Why did you hide this from me?" she asked, wringing her hands. "He's my son too."

"You know how you react, Ima," Mahlon said, leaning back in his chair. He exhaled slowly. "We knew *this* would happen."

Naomi's heart beat hard against her chest. *Is this what the people of Moab have done to our family? Created deceivers? Infiltrated our home? Our sacred space?*

"It's fine," Naomi said, attempting to remain calm. "I'll talk to Cajsa in the morning."

Elimelech frowned. "What do you mean?"

"Ruth is a nice girl," Naomi replied. "But I'm not interested in having a Moabitess for a daughter."

"It's not Ruth," Mahlon interrupted, fiddling with the rim of his bowl. "It's Orpah."

Naomi stared at Mahlon; her eyes wide as she tried to remember who Orpah was. She'd heard the name before. Her eyes shifted to Elimelech's face, searching for signs that they were only teasing her.

There were none.

"You – you – promised," Naomi said, her voice faltering. "You swore you would keep our boys safe." Her face crumpled as the comprehension of the situation sunk deeper. "Why are you encouraging this behaviour? You know I want our sons to marry damsels from Ephraim. You *know* that!" Hot tears filled her eyes. She wiped them away in frustration, and glared at Elimelech, waiting for his reason. He always had a reason.

"If you hadn't forgotten, Naomi," Elimelech replied, his voice unusually stern. "There's a raging famine in Israel. What do you want the lads to do? Wait for the famine to be over before they wed? That could be twenty years away!"

Naomi shook her head. "But a Moabitess?" The room closed in around her. Each inhale of breath as heavy as a sack of grain pressed against her chest. "Couldn't they travel back to Israel and bring brides here?"

Elimelech scoffed. "Who would let their daughter leave Israel for Moab?" he asked. "Everyone in Israel is the same as *you,* full of racial pride."

Naomi pressed a hand against her chest. His words had stung, adding to the turmoil that was boiling up inside her.

Chilion pushed through the front door. A tune whistling on his lips. His eyes narrowed as he shut the door and surveyed the room. "What's going on?"

Naomi bit her lip. His face, to her, was so like a small child. *My precious boy.*

"You are not to visit Orpah anymore," she said. "She is not the woman you want to marry."

Chilion snorted. "What?" He glanced at Elimelech.

"I don't want to argue with you, Chilion," Naomi replied. "You will marry a Hebrew woman when we return to Beit-Lechem." She turned towards the fire, unable to watch the pain rip across Chilion's face.

"But, Ima," he said. "You must meet Orpah, and you will change your mind, you'll see."

"That will never happen," Naomi replied.

"You are happy to have Cajsa and Ruth in this house," Mahlon interrupted. "Orpah is no different."

"Orpah *is* different," Naomi said, turning to face them. "Cajsa and her daughter are healers. That's why I allow them inside. But they are not part of our family and never will be."

"You speak nonsense!" Chilion choked. "How quickly you have soured!"

Naomi's face flushed red.

Chilion paced the floor. "Abba, reason with her!"

Elimelech pushed his stool back and stood tall. "If the woman is willing to take on our name and beliefs, I say Chilion can marry whomever he wishes."

"What? No!" Naomi said, raising her hands. "Orpah may say she'll change but the minute we let our guard down there will be idols in the house!"

"Why do you hate them so!" Elimelech roared, slamming his fists on the table, scattering the bowls and cutlery. Veins threatened to spring from his forehead.

Naomi recoiled. She'd witnessed his anger before, but this was different.

"You never stop," Elimelech said, running his hand through this hair. "This incessant assault on people you've never met. You leave a vile taste in the air as you speak the words. You would choose to uphold your own righteousness over your children's lives!"

"How dare you!" Naomi snapped. Her body shook uncontrollably.

Mahlon cursed and stormed outside, slamming the door behind him.

Chilion raised his hands and lowered his head. "Ima, Abba, stop this. I will find a wife in Israel."

Elimelech kept his eyes on Naomi as his chest rose and fell rapidly. Beads of sweat laced his brow. "I've made my decision on the matter, Naomi," he said, as he caught his breath. "He can marry Orpah."

Naomi raised her face in defiance. "I will not be bullied," she said. Her heart threatened to break as she pointed an accusing finger at her husband. "*You* are the one who wanted to move here when I didn't, but *I* followed because you are my husband. Then *you* swore that you would keep our boys safe. And now you're breaking that promise."

The muscles in Elimelech's face moved as he clenched and unclenched his jaw.

"*You* may have swayed in your faith," Naomi said. "But I will not stand by and watch my sons be devoured by the hungry gods of another nation!"

"For once in your life stop trying to control everything!" Elimelech snapped. He pushed past her and stormed outside into the night air.

"You are wrong!" Naomi screamed out after him.

Her heart raced. He'd never walked off during an argument, but they'd never had a quarrel as heated as this one. She sat at the table and closed her eyes, paying close attention to her breathing as she tried to calm the beats of her heart. She knew she was right, that it was for the best. It had to be.

Chilion's footsteps of retreat filled her ears as he, too, left the house.

Naomi laid her head in her hands, massaging the tension in her skull, attempting to hold back the sobs that threatened to spill out of her. She hated the quarrelling. Elimelech wasn't only her husband. He was her closest friend. They had been through much together. And she loved him. Too much to let this anger linger. They'd had their share of disagreements before. This would be no different. They could work this out.

The stool squeaked on the floor as Naomi pushed against it to stand up. She grabbed a shawl off a hook near the door and made her way into the night.

Outside, the surrounding trees shrouded the house in darkness, despite the fullness of the moon. A flicker of light caught Naomi's eye. Flames from a fire in the distance. Near enough for Naomi to see Mahlon and Chilion sitting around it, but far enough away for the air to keep secret the words they spoke.

She pushed off against the rough stone wall of the house and stepped in the opposite direction to find her husband.

....

Elimelech sat alongside an old well, his back pressed against the cold rocks.

"What are you doing out here?" Naomi asked, stepping closer. Shivers ran through her body as she inhaled crisp night air. "It took me an age to find you."

The humidity from the day had settled on the soil. Moisture moved from the earth into her clothes as she sat beside Elimelech.

"I'm sorry I yelled at you," Naomi said, rubbing her forehead. *Stay strong.* Her fingers played with the fringes that ran along the edge of her shawl. "You are my rock, you know that?"

A bat flapped past overhead, heading towards fruit in the valley below.

Naomi adjusted her shawl, tightening it around her shoulders, and pulled it under her elbows. "I can't bear the thought of losing our sons."

Elimelech didn't reply.

Speak to me. I hate it when you shut me out.

She turned her face to the star covered sky. The heavenly ambience unnoticed as her mind wandered. *Tell me what you are thinking.*

"I know you're angry," Naomi said, placing a hand on his arm. "But you'll understand when we move back to Israel." She moved her hand down his arm and laced her fingers in his. "Just imagine all the Hebrew grandchildren we'll have."

Elimelech's familiar scent filled her nostrils as she lay her head on his shoulder, waiting, resting on him in the quiet darkness.

A dull ache formed in her chest as his silence continued. Their quarrel greater than she'd comprehended.

Naomi exhaled. "I'll be inside when you're ready to talk."

As she braced to stand, Elimelech folded and fell forward into her lap.

"El?" Naomi raised his head in her hands, struggling to sit him up. "Elimelech?"

There was no response.

Naomi slapped his face, anticipating a reaction. Elimelech lay limp in her arms. A soft whimper rose in her throat as she stood up and rolled him onto his back, kneeling beside him, bringing her ear close to his mouth.

No breath. No condensation rising in the night air.

"Mahlon!" Naomi's cry tore across the field. "Chilion, help me!"

Her chest tightened; each inhale becoming more laborious than the last. She moved Elimelech's fringe off his face and leant down, pressing her lips against his forehead.

"Don't leave me."

....

A thick fog consumed the hills beyond the Dead Sea, covering the highlands in a warm blanket as the temperature dipped. Above, a ceiling of indigo spread across the sky; first hints of an approaching dawn.

Naomi sat against the well. Elimelech's lifeless body lay in her lap. She cradled his head in her arms, her forehead pressed against his. Tears had ceased to flow, sorrow long exhausted, but Elimelech's face shone with her salty grief.

Nearby, rocks crushed underfoot.

Naomi raised her heavy head. A throb pound between her ears, cycling through each side of her head in a constant rhythm.

Mahlon appeared as rays of burnt orange poked through the horizon and pushed against the indigo sky. He called over his shoulder, words Naomi didn't understand. Something about Chilion.

Mahlon ran to Naomi and fell to his knees beside her. "What are you both doing out here, Ima?" he asked, reaching out to touch her. "You're freezing." His eyes surveyed Elimelech in Naomi's lap. "What's wrong with Abba?"

Naomi shook her head and reached out to stroke her son's warm cheek with the back of her hand. "Abba isn't here Mahlon," she said.

"Let me take him," Mahlon said, attempting to pull Elimelech's head out of Naomi's arms. "He needs help."

Naomi refused to release her grip.

A cry of frustration escaped Mahlon's lips. "Ima, let go," he said. "We need to take him to Cajsa."

"Your abba isn't here," Naomi replied, her voice slow and distant.

Chilion ran towards them. A loud cough rattled from his lungs. "What is it?" he asked. His eyes widened as he watched.

Mahlon moaned loudly, his body shaking with sobs. "Let me take him, Ima!"

Naomi peered up at Mahlon, her eyes red and swollen. *Take him? No, I won't part with him. You can't have him, Mahlon.* A hot sting burst through the muscles in her arms, as she strengthened her grip around Elimelech.

He's mine. Mine forever.

....

Sunlight streamed through an open window, catching dust particles as they floated with ease throughout the room.

A sharp pain exploded in Naomi's head. She moaned softly, rubbing her temples.

Someone was nearby. She sensed it, but her eyes refused to open. Whoever it was would have to wait. She was too tired. Too sore to concern herself with the problems of someone else today.

She couldn't think what had brought on the weariness, or the headache, but the warm touch of the sun assured her that all was well. *A bad night's sleep is all it must have been,* was the lingering thought on her mind as she disappeared back into the gentle embrace of slumber.

....

A crowd gathered around her; their stares intense on Naomi as she sunk deeper into the bed. She pulled the blanket up over her chin. Mixed races, of all skin colours, different apparels, a range of jewellery, tattoos and piercings. No words were uttered. They stood in silence; eyes fixated on Naomi.

What are you people doing here?

A haze cleared from Naomi's eyes, and the multitude disappeared, leaving Mahlon and Chilion kneeling beside the bed. Cajsa and Malack stood behind them.

Naomi reached out and ran her fingers across the crumpled sheet on the bed beside her. "El?"

Chilion shifted his gaze to the floor. The muscles along Mahlon's jaw clenched, as Cajsa moved towards Naomi and knelt beside her, taking Naomi's hand in her own.

Naomi rolled onto her side and peered into Cajsa's eyes. They were moist and pink.

Where is Elimelech?

Cajsa stroked Naomi's hands. "We're here for you."

The wobble in Cajsa's voice raised an alarm in Naomi.

"Where is Elimelech?"

Cajsa swallowed. "He's gone, Naomi."

"Where?" Naomi asked, pulling her hand out of Cajsa's. "Who's taken him?"

Cajsa's chin trembled, and her forehead crinkled as she fought back emotions. "Don't you remember?" she asked. "He passed away Naomi. Last night. You found him. From what I can tell, his heart gave up."

What are you talking about?

There was a pause. Naomi glanced from one pain-stricken face to the next. Then the memory of the night's events returned to her mind, forcefully, as the warm reality she'd created collapsed around her.

The argument. The harsh words. The anguish.

Naomi's wail filled the room as an ache built up in her chest. *No, it can't be true!*

Cajsa moved aside as Mahlon took Naomi in his arms.

Tears ran down Chilion's cheeks, soaking his blond stubble. "I'm so sorry, Ima," he said. "Can you forgive me?"

Naomi's heart broke even more. "Oh Chilion," she said. "You are wrong. This is not your fault." She reached out and pulled her sons in close as they huddled together, fused by sorrow. Their pain, enough to fill all the seas in the world.

....

Each morning Naomi would wake to find the space beside her empty. First, she'd wonder why. Then she'd remember. An unrelenting anguish.

Three months had passed since Elimelech's death.

Naomi wished she knew how long it would take to move past this morning cycle of confusion, then despair. She missed her Elimelech. So much. Some days she didn't know if she could keep going. But then, for some reason, something always pushed her to stay strong. Stay alive. So, she did.

She knew her sons were suffering in the same way, although they didn't speak about Elimelech much. Naomi assumed it was out of concern for her, worrying they'd upset her.

Elimelech's last words continued to haunt her. He wasn't worried if Chilion married a Moabitess.

Naomi couldn't shake the thought that perhaps it was the will of El Shaddai that Chilion marry Orpah. To bring her into their lives, for her to learn to love their god as her own.

If you want this marriage, was losing Elimelech the only way you could open my eyes? Is this my fault? Was it because I am too stubborn? Is that why you took him?

There were too many questions, all of which held answers too painful if she dared to address them.

After wiping the moisture from her eyes, Naomi climbed down the ladder from her bedchamber. Her head ached as she set about making herself breakfast.

Chilion appeared through the front door. "You're up," he said, a smile spreading across his face. "And its only midday."

Naomi glanced up as he strolled over to her. She soaked up the warmth of his arms as he wrapped them around her shoulders. His body was wet with sweat, and stench clung to him from the hot day it had become.

Naomi resisted the urge to push his filthy body away from her own. She needed the embrace as much as he did.

"I love you, Ima," he said, squeezing her tighter.

"I love you too," Naomi replied, reaching up to stroke his head. "I'll always love you." She pulled away and held him at arm's length. "There's something I need to talk to you about."

Chilion let his arms fall to his sides as his eyebrows knit together. "What is it?"

Naomi closed her eyes and rubbed her chin. "I think…" She paused, then opened her eyes, inhaling deeply. "I think … if you know your damsel – Orpah – has a good heart, and you will not be swayed by her gods … then I think I am happy for her to become part of this family."

Please El Shaddai, hold my sons in your loving arms and do not let go.

Chilion's eyes lit up, as his body surged with a newfound energy.

"You *think* you are happy, or you *are* happy?" he asked.

"I don't know," Naomi replied, gazing into his eyes, seeing only a small boy, not the man he had become. *I actually don't know how I feel.*

"She is the love of my life, Ima," Chilion replied, his voice quiet. "When you meet her, you will see how much she wants to learn about our god." He pulled his ima back into his embrace and bounced on his feet.

Naomi lay her chin on his shoulder and smiled. Joy and love flowed out from her son like fluid gold. She was surprised at the overwhelming relief she suddenly experienced. In her opinion she would have always said that she believed El Shaddai was in control, but now she realised she'd never fully let him have control of her family.

As the scales of her prejudices fell away, she understood how her determination to protect her sons had blinded her. El Shaddai could use these circumstances, however undesirable to her, to fulfill her desire for a larger family.

....

"Are you hungry?" Naomi asked Orpah. "It's almost supper time and the men will be home soon."

Naomi expected Mahlon would arrive first. Chilion had been busy in the last month, working overtime to pay the mohar, an agreed price by Israelite tradition, to give Orpah's abba in return for his daughter.

Orpah's ima, had arranged to visit Naomi several times, but each time Naomi had been left waiting. There were never any explanations, excuses, or apologies. Naomi had thought it best to visit Orpah's home, but this was met with resistance, and the assurance that the next organised visit would happen.

During the sole occasion that Naomi met Orpah's abba, she deduced he was a devoted worshipper of false gods, but he was gentle and kind-hearted. This left confusion in Naomi's heart, unable to combine the two attributes in her mind.

Orpah, on the other hand, had become a regular visitor to their home. She would come, and sit across from the table, day after day, learning about El Shaddai, the history of Israel, and their worship. Naomi described in detail Israel's escape from slavery in Egypt, the miracles and curses that occurred, and the arduous journey to the promised land.

During their time together, Naomi observed Orpah, wondering what the young woman thought of it all. She couldn't figure Orpah out. There were too many barriers. She wished she could move past the nervous, but strong, exterior to know the real Orpah.

Naomi knew Chilion must have managed to break through and hoped he continued to teach her about Israel in their time together.

Orpah fiddled with the tassels on her tunic. "I won't stay for supper," she said. "I have to leave before it gets dark." Her gaze found the floor. "My ima will have chores for me but thank you again for your kindness."

As Orpah stood to leave, Naomi sensed a nudge in her mind to tell Orpah the truth about Chilion. She hadn't had the bravery to face it before, but they would be married in a week.

"Orpah."

Orpah turned, pulling a cloak around her shoulders.

"I need to tell you something about Chilion," Naomi said. "He's never been quite well."

Orpah's brows narrowed. "What do you mean?" Suspicion clear in her voice.

Naomi walked towards her. "Oh, there's nothing wrong with his mind," she said. "It's his health. Ever since he was born, he has been unwell. Often. Like what you witnessed not long ago. Sometimes his sicknesses take him close to death." Naomi laid a hand on Orpah's shoulder and squeezed gently. "I wanted you to know that before you marry him. I don't know if your children will have his weakness, but I pray El Shaddai will bless your children with your strength."

Orpah smiled weakly. "I appreciate you telling me." She shifted uneasily between her feet. "But there is nothing you could ever say that would change my love for him."

"I'm not trying to break you apart, Orpah," Naomi said, her voice gentle.

"Are you sure?" Orpah asked, fidgeting with her fingers. "I know what you thought about me before Elimelech passed."

Naomi sighed. "It wasn't you," she said. "And I am sorry now, how I treated the situation."

"If it wasn't me, what was it?" Orpah demanded.

The usual passive, quiet Orpah appeared taller. The towering walls of defence she had put in place around her spoke for themselves. Defiance edging to the surface.

"I was fearful for my sons," Naomi replied, raising her hands in surrender. "All my life I have heard nothing but evil about Moab. I was brought up to believe that El Shaddai hated *all* Moabites and wanted every single soul destroyed."

"Why did you believe that?"

"Because that is what I was taught from a child," Naomi said. She shrugged. "And now I'm old. These are ideas that have been deeply rooted into the *who* of what I am. Not easily bent or broken."

Orpah shook her head. "I don't understand."

Naomi scratched her forehead. "That's something I've been experiencing a lot these days," she said. "Elimelech could always see further than I could." Naomi sighed and stared out into the dusk-coloured sky. "I wished I'd realised it before he was taken."

RUTH

MOAB – 1194 BC

The midday sun broke through the retreating clouds and beat against the freshly showered pastures, signalling insects to rise from their hiding places. They took to the sky in swarms, energised, creating a gentle hum in the humid air.

Malak wiped beads of sweat from his brow. "I'm sure Orpah hasn't been doing this type of farm work since she married." He pulled on a rope which hung above a well, hand over hand. A slow and tedious process.

The flat surface of stone was rough against Ruth's fingers as she moved her hand across the lip of the well.

"You should get married if you're tired of working," Malak said, wiping his mouth against his shoulder.

Ruth groaned loudly.

Malak's throaty laugh shook his body. "Why not have a husband care for you?"

A small fly flew towards Ruth's face and narrowly missed her hand as she swatted it away. "Well, I would get married," she replied, rubbing an itch on her arm. "But you know there's no man alive who will have me."

Malak pulled a bucket of water from the well and sat it on the ground. He paused and leant against the well, catching his breath. "What about that Hebrew boy, Mahlon?" he asked, wiping sweat from his beard. "He's not bad. You could do worse."

Ruth scoffed and shook her head. "I barely know him, Abba," she said. "Besides, he hasn't looked twice at me."

"Your intimidation can't be helping," Malak said. "Especially with that mess you call hair swirling around your face."

Ruth feigned offence and punched Malak in the arm.

"Ow," Malak laughed, rubbing at the pain. "Leave the old man be."

Ruth pulled her hair into a rough knot at the back of her head. "Better?"

Malak clasped his hands together. "Oh, mighty Chemosh," he said, raising his eyes to heaven. "Give Ruth the help she needs." He chuckled and handed his smirking daughter two full buckets to carry.

Ruth followed Malak as he trekked to the water troughs. Sweat trickled down the soft skin of her back, itching as she walked. Her eyes locked onto Malak as he carried his load before her. Greying hair floated around his head, drifting in the humid breeze as they stepped along the rocky path. An intense burst of love filled her chest. *What would I ever do if I lost you?*

She couldn't imagine the pain Naomi's family had endured as they came to terms with losing Elimelech. Malak was a good ten years older than Elimelech, so Ruth knew it was only a matter of time.

"Fine," Ruth said, as they approached the first water trough. "I'll visit my *married friend* more often at the Hebrew house and see if Mahlon will talk to me." She leant forward and threw her water in the trough. "But I warn you, I know I am right. He's not interested."

Murky water splashed back into her face as she emptied the second bucket. She spat with disgust, wiping her lips on her clothes.

After they'd emptied all the water into the trough, they turned back to the well. The work was hard, trudging back and forth over the uneven ground.

Ruth moaned and threw her head back, letting her arms sag by her sides in the stance of a whining child. "Why weren't the troughs built closer?" She sat an empty bucket on the lip of the well and crossed her arms over it, resting her chin on her hands. A thought popped into her mind. "Why do you worship Chemosh, Abba?" she asked.

Malak lowered a bucket into the well. The rope slid through his calloused fingers as he stared into the distance. "Because I want food in my belly and a roof over my head," he said. Sweat trickled down his sunburnt nose. "I also want someone to keep an eye out for you and your ima." He frowned, eyes watching the bucket descend. "Why do you ask? Have the Hebrews got into your head about that god of theirs?"

Ruth squinted under the glare of the sun. "No, I don't believe in the gods." She ran her fingers along the timber grain in the bucket she held, debating whether now was the right time to tell Malak what she'd witnessed outside the village. The memories of that night had lessened in their hauntings, but the desire to speak about it remained.

Ruth lowered her head. "I went to a Chemosh ceremony near the village," she said.

"What?" Malak's eyes narrowed. "When did you go?"

Ruth inhaled, noticing the anxiety rise in her chest. "Over a year ago."

"But why?"

"Because you and Ima never let me," Ruth replied. The muscles around her throat tightened. "You never told me what happens." Emotions which had been pushed down for the last year broke from their cage. "And I wish you had told me! What I witnessed has ripped my soul in two." Tears pricked at her eyes. "I've been broken ever since, and I don't know how to fix it." Her chin trembled as she peered up at her abba.

"Oh, little one," Malak said. He let the rope slip through his fingers and pulled Ruth into his arms, rocking and hushing as he did when she was little.

After a minute, he released her from his grip and wiped the tears from her face.

"I will never, *ever*, understand why people sacrifice their children," he said, pushing Ruth's mattered hair away from her cheeks. "But it's the price some people will pay for safety and prosperity."

"It makes no sense," Ruth said.

Malak sighed. "Have you noticed how Moab has an abundance of rain and good fortune?" he said. "But across the Jordon River, there is famine and bad luck at every turn?"

Ruth nodded.

"We worship a different god to Israel," Malak said. "And Chemosh rewards us with things such as rain in return for our sacrifices."

Ruth thought about this. "Then why doesn't Israel's God give them rain?"

Malak shrugged. "I don't know. Maybe it's because they only sacrifice animals. Who knows. Although in this drought, I doubt they have anything alive left to sacrifice." He scratched at his beard. "I have heard that their god did ask for a child sacrifice in the past. One of their ancestors was asked to do it. But as far as I know, they only sacrifice animals now."

Ruth stared into the open pastures, tossing a question around in her mind that had nagged her since the night in the village. A question she wasn't sure she was ready to hear the answer to. Her heartbeat increased as she stared at the sandal straps on her feet.

"Did *I* have any sisters or brothers?" Ruth asked, her tongue tying in knots as she tried to speak past the emotions which threatened to spill out. "That you used for blessings?"

"Oh, Ruth," Malak said, placing his arm around her shoulders and pulling her close. "No, you are our only child. And we would never do such a thing."

A huge weight lifted from her heart as she laid her head on his shoulder.

"Do you know how many babies Ima has delivered that were offered to Chemosh afterwards?" Malak asked.

Ruth shook her head.

Malak ran his hand through his hair. "It's more than she can count."

"Then why does she do it?" Ruth asked. "I couldn't bear helping new life into the world if I knew its only purpose was to die."

Malak exhaled. "You'll understand one day," he said. "That's the thing about life; there are always difficult decisions. Hurt or help. Fight or run. Go or stay. Ima chose to deliver babies so that in the short moments after birth she has a chance to convince parents how precious and irreplaceable their child is. Hoping to change their minds." He pushed loose strands of Ruth's hair out of his face as the breeze blew them against him. "It's not without risk," he said. "If anyone reported her to the prophets of Chemosh, they would rip her apart."

Ruth swallowed as this new realisation of her ima sunk in.

Malak turned and hauled the bucket up from the well again. "There is something else you need to know," he said. "About your birth."

"What is it?"

"Ima will tell you," Malak replied, pulling the newly filled bucket towards his chest. "When she is ready."

....

"Oh Ruth, my life is so much more than I could ever have imagined!"

Ruth smiled. It was hard to miss the happiness that was forever sketched across Orpah's face. In all their childhood years together, Ruth had never seen Orpah this joyful. The tension that previously surrounded Orpah's essence had left, and her complexion had changed, become healthier, as the time she spent in her ima's home became a distant memory.

"I know," Ruth said as she reached across the table and held her friend's hand.

"You should visit more often," Orpah said.

"In this Hebrew house?" Ruth asked. "You can always visit *me* now you live closer."

"Ruth," Orpah laughed. "Spend some time with Mahlon. He needs a wife, and you need a husband."

Ruth smirked and flicked a few long curls over her shoulder. "You sound like my abba."

Orpah smiled. "Would it be that bad to be related to me finally?"

The floor rustled above them as Naomi climbed down the ladder, one staggered step after the other, from the sleeping quarters. She held her back and groaned as her feet touched the ground.

"More talk of marriage?" Naomi asked, reaching for the staff which leant against the wall.

The temperature rose in Ruth's cheeks. "No marriage," she said, shaking her head. "I've passed my twentieth summer. I'm basically an old maid."

Naomi leant on the staff and stepped towards them as an all-knowing smile spread across her face. She hummed a Hebrew tune, hobbling over to place a frail hand over Orpah's abdomen. She muttered something before moving outside.

"What was that?" Ruth asked, motioning to Orpah's stomach once Naomi was out of earshot.

"I desperately want a baby," Orpah replied. "Chilion and I have been wed for over a year now, but I'm still not with child." She sat back and rubbed her eyes. "I'm making swaddling now, hoping that will get me pregnant."

Ruth raised her eyebrows. "That's not how …"

"No, I know," Orpah laughed as her cheeks reddened. "I know something is blocking a child from growing inside me. One of my cousins pretended she was pregnant, started the whole process of preparing clothes and swaddling, and it happened."

"Sometimes it takes time," Ruth said, giving Orpah's hand a squeeze. "I'm sure you'll have one growing inside you in no time."

Orpah nodded with a smile. "I know, you're right," she said. "El Shaddai has blessed me in many other ways. I'm sure the God of Israel will bless me with a child."

Ruth's eyes narrowed. She released Orpah's hand, unsure of this new development. This wasn't the Orpah she knew. "What's this about Hebrew gods and blessings?"

Orpah shook her head with a grin. "I knew you would be like this!" She sat up straight, her face solemn. "I've taken on the Hebrew god as my own, and I have to tell you, it –"

Ruth stuck her fingers in her ears to block Orpah's words.

Orpah giggled and reached over to pull Ruth's hands down. "Oh, stop it! You're acting like a child."

Ruth surveyed her friend, her face serious. "I cannot believe you've converted." she said. "I don't even know what to say."

Orpah glanced around the room, then leant across the table, closer to Ruth. "I'm not *actually* converted," she said, her voice low. "I put on this facade because I love Chilion so much, and he does worry what his ima thinks of me. For now, I have become a blessed Hebrew. Please don't say a word to Chilion."

Ruth chuckled. "I think you've lost your mind," she said. "But my friend you shall remain. Even if you are a fraudulent blessed Hebrew!"

....

"Come downstairs Ruth!" Cajsa bellowed.

Ruth rolled onto her stomach and smothered her face in the pillow. She had no intention of leaving the warm and welcoming sanctuary of her own bed. It was too early. And the last day of the week. The day she was not required to do any farm work. *What could you possibly want right now, Ima?*

"Ruth!"

Ruth groaned loudly, determined Cajsa would hear her disgust and protest from downstairs. She raised her head, hands still tightly gripping the pillow. "What do you want?" she yelled back.

"Please come downstairs," Cajsa shouted.

With more drama than was necessary, Ruth pulled herself out of bed. She fumbled with her robe, irritability rising as her arms refused to go where they were supposed to. She then stormed to the stairs, landing heavily on each step to the ground floor, displaying her frustration. With the finest glare she could muster, she turned the corner, preparing to face her nagging ima.

Mahlon stood by the front door.

Heat rose in Ruth's cheeks as she contemplated retreating up the stairs, but the mockery on Mahlon's face fed her determination to stand her ground.

She shrugged him off. "Come for breakfast, have you?" she asked, raising an eyebrow as she walked past him, barefoot, towards the kitchen, tugging her robe more tightly around her.

Mahlon glanced at the floor and fiddled with the fibrous bracelet on his wrist.

"Ruth!" Cajsa demanded, as she followed her daughter into the kitchen. "Where are you going?"

Ruth held her hands up in defence, shaking her head. "I was only joking." She sat down at the table and reached for a slice of freshly baked bread.

Cajsa continued to glare at her.

Ruth shot her ima a look of confusion. "What?" she whispered.

Cajsa held an open hand in the direction of Mahlon.

Ruth rolled her eyes. "Come and join us, Mahlon," she called out.

Cajsa exhaled slowly and moved aside for Mahlon to enter.

Ruth pointed to an empty stool opposite her. "You can sit there if you want."

As Mahlon sat down, Ruth peered up from under her eyelashes to survey the stranger in their house. She hadn't seen much of him before. He was never home at the Hebrew house when she visited.

His appearance was dark and brooding. Shoulder length hair of chocolate brown grew from his head, and a short beard surrounded his tanned olive skin. Not a cheerful countenance, but in this proximity, Ruth decided he was brutishly handsome, and appeared younger than the age her abba had told her.

His eyes met Ruth's intense stare. She immediately turned her head, hoping he didn't see the blush that had spread across her cheeks. She hadn't meant to analyse him so obviously and was unsure of the small tugs of attraction inside her.

Cajsa leant on the table, focussing her attention on Mahlon. "We have goats' milk, bread, cooked grain …"

"I don't feel great, Ima," Ruth said, standing. The stool fell over behind her, landing on the dirt floor with a thud. "I think I'll go outside for a walk to clear my head."

Before Cajsa could protest, Ruth righted the stool and grabbed her cloak before hurrying out the door.

Outside, Ruth fanned her face with her hands and exhaled slowly. She could hear the others talking inside.

"Thank you, Ima Cajsa," Mahlon said. "But I have already eaten."

Ruth's face wrinkled in disgust. "Ima Cajsa?" she whispered to herself. After strapping sandals on her feet, she stepped towards the path, beginning the trek to her sanctuary.

....

The rays of morning sun warmed her face, and the breeze teased Ruth's curls as they swirled down her back, bouncing as she walked.

The fragrance of the moist ground elevated her spirits. She inhaled deeply, connecting to the earth again as the controlling expectations around her peeled off, leaving her light and free.

She hadn't walked far when she sensed the presence of another and turned to find Mahlon thirty cubits behind her.

Of course it is you.

"What are you doing?" she asked, continuing to walk up the path.

"I thought that was obvious," Mahlon shrugged, his breath laboured. "I'm following you."

Ruth increased her speed. She knew this route, knew the effort it required. Maybe he'd pass out soon, leaving her to continue in peace.

"How could I not follow you?" Mahlon said. "Your beauty leaves me breathless."

"That's not my beauty," Ruth replied. "But your lack of physical fitness."

Mahlon laughed and ran to catch up to her side. His face became serious. "Would you allow me to see you regularly?" he asked, sucking in mouthfuls of air as he slowed down.

"Is this my parents' idea?" Ruth asked, stopping to face him. "Or your ima's?"

"Why couldn't it be *my* idea?" Mahlon replied, laughing as he bent over, placing his hands on his knees.

"What would be in it for me?" Ruth asked. "My family has an abundance of wealth. I would become poor if I wed you."

Mahlon stood up straight and stretched his back. "I admit, I have nothing *here* in Moab," he said. "But I will inherit once we return to Beit-Lechem."

"An inheritance which is?"

Marrying into a lower class didn't concern Ruth. Malak would provide, no matter where she ended up. But she was curious to hear what this Hebrew imagined he possessed that would be even remotely enticing.

"A large house," Mahlon said, stepping closer. "Enough pasture to fill with fifteen homers of barley seed." He moved closer. "Respect amongst the people." Another step. His face was inches from her own. "Would that tempt you, Ruth?"

Ruth peered into his eyes, straining to keep the muscles in her jaw tight, but she couldn't hold it. Laughter poured from her lips. "I'm about as tempted to inherit famine riddled farmland as I am to go fishing in the Dead Sea."

Mahlon's eyes narrowed as he let out a sigh of defeat. "Was worth a try," he said, as he turned to head back down the hill.

Ruth bit her lip and cleared her throat, watching Mahlon's back. Something stirred in her mind. *I'm twenty years of age now … maybe this is the last offer I'll ever get.*

"Fine," she called out, not believing the words as they left her mouth. "Visit me whenever you wish."

Mahlon turned around and smiled, before bowing low to the ground.

Ruth ran her hand through her hair. Her fingers caught a knot, and she cursed in frustration.

What am I thinking? A Hebrew boy?

....

"You can't tell anyone about this place," Ruth said. She lay beside Mahlon, high in the hills, overlooking the sea. "If you do tell anyone, this thing between us will be over."

In the weeks since Mahlon had asked to see her, Ruth's life had completely changed. He would visit almost every day and surprise her with gifts. He made her feel like the only woman on earth. Her heart melted every time she spied him approaching her home. If this is what love was, then she never wanted it to end.

Mahlon laughed. "Who am I going to tell?" He tickled her nose with a tip of wheat.

Ruth pushed his hand away and rubbed her face. "Tell me about this god of yours."

"Is that what you want to know?" Mahlon asked, rolling onto his side to face her. "Wouldn't you rather spend our time getting to know *me* better?"

"I'm only curious," Ruth replied. "Orpah appears to be all wrapped up in it." She knew the depth of Orpah's commitment but kept that secret from Mahlon.

"Fine," Mahlon said. He propped his head up with his hand. "What do you want to know?"

Ruth stared up into the blue sky and opened her arms wide into the air. "I want to know everything."

Mahlon twirled a stalk of wheat between his fingers. "El Shaddai *is* everything. He was, he is, and he is going to be."

Ruth snorted. "That makes no sense."

"That's because you're trying to grasp the reality of a supreme being in the strength of your limited mind." Mahlon replied, poking her forehead.

"Because I have a woman's mind?"

Mahlon laughed. "That'll do it."

Ruth pushed his shoulder, knocking him onto his back.

"I'm joking!" Mahlon said. "None of our minds can comprehend anything about the creator. Can we talk about you now, and your beautiful face." He reached out and touched her chin.

"Why Israel?" Ruth said, brushing his hand away. "What made your god pick Israel over other nations?"

"Does it matter?" Mahlon replied. "All you need to know is that we are a special, chosen people."

"So, what's your god going to think about you chasing after a foreign woman?" Ruth asked, poking him in the ribs.

"I'm happy to risk it," Mahlon said. "Besides, Israelite women are in short supply in Moab, so I doubt El Shaddai will mind." He chuckled as he saw the frown on her face. "Don't worry," he said. "If I married you, you wouldn't be a Moabite anymore. You'd be part of Israel."

Ruth thought about it for a minute.

"What about the famine?" she asked. "If Israel is so blessed, why is your god withholding the rain?"

"Who knows," he replied, tucking his hands behind his head. "Probably one of those things El Shaddai does to see if we will still worship."

Ruth watched puffy clouds slide across the blue. "What else?" she asked.

Mahlon shrugged. "I can't tell you about our whole history in a day," he replied. "But the short story is our ancestor Avraham was told by El Shaddai to leave his homeland. His descendants became slaves of Egypt. Moshe convinced Pharaoh to let the Israelites leave. They crossed the Red Sea and escaped into the wilderness." Mahlon scratched his beard. "Eventually they arrived in these surrounding lands, and, one by one, the cities which inhabited this land were destroyed."

"Seems barbaric," Ruth said. "For a god who is supposed to be different."

"Who are we to question," Mahlon replied.

"I don't know," Ruth said. "*Who are we to question* seems like a convenient line to use when you don't know the answer."

The surrounding wheat swayed as the breeze pushed through the tops. Ruth reached out her hand to touch them. She had convinced herself that gods were fear inducing stories that were told to children. Beliefs that followed them into adulthood to pass on to their own children. An eternal cycle of fear. What made the god of Israel any different?

"Am I boring you?" Mahlon asked.

Ruth smiled. "No. I was just thinking."

He reached across and placed his hand over Ruth's, entwining his fingers with hers.

"Will you marry me?" he asked. The muscles in his jaw tensed. Creases lined his forehead.

Ruth stiffened. "What … now?" she asked. Her mouth became dry.

Mahlon chuckled and caressed her cheek with the back of his hand. "No, not right this second," he said. "But how about soon?"

A million thoughts rushed into Ruth's mind. She sat up and stretched her arms in front of herself. Her affection for Mahlon had grown during their time together, but something felt odd. Rushed. And what if the famine in Israel ended? Would she have to move to Israel, away from her family, her people, her life? She glanced at Mahlon. His playful brown eyes teased her.

Why is he perfect? Maybe that's my answer.

Mahlon picked loose chaff from her hair. "I'll talk to your abba when we get back."

Ruth laid her hand on his arm. "Let me think about it," she said.

"What's there to think about?" Mahlon asked. He stood and pulled Ruth to her feet and into his strong arms. "We are made for each other."

Ruth laughed. "I will give you my answer in the morning."

....

Ruth lay on her back, staring up at the unfamiliar thatch ceiling which spread out above her. The first hints of dawn poked through the cracks in the eaves as she mulled over the previous day's events.

Her marriage to Mahlon had been beautiful, taking place amongst the aromatic olive trees, heavy with fruit, which grew on her parent's farm. A breeze from the sea below swirled around the trees, light and easy.

Ruth had made herself a long tunic from soft white linen. It flowed effortlessly around her slender legs as she walked. A crown of yellow wildflowers and black berries sat atop her hair, which held in place a long veil, lined with white beads from the land of Edom.

Malak had showered her with Egyptian jewellery; intricate designs of gemstone studded gold. Cajsa disapproved of the indulgence.

"We only get to do this once," Malak had laughed.

Ruth smiled as she continued to stare at the ceiling, remembering the admiration on Mahlon's face as he first caught sight of her in her wedding garments and adornments.

"You're beautiful," he had whispered in her ear, pulling her close. In that moment, she felt as though the joy in her heart might burst through her chest. Mahlon couldn't keep his eyes off her all day, and into the night, throughout their feast and dancing under the lanterns in the trees. Ruth couldn't remember a happier time in her life.

But now, in the early hours of the next morning, something felt off.

The consummation of their marriage had been awkward and uncomfortable, with nothing but a loose cloth separating them from the other sleeping occupants of Naomi's second floor. Afterwards, Mahlon had rolled onto his side, his back to Ruth, without a single word. No kiss or touch of affection.

In the few hours since, Ruth had been unable to sleep. *Had I not been wife enough for him?*

The idea of rising early, to walk and clear her head, crossed her mind several times, but fear of waking the others prevented her.

She lay on her back, unsure of what to do.

Ima, you could've given me some instruction. Anything would have been nice.

She sensed Mahlon move beside her and nestled herself into his back, wrapping her arm over his waist as she breathed in the smell of his skin.

Mahlon pushed her arm off his side, cursing.

"What's wrong?" Ruth whispered.

Mahlon rolled over, his face dark with fury. Pain shot through Ruth's jaw as he grabbed her chin between his thumb and fingers.

"Stop," Ruth pleaded, struggling to pull out of his grip. "You're hurting me!"

Mahlon refused to let go, bringing his face close to hers. "Shut. Up," he whispered.

The heat of his breath washed across Ruth's face as he glanced around, checking to see if anyone had stirred. Soft snoring filled the top floor.

"I wasted the whole day yesterday keeping you happy," Mahlon said, his voice barely audible. "Now it's your turn. Leave me alone so I can sleep." He released her chin, then rolled away from her, pulling the sheet over his shoulder. Within minutes, he was snoring.

Ruth lay on her back, paralysed. Panic surged through her body.

As her husband's snoring became louder, she found the strength to shuffle onto her side and pull her knees up into her arms.

He's tired. I shouldn't have disturbed him. Tomorrow will be better.

....

Orpah sat behind Ruth, her hands deep in Ruth's hair as she braided the red curls outside in the sun's warmth.

"I honestly thought you'd be deliriously happy married to Mahlon," Orpah said. "He's such a nice man. But you never smile at him anymore." A grin formed on her lips. "Are you that hard to please?" she teased.

Ruth's face crumpled as an ache seared through her soul. Stinging tears blurred her vision, but she blinked them back before Orpah had a chance to notice. The bruises on her back were easily hidden under a robe, but tears on her face would reveal the truth.

So many times, in the past four months, Ruth had been tempted to divulge to Orpah the treatment she had experienced at the hands of Mahlon. But if Orpah, or even Naomi, knew the truth, Mahlon's rage would likely end her.

Ruth inhaled deeply and cleared her throat, taking a moment to calm her thoughts. "I *am* happy," she said, fiddling with the hem of her robe. Another thought occurred to her. "You haven't said anything about your suspicion of my unhappiness to Chilion have you?"

Orpah shrugged, continuing to pull strands of Ruth's hair to the middle. "We talk about everything, so yes," she said. "But Chilion was the one who was concerned. I thought you were missing your parents, but *he* thinks you're displeased with your match."

Ruth's heart sank as she imagined her life dissolving around her.

Have I been that careless? What if Chilion tells Mahlon?

There had been no beatings during the first weeks of their marriage, only verbal disdain. He reminded her that she was a dirty heathen, who would never reach the status of even the lowliest of Hebrew damsels. How useless she was as a wife. There were the false accusations of promiscuity and being told to cover up her skin. Then suddenly, mixed between the insults, he would surprise her with overflowing love and kindness, making her believe the real Mahlon was back to stay and perhaps it wasn't all that bad.

But a month after their wedding, Mahlon tripped over Ruth's leg as he stepped out of bed, and fell down the ladder, spraining his ankle. Nobody had been home at the time, and Mahlon beat Ruth in retaliation so badly she could barely walk.

There had been much concern when each member of the family had assessed the damage to Ruth's face. Mahlon hovered nearby, relaying the dramatic story of her fall from a rocky ledge whilst picking wildflowers.

"How silly is my beauty," he'd said, tenderly kissing Ruth on the forehead. "Especially since she's grown up in this area and knows the dangers."

They accepted his loving truth, whilst all Ruth could see was the threat in his eyes not to speak a word.

From then, his lust to inflict pain on her continued, although he was careful not to hit her face again, and only when nobody else was around.

Ruth became a shadow of the woman she once was. Spending most of her waking moments trying to stay two steps ahead of Mahlon's moods to avoid the pain of his fists.

"Here's another thought," Orpah said, tugging on Ruth's hair. "Since you won't tell me what is bothering you, why don't you pray about it?"

Ruth stared into the distance as her eyes glazed over. Her body completely numb, seeing no way out of the darkness her life had become.

"Pray to who, Orpah?" she murmured. "There's nobody out there."

BOAZ

ISRAEL – 1192 BC

Enosh shifted uncomfortably on his feet, unable to raise his eyes to meet his master's intense gaze.

Boaz waved a fly from his nose. "What's going on?" he asked, walking towards Enosh under the shade of the pillared facade in the courtyard entrance. He pulled up a stool and sat, resting his knee as he watched his scrawny overseer squirm in front of him. "This is the second time in two years you've fired workers without my authority. The first time I heard from Devorah and this time I hear it from people in the city."

Enosh pulled at the wiry grey beard on his chin and glanced at Boaz, squinting under the reflection of the bright sun against the sandstone wall. "We are running out of grain to pay the workers," he said, his voice raspy. "We had to let some go." He wiped perspiration from his brow.

Boaz studied his old overseer. Fifteen years older than himself, Enosh's skin hadn't fared well in the sun. Rough, uneven lines marked his face, and broken capillaries spread over his large nose and cheeks.

"How will they feed their families now?" Boaz asked. He tapped the stool beside him, signalling Enosh to sit. "They will be on the street begging before the week is finished."

Enosh bowed his head and sat beside Boaz. "With respect, your own family would have ended up on the street if we had kept those labourers on the farm."

"Ah, *my* family," Boaz smirked. He placed his hand on Enosh's thin shoulder. "There are ways around these issues," he said, giving the overseer a squeeze. "But you need to come to me, otherwise I can't fix them."

Enosh raised his head, shame in his eyes. "How can you possibly afford to keep them on the farm?"

"I have *things* I can trade in other lands for grain," Boaz replied. "Jewels, fine apparel. Belongings I won't be taking with me after I die."

"Then you will no longer be rich," Enosh said, scratching his beard.

Boaz smiled. "That depends on what you think rich is, my friend."

Enosh raised his eyebrows. "Do not think badly of me," he said. "But these workers are the lowest of the low. Do not sell your fine things. They are precious to you. The labourers will find work elsewhere, I am sure."

"What type of steward would I be," Boaz said. "If I didn't use the blessings I have been given to care for those in my power to help."

Enosh tilted his head, eyes narrowed.

Boaz laughed. "I'm saying I will provide for my labourers, yourself included, until I have nothing left to trade," he said. "Even if it means I end up with nothing!"

Enosh wriggled on the stool. He pulled off his old hat to scratch at the thinning hair on his scalp.

"What are you waiting for?" Boaz asked, as he stood. "Go. Take my horse if you must and tell my labourers to come back!"

Boaz turned to see Shoshanna approaching. He lowered the beehive cover in his hand. "Shalom Shoshanna."

"Shalom Boaz."

He watched the young woman draw near. "When did you arrive back in Bet-Lechem?" he asked, returning his gaze to the beehive. "Did you come with Dalia?"

There was something different about Shoshanna. It had been two years since Boaz last saw her, and he'd been thankful, assuming Dalia had given up on that match.

He glanced up again and realised what the difference was. He'd seen a few of the wealthier Hebrew women doing it. A mud of some sort, rubbed onto the skin of their faces. Devorah had been more than happy to tell him all about it when he asked.

Boaz didn't see the appeal or understand the finer details of this new beauty development. All he saw was the majority of Israel facing starvation, their faces filthy from the dust as they searched for food. Then there was the small minority of Israel, who had enough surplus money to purchase a special dirt to cover their faces deliberately.

"You shouldn't come any closer," Boaz told Shoshanna. "There aren't many bees left, but the ones that are still alive are quite feisty."

Shoshanna stopped in her stride, her eyes narrowing. "Is that what those clay tubes on the ground are?"

"Beehives," Boaz nodded. "The bees build their comb inside. One end is sealed off, and this end …" he said holding up the cover, "… is removed to check the hive." He watched Shoshanna surveyed the rows of long cylinder pots.

"How do the bees get in and out?"

Boaz pointed to the end of the cylinders. "There's a small hole at the back."

"Ah," Shoshanna said, fiddling with her hair. "I didn't know we still had honey in Israel."

"There's not as much as there was before," Boaz said. He pushed the cover back into place on the open hive. "Out of all these hives, only two have bees in them."

"That's sad," Shoshanna replied unconvincingly.

Boaz's eyes rested on the young woman, wondering if there was more depth to her soul than she was showing. There was no denying she was attractive, and he pondered if his aunty had been right to introduce the two of them after all. He was surprised Shoshanna hadn't been snatched up in the years since he'd seen her. There would be fewer opportunities presenting themselves the older he grew, and the more Boaz thought about it, the more he realised he was in denial about his age.

"I'm sorry about the last time you were here," he said, walking towards Shoshanna. He removed a veiled hat from his head. "I shouldn't have said what I did."

Shoshanna smiled and reached out for his hand as he approached. "It wasn't your fault," she said. "I think something I ate turned foul."

Boaz hesitantly let her take his rough hand in her own. Shoshanna was the boldest woman Dalia had ever brought to meet him and a sudden fear gripped his stomach. He withdrew his hand. "I'm sorry."

Shoshanna's lips dropped into a pout.

"I have work to do," Boaz said as he turned to walk off. He stopped after a few steps and turned to face her again. "I don't know what my aunt Dalia has put in your head," he said. "But I don't think this will work."

"What do you mean?" Shoshanna asked, catching up to him. "I enjoy money and you have a lot of it. It's as if El Shaddai arranged this match."

Boaz's heart sank as the seriousness in her voice confirmed what he feared. "We're two different people," he said. "Yes, I am rich, but I *have* riches because I don't try to hold on to them."

"See, we're perfect," Shoshanna gushed. "I'm more than happy to offload some riches for you."

Boaz groaned. "You don't see people the way I do. To you people are dispensable, a means to an end. To me they are vessels, each holding a portion of the untouchable spirit of life within them."

"I had heard you give food away for nothing," Shoshanna shrugged. "I won't mind if you give a small amount away."

Boaz laughed nervously and shook his head. "It wouldn't work."

"Should I leave for home then?"

"If that's what you desire," Boaz replied. "Or you are welcome to stay and spend more time with Devorah."

Shoshanna crossed her arms. "I can't stand Devorah."

"That's fine, decide whatever you want to do. But this –" Boaz said, signalling at the air between them. "– this is not going to work."

"It's a shame you prefer the company of people below your rank more than the ones in your own high standing." She ran her eyes up and down his body, clicking her tongue. "Such a waste."

Boaz gazed at his feet, attempting to hide a smirk. *Dodged a spear.*

"Come with me," he said, sensing the air lighten between them. "I want to show you something."

They walked past the main living quarters and towards the store house. Inside were sacks of grain, leaning against the wall in the far corner.

Boaz walked forward and grabbed a full sack, swinging it over his shoulder and onto his back. "Take one," he told Shoshanna, who had followed him in. "They won't be too heavy for a young woman like you."

Shoshanna's face flushed. "Do I look like a servant?" She waved him off and walked back through the store house doorway.

"Fine," Boaz muttered. He grabbed another sack with his free hand. Pain shot through his knee, but he ignored it, knowing it would be momentary. He threw the sacks onto a small timber cart that had been left outside the store house. The sacks landed with a thud, sending billows of dust into the air. Boaz ducked back into the store house and grabbed two more sacks to add to the cart.

"Now we head outside," Boaz said, as he wrestled the cart in the direction of the front gate.

Shoshanna trudged behind him as he pushed the cart towards the entrance of the courtyard. They stopped at the edge of the open gates and waited in the cool of the shade. Boaz wiped sweat from his face as he caught his breath. "We're not there yet," he said, pointing to the road that passed his farm. "We'll wait by the old cypress trees over there."

After they reached the entrance to the farm, Boaz groaned, letting the cart come to a standstill.

"Now what?" Shoshanna asked. She leant against the cart and pushed bothersome loose strands of hair from her mud-covered face.

Boaz searched the sky for the sun, his eyes squinting under the glare. "Going by the angle of the sunlight, they should be here any time now."

"They?" Shoshanna asked.

"They," Boaz repeated, pointing into the distance.

Just as he predicted, a person appeared; a speck on the road further down the hill; their silhouette dancing on the road under the heat of the day. Then another individual, and another, until about fifty people advanced towards them.

As they drew closer, Boaz observed Shoshanna, hoping to see an ounce of humanity.

"They're beggars," Shoshanna gasped, raising a hand to her mouth. "We're going to be attacked."

Boaz laughed. "Stop being dramatic. The little energy they have, they are using to walk up here to get food. They're not going to waste any energy attacking."

As the people approached, Boaz took a knife from his garment and sliced open a sack of grain.

The heavy aroma of unwashed men and women flowed up the hill, surrounding them in a layer of stench. Their clothes were in tatters, having lost all colour and shape from years of wear.

Boaz's eyes narrowed as Shoshanna took a few steps back, her hand tightly over her nose.

"Now I know why you're running out of grain," she said, before storming back towards the house.

The muscles in Boaz's jaw clenched as he watched her leave. This was one sight he was sure would light a flame of compassion in Shoshanna's heart. It had in his own so many years ago.

An older man, who led the crowd, reached him and stepped into the shade, exhaling loudly.

Boaz placed a hand on his shoulder. "Rest here weary man."

The old man smiled, revealing a mouth of mostly gums. "El Shaddai bless you, Boaz." His frail hand shook as he lowered his small bag to be filled with grain.

One by one, each impoverished man, woman and child filed past and were given all the grain they could carry.

Boaz watched them trudge back down the hill; his heart heavy with the suffering they carried. Many of them had owned farms before the famine hit. Now they, like the poor of Beit-Lechem, lined up for his grain.

Out of the corner of his eye Boaz saw one of his servants running towards him.

"It's your ima, Boaz," the servant said. "Come quickly."

....

"You need to eat, Nephew," Dalia said, running a hand over Boaz's tangled hair.

A small sigh left her lips as she laid a plate of bread and meat on the table between his arms. She sat down beside him. "The servants told me you've been turning back every meal they bring you. Is this true?"

Billowing white linen, which hung loosely over the open window in his bedroom, blew inwards into the room, allowing warm air from outside to sneak in.

"I'm not sure I can keep going," Boaz said, staring into his aunt's eyes. "Not with Ima gone. I have been stripped of my thirst for life." The hole in his chest grew as renewed grief clutched his heart. "I thought caring for the lost and weak would distract me, but I can't bear it."

Dalia squeezed his hand. "It will get easier," she said, a small shake audible in her voice. "When I lost *my* ima, I held the same pain. But time will heal the wound. You'll see."

Boaz shrugged. "It's been two months since she died, and I see no light on the horizon."

Dalia sighed. "You do know your ima had power in her death, don't you?"

"What do you mean?" Boaz asked.

"I went into Beit-Lechem yesterday," Dalia replied. "The news of Rahab's death has spread through Israel."

"How?"

"It must be the trade routes," Dalia said. "But it has reignited the memories of Jericho."

"What do you mean?" Boaz asked, scratching his chin.

"Whilst you've been here, hiding in your grief," Dalia said. "The whole nation has been grieving with you. Fasting, heaping ashes on their heads; weeping in repentance to a god they have forgotten, and the woman whose death has reminded them. Your ima."

Boaz stared out the window as this new information sunk in.

Dalia peered across him at the sheets of papyrus beside his hand. "What are you writing," she asked, standing to reach for one.

Boaz's awareness returned to the room. "The meditations of my mind."

Dalia scanned the front, then the back, nodding in satisfaction. "May I read it aloud?"

Boaz shrugged, not caring what she did with it. He had been private with his writings before now, but that was before his ima had passed. Now, he wasn't sure if he cared about anything.

"I have searched the land for you," Dalia read. *"But you hide. My pain is bare before you, yet you continue to ignore my cries. Have you forgotten me? Am I as distasteful to you as the people who sneer at me?"*

Dalia stopped. "Who is sneering at you? It's not Devorah, is it?"

A crooked smile crossed his lips as Boaz shook his head and reached to take the papyrus from her. "No, it's not," he said. "You don't need to read the whole lot."

Dalia held it out of his reach. "I want to finish it. Can I?"

Boaz groaned, resting his head in his hands.

"They sneer at me through false smiles. In light pretending to be one thing; in darkness they are another. They desire not a pure heart, the sphere of encompassing love, but a heart that will worship only the sorrow they bring to others."

Dalia glanced at Boaz. "And those are more?" she asked, pointing to the small pile.

Boaz nodded. "Every thought I have somehow makes it onto the papyrus."

"I never knew you *felt* so ... deeply," Dalia said, laying the papyrus on the table. She tapped it with her finger. "You have a deep and beautiful soul under that hard shell you've built around yourself." She patted his shoulder with affection. "Maybe it's time to take the shell off."

The curtain beside them stopped billowing and dropped quietly against the sill. Boaz pricked up his ears but couldn't hear anything, other than the faint murmuring of servants below. An odd sensation of calm settled in the bedroom.

Dalia's nostrils flared. "Can you smell that?"

Boaz watched as the soft curtains moved again, before they were pulled out of the window, sucked into the breeze as it changed direction. They flapped around, trying to get loose from the inside.

Boaz glanced at his aunt. "I *can* smell it!" He pushed the stool back and raced for the door. Pain seared through his knee with every stride down the stairs, but he didn't care. He remembered that smell from long ago. Nothing would stop him heading outside.

The courtyard darkened under an eerie shadow as Boaz stumbled outside onto the gritty dirt. He crossed his arms tightly, shivering as the temperature drop rapidly.

A large cloud mass towered above them, ominous in appearance. A head of purest white, glistening under the sun's rays, with a belly full of dark shadows. The hairs on Boaz's skin stood on end, as energy travelling through the air triggered cells in his body.

A thick wall of rain moved towards them, falling from the clouds above. It devoured one thirsty farm after the other, then hid them from view as it advanced over Beit-Lechem.

Boaz laughed hysterically, pounding his fists at the sky. "The drought has broken!" he hollered as he fell to his knees. Tears poured from his eyes; years of pent-up anxiety released. "Oh, how the creator listens!" He bowed himself to the ground, his forehead hard against the dust, as he stretched out his arms.

"Look at it!" Dalia screamed out from Boaz's window above, her hands outstretched to the skies. "Oh, I wish Gad were here!"

Servants rushed outside; frenzied cries and praises sprang from their lungs as they leapt around the courtyard, delirious with excitement.

A smile crossed Devorah's face as she stood by the pillars of the house, her hand resting against the cool sandstone. The wind picked up, whipping the long flowing fabric of her tunic around her legs.

Within minutes heavy droplets of water arrived, pounding the surrounding ground, hammering off the roofs and creating new rivers across the hilly farmland. Echoing hollers of happiness echoed up from the fields below them, as Boaz's drenched labourers hurried towards the house.

"Come inside Boaz!" Dalia called out. "This is no ordinary storm. There's ice coming."

Lightening whipped across the sky and thunder cracked through the air, but Boaz stayed where he was, bowed low to the ground, muddied water splashing against him. The cold stung his skin, but he didn't move, wanting to live this moment to the fullest. He wouldn't retreat, even if the sky did release its ice.

ORPAH

MOAB – 1186 BC

The lingering aroma of barley bread, beans and garlic hung in the air as Orpah removed the last dirty plate from the table. Her body worked on the task at hand, but her eyes focused on Ruth.

Ruth's blank stare fixated on the hardened dirt floor at her feet, as if watching something just below the surface. Mahlon sat beside her at the table but appeared not to notice; his conversation with Chilion consuming his attention. Between the loose waves of red hair, Ruth's thin face was void of expression, her mind somewhere in the distance. Dark circles lined the soft skin under her eyes.

Orpah's gaze dropped from Ruth's face to her shoulders, and she swallowed, realising the bones had become visible under her skin. *It was no wonder*, she thought, as tonight as many other nights before, Ruth had barely eaten anything for supper.

Tell me what is wrong, Ruth. Are you barren too? Orpah had made peace with a childless future. Choosing to live her time on earth loving the man who made her whole, instead of wishing for something she would never have.

After placing the used plate on the dirty pile, Orpah wiped her hands against her apron, continuing to watch her friend, wishing Ruth could experience the same contentment she had. *Perhaps you cannot find peace without children, Ruth?*

For Orpah, the pain of her past had mostly disappeared in the ten years she'd been married. Chilion knew what she'd been through. He had seen the scars over her body during their wedding night. The shock in his eyes had filled her with shame. But he had pulled her close and kissed away the trauma and sorrow; loved her and protected her, refusing to let her face the torments again. In all her years, Orpah had never known such a peace existed.

If I've only known happiness since joining this family Ruth, what are you hiding?

Naomi hit a staff against the table, pulling Orpah from her thoughts.

Ruth's presence returned to the room and her lips moved into a faint smile as she glanced up and noticed the concern on Orpah's face.

"It is time to journey back to Israel," Naomi said, swivelling the staff in her hand.

"For what purpose?" Mahlon asked, leaning back on his stool. "As far as we know the famine is still raging. Just because the drought is over doesn't mean there's food. It's not worth the effort."

"I can't explain it," Naomi replied. She closed her eyes and tapped a wrinkled finger against her chest. "But something is tugging at my heart, telling me it is time to go home. I've even heard people say the rains returned as far back as six years ago."

Orpah glanced at Chilion. His eyes were on her. A smile crossed her lips. *I don't care where we end up as long as you're there.*

A wide grin spread across Chilion's face, and he winked, causing the temperature to rise in her cheeks.

"No, we should stay here," Mahlon said, tapping his fingers on the table. "I've also heard rumours that the drought ended years ago but I don't believe Israel has recovered yet. El Shaddai promised us a land flowing with milk and honey, and Moab is where it's flowing. Israel has all the promise of an old wet nurse. Completely dried up."

"Mahlon!" Naomi said.

"It's true," Mahlon replied. "And even if Israel has had rain, I don't plan on leaving any time soon. The master of the farm I work at, this morning, promoted me to overseer."

Chilion laughed. "How did you manage that?"

Mahlon shot him a glare of disgust.

"Won't that mean you'll have to work longer hours?" Naomi asked, the lines on her forehead becoming more pronounced. "And you'll have to live on the farm?"

"It may come to that," Mahlon replied, clasping his hands together. "But I'm sure you'll all survive without me for those stretches of time."

Orpah's heart went out to Ruth, certain this new piece of information would finally break her. A jolt of panic hit her stomach as she watched a flash of relief cross Ruth's face.

What is going on!?

As the brothers commenced a conversation between themselves, Orpah seized the opportunity and signalled Ruth to follow her outside into the night air.

"What's wrong?" Ruth asked, wrapping a thin shawl around her shoulders, grimacing as loose strands of her hair caught under it.

"What do you mean, 'what's wrong?'" Orpah asked, her eyes widening. She shook her head. "Something is very wrong. You need to tell me, my friend."

"I'm fine," Ruth said, squinting in the darkness. She glanced at the doorway then back to Orpah. "I'm just tired."

"Probably because you haven't been eating much."

"The sight of food makes me nauseous sometimes."

"Are you with child?"

"No," Ruth chuckled softly.

Confusion surfaced in Orpah's mind. She surveyed Ruth's face, watching for clues. "Why aren't you displeased at Mahlon's news?"

Ruth reached out and held Orpah's hand. "He's been working late for weeks now anyway," she said. "It won't be any different."

"But you looked relieved!"

"I was relieved it wouldn't affect us, any more than it has already been."

Orpah gripped Ruth's hands tightly. "Please help me understand!" she begged. "I would be devastated if I had less time with Chilion. Tell me what's going on."

"Nothing is going on," Ruth said, her voice soft. She glanced past Orpah towards the door again.

A familiar sensation rose in Orpah's chest. An awareness that had been absent for a long time. For the last decade it had been silent, subdued by Chilion's love, and held back by the strong chains in Orpah's mind. But Ruth's reluctance to share her suffering had awakened new life into it.

Did you really think she'd confide in you? Why would she want to share her problems with a complete idiot? You've never been helpful. Useless.

Orpah shook her head in frustration, pushing her fingers hard against the sides of her forehead, silently begging the voice to leave.

"I promise there is nothing going on," Ruth said, gently pulling Orpah's hands down.

"But you weren't this way before you were married," Orpah said. She paused as her own words sunk in. "Is it Mahlon?"

"No," Ruth replied, drawing Orpah into her arms. "We have our disagreements, but I know Mahlon loves me. He tells me all the time, so I know it must be true. He's not perfect, but I know he tries. What else could a wife ask for?"

The warmth of Ruth's frail body seeped past the fabric of Orpah's tunic and against her skin.

"I'm glad you're here with me," Ruth replied. "I don't think I could ever bear to be apart from you."

A scuffing on the wooden doorstep behind them caused Orpah to turn.

Mahlon leant against the door frame, shooting her a boyish grin. "You've had her long enough now, Orpah," he said. "I hardly get to see her."

Ruth's body stiffened in Orpah's arms.

Mahlon raised his head. "It's time to retire, Ruth."

After pulling herself from Orpah's embrace, Ruth kissed her lightly on the cheek. "I'll finish discussing the garden layout tomorrow," she said loudly. "I'm sure we can find somewhere to plant those garlics."

Orpah's mind raced as she watched Mahlon lead her friend inside, his hand resting on the small of her back as she stepped over the threshold.

It must be Mahlon. But that doesn't make any sense.

He loved Ruth, doted over her, just as Ruth said.

Orpah shivered, struggling to comprehend how a person such as Mahlon had managed to strip a woman of her joy. No one would deny he was good natured, generous and funny. Maybe it wasn't Mahlon. Maybe there was something wrong with Ruth.

Not that you can help, Orpah. You can't even grow a child in your belly. Useless.

....

As the months sped past, winter visited the land of Moab briefly, then left for other lands, leaving spring wildflowers to carpet the hillsides with colour and fragrance. Down below, the Dead Sea sat quietly, a pool of aqua, sending up the occasional breeze to remind them it was still there.

"Are you going to join us?" Ruth called out to Orpah from under the towering old oak.

Orpah ran her hand through her hair, using fingers to comb out the tangles. A smile formed on her lips as she watched Ruth's insistent face. "Yes," she replied. "I'm coming."

Ruth's health had improved during Mahlon's extended absences. She had kept silent on the matter but there was no question in Orpah's mind now. Mahlon was somehow responsible for Ruth's decline.

She tucked the thoughts away as she strolled over to Ruth and Naomi and settled in the shade on the woollen blanket beside them.

Naomi stretched her neck back and groaned. "So horrible to be old," she said. "Thank goodness I have you women to keep me young."

Ruth laughed and the sweetness of it filled Orpah's heart. A sound she hadn't heard in a long time.

"What wisdom are we discussing under the great tree today?" Orpah asked.

Naomi reached out and squeezed Ruth's shoulder. "We weren't talking about it, but I've been impressed by Ruth's positivity. How truly amazing it is that she's managed to find happiness, despite her absent husband."

Orpah watched Ruth's gaze drop to the grass.

"And your health is returning," Naomi said, rubbing Ruth's arm with a weathered hand. "Doesn't she appear well Orpah?"

Ruth picked at the blades of grass under her ankles as red curls slid down, covering her face from view.

Orpah nodded, wishing to steer the conversation in another direction. "It is good to see."

"I may be old, but I have a suspicion I'll be holding a newborn before I die," Naomi said, nodding. She stretched her weak arms towards the sky. "I just know it."

Orpah's heart skipped a beat. Could it be true? Naomi had a knack for sensing things.

Enjoy your happy little moment whilst you can. You know it won't last.

"There are many other things to enjoy in life besides children," Ruth said, pulling her hair back over her shoulders.

"Rubbish," Naomi chuckled. "My intuition has been wrong before, but if one of you girls don't have a baby soon, I think I *shall* die."

Ruth leant back, resting on her elbows as she rolled her eyes behind Naomi. A smile spread across her face.

Orpah grinned, unfazed by Naomi's tactless comments. The pressure to provide Naomi with grandchildren was never-ending. But in that moment Orpah didn't care. Too sidetracked with relief that Ruth had resurfaced into the land of the living.

....

She'd slept in. Going by the sun's position in the sky she guessed it was already midday. Everyone had eaten and left, leaving dirty dishes in the pot.

The bones in her spine cracked as Orpah stretched out, leaning to the side as she yawned loudly. She stretched again to the other side, surveying the view through the open kitchen window. Her ear caught Naomi's voice from outside.

Her eyes narrowed. They weren't expecting visitors today.

Stepping lightly on the dirt floor, Orpah moved to the door, staying out of sight behind the wall. A dull pain grew in her chest as familiar vocals pushed through the walls of the house.

She hadn't spoken with her ima for ten years. Wanting to be rid of the memories of her hellish childhood, she had shut her family out shortly after she wed Chilion. It had been an easy thing to accomplish. Ima had no interest in visiting, Abba was too busy, and her siblings resented her for leaving them with all the work.

But now, the unwelcome dark cloud of her past had returned.

"Orpah!" Naomi called out.

The sun sent a warm glow over the hairs of Orpah's head as she stepped outside. A shaky exhale passed her lips.

"Shalom, Ima."

Izevel's lips tightened. "Shalom?" She turned to Naomi. "I see you've managed to turn her into a Hebrew."

Orpah wrung her hands. "Why are you here, Ima? You've never visited before."

Izevel scoffed. "Is this how you greet your ima?"

Orpah studied Izevel's face. She had aged during their years apart, but unlike Naomi who had become frailer and finer as time passed, Izevel had increased in size. It was possible she was with child again, but there was no way of telling due to her large frame.

"Don't worry. I'm not staying," Izevel said. "I know you think you rank above your own people now you've married a Hebrew."

"Ima … it's not …" Orpah shifted on her feet, uncomfortable with the power her ima held over her, even after all this time.

"But just remember you're not," Izevel said. She held up an accusing finger at her daughter. "You'll always be a Moabite."

Orpah trembled at her words, desperate to be free of their truths, but the taunts continued.

"And what are you wearing?" Izevel asked, eyeing Orpah up and down. "These robes aren't what we Moabites wear. Why so plain, so colourless?"

"That's enough," Naomi said, reaching out for Orpah's hand. She clasped it tightly. "Is there a reason why you're here Izevel?"

Izevel sniffed, disinterested. "I came to tell Orpah her abba has died."

The muscles around Orpah's ribs squeezed tight. "What?" she

whispered.

"I knew he favoured you," Izevel replied, blinking at the sky. "I thought you should know."

Orpah pulled her hand out of Naomi's. "I don't believe you."

"You can believe what you want," Izevel snapped. "He's dead. And now I have no one to care for me. I thought maybe you could move back home and help your ima. Bring your husband too."

"How did he die?" Orpah asked. Tears pricked at her eyes as her face threatened to crumple.

"Does it matter?" Izevel replied, throwing her hands in the air. "My guess is it was from a broken heart, given his favourite daughter left home and never returned."

Orpah gasped and collapsed to the ground. Her breathing laboured as cries of anguish shook her body. Her face contorted as she climbed to her feet, muttering erratically.

She needed to leave. To be anywhere but here. Without a second thought Orpah turned and ran.

Behind her, Naomi's raised voice called out. The words blurred into random sounds, overridden by the heaving gasps for air and the thumping between her ears.

The higher she climbed the rougher the terrain became. Low bushes scratched at her legs and small stones cut her bare feet as she pushed past, refusing to slow.

A stinging sear shot through her lungs as she stumbled into a small hollow in a rocky outcrop. The surface was rough but cool against her back. Her chest rose and fell rapidly as her legs gave way. As she slid down the stone wall, her tunic caught on the coarse grit, pulling threads loose.

Why did you desert your Abba? He was the one who had taught her there was light and love in this world of darkness. How she wished she had seen him one more time.

She wept, and the memories of her childhood rose to engulf her, unleashed from the vault she'd created in her mind years ago. The beatings, the starvation, the truth she wasn't enough. Wasn't worthy of love.

It's your fault Abba's dead. You broke his heart. It should have been you that died, not him.

"Be quiet!"

Orpah whimpered and slapped the sides of her head with her hands, determined to stop the voice that jeered at her.

Chilion will be better off without you.

Chilion. Guilt clutched her heart. He would begin searching for her when he returned from the farm, she knew that, but she couldn't go back. Couldn't face her ima again.

What had she been thinking, to marry Chilion? A beautiful man who deserved a wife who could give him more children than he could count. Maybe going back to her Ima was what she deserved.

Finally, you're understanding. You're worthless.

She cried again, wishing to be free of the hateful voice in her head.

....

The ground swirled beneath Orpah as she climbed to her feet. She placed a hand on the wall to steady herself. Her head throbbed and her back ached. As the scenery around her came into focus, Orpah realised the faint light touching the landscape wasn't that of dusk, but of dawn. Vague memories of a sleepless night filled with unfamiliar sounds arose in her mind. Why hadn't she returned home?

The sun had yet to rise, but the soft glow on the horizon indicated it was only a matter of minutes.

Orpah rubbed her head and groaned as the memory of her abba returned. She pushed off the stone wall and stepped outside to trudge down the slope.

She hadn't realised how far she'd travelled until she began to tire and realised there were no familiar landmarks.

Finally, the big oak came into view. Ruth stood beside it, waving her hands frantically as she jumped. Once again guilt gripped Orpah. Surely, they would be furious with her.

Ruth hitched her long robe up around her knees and ran towards Orpah, dodging rocks that squeezed out of the earth.

As she approached, Orpah collapsed into Ruth's outstretched arms.

"Oh Orpah, where have you been?" Ruth said as she sat and let Orpah's head rest on her lap. With gentle fingers she moved the knotted brown hair off Orpah's face. "I'm so sorry."

Orpah rubbed her eyes. A flow of nausea filled her stomach. "I'm sorry I didn't come home last night."

Ruth's chin trembled as she shook her head. "You have nothing to apologise for," she said, lacing her fingers in Orpah's. "I'm sorry I didn't find you in time."

"In time?" Orpah whispered. Her lips tightened as she turned away. Had Ruth known her abba was unwell and kept it from her? Why hadn't she warned her?

She is no friend of yours. And you can't blame her ... who would want you?

"It happened so fast," Ruth replied, continuing to stroke Orpah's hair. "He called for you, and I searched everywhere I could think."

Orpah paused. She stared up at Ruth, wide eyed. "What do you mean it was fast?"

"One minute there was nothing wrong with him," Ruth replied. "And the next minute there was."

Orpah sat up and grabbed her friend by the arms. "How do you know what happened to my abba?" she asked. "Where you there when he died?"

"Your abba?" Ruth's eyes narrowed, then her face softened. Her shoulders hunched forward, and she covered her face in her hands as her cries filled the air. "No, not your abba. Oh, Orpah, I'm sorry. He loved you so much." She wiped tears from her cheeks. "Till the very end you were the only person on Chilion's mind."

Orpah's eyes darted back and forth, as the truth dawned on her. She shook her head. "No ... no ... you can't ..." She gasped for air as the weight of the mountains surrounding them closed in on her. "Say it isn't true!" Her vision blurred as tremors surged through her body.

It's your fault.

RUTH

MOAB – 1185 BC

She needed to escape. Up to her mountain, where peace flowed easily. Her chest ached with sadness, and she detested it, wishing to be free of the grip it held on her heart.

Snuggling into Orpah's side, Ruth wrapped her arm over her friend, careful not to wake her. In the hours before, Orpah had wailed; her face hard against the dust as she doubled over, pounding her fists against the earth, begging Chilion to return.

Now Orpah's chest rose and fell in a slow rhythm, as exhaustion overcame her sorrow. She had begged Ruth to tell her what happened, but Naomi had shaken her head.

As far as Orpah would ever know, Chilion had passed away peacefully in his sleep. There had been no indication his health was failing and there had been no suffering. He had gone to bed and had never woken up.

Ruth kissed Orpah's arm softly as slithers of sun light poked through the cracks in the window. She would hold the truth in her heart. The truth that Chilion had died painfully; a drawn-out torture that had lasted into the early hours of the morning.

Chilion had returned from work to discover Orpah's absence, and the retelling of her abba's death. In a panic, he left the house on foot to find her. Hours after he'd left, and the moon had risen amongst the stars, Naomi became unsettled and sent Mahlon out to find his brother. He found Chilion lying on his side, not too far from the house, struggling to get much-needed oxygen into his lungs.

Despite the warmth of their home, his health continued to decline, as each uncontrollable bout of coughing tightened his airways. He had clutched his chest and continually called for Orpah in breathless vocals.

Cajsa was sent for, but as the first flecks of blood sprayed from Chilion's mouth she had known it was the end.

"All we can do now is make him comfortable," Cajsa had said, as her eyes moistened. "I have a mixture that will take away his pain, but he mightn't remember who you are whilst he is on it."

"He has been this sick before," Naomi pleaded, "and you healed him then."

Cajsa shook her head. "This isn't the same as last time." She placed her hand on Naomi's arm. "I'm sorry, but I can't help him."

"No," Naomi whispered, pulling Chilion into her arms. "You cannot leave me." She lay her head on his blond curls as tears formed in her eyes.

Mahlon leant against the wall, staring at Chilion's pale body, his eyes empty of emotion as he clenched his teeth.

In that moment Ruth had experienced a surge of compassion for Mahlon. The only man he could call brother was dying. A desire filled Ruth to stand and embrace Mahlon; to assure him she was here. But she stayed, sitting quietly beside Naomi, uncertain of what his reaction would be.

Ruth blinked, her thoughts resurfacing in the present as Orpah stirred under her arm. She squirmed, then settled back into soft shallow snoring.

Ruth waited. Her bones ached, stiff from the hours she had lain still beside Orpah. A heavy layer of fog hung inside her head. Lack of sleep and emotional turmoil pressed in against the sides of her temples.

The bed moved slightly as Ruth pushed herself up. She grimaced, sure she had woken her friend. There was no response. She backed away from the bed and climbed down the ladder. The rungs creaked under her bare feet prompting Ruth to curse under her breath.

Naomi sat at the table, hunched over, her head in her hands, unaware of Ruth's presence. Ruth stopped, as empathy overcame her. How could she relieve the distress in the old woman's heart? How could she take the pain away?

Ruth found her sandals and tip toed to the front door.

Outside, Mahlon approached the house. The midday sun beat down on his head and beads of sweat lay on his forehead. Despite the way he treated her, Ruth pitied him. He'd lost his twin, and he had loved that man. Perhaps the only person in the world who achieved Mahlon's true love.

Mahlon scratched his beard, watching Ruth bend over to slide her foot into her sandal. He opened his mouth to say something, then stopped, and walked past her through the front door.

Today he hadn't ordered Ruth to follow him inside. Today, she was that pagan who wasn't invited into the privacy of their home.

Ruth finished tying the cords of her sandals around her fine ankles and glanced up at the sky as a coolness overcame her. Clouds were gathering.

....

Yace, the grey mule, appeared happy to see Ruth as she wandered into the stable. It smelt of damp hay and horse manure. He stood still as she slid the bridle over his head, but after Ruth pulled herself over his round back, he dropped his head and sidestepped, readying himself to remove her.

"Oh no you don't," Ruth said, pulling his head up with the reins. "You're supposed to be a nice boy."

Yace tossed his head, moving forward reluctantly as Ruth squeezed her legs against his sides. As he picked up speed, Ruth allowed herself to relax, inhaling deeply. The fresh air that rushed past and the movement of Yace's unusually smooth trot calmed her. It reminded her of her days with Harnepher.

Mahlon had refused to let Ruth bring Harnepher to their stable, insisting there wasn't room. Her heart had broken, knowing there was space enough for two extra beasts. When she brought it up the second time, Mahlon said he didn't want her riding anymore. Harnepher passed away two years later.

But a year ago, Chilion had brought a new mule to the stable. One he promised possessed a gentle soul.

Ruth's face crumpled as she recalled the conversation.

"His name is Yace," Chilion had said, running his hand over the mule's soft nostrils. "He's as placid as they come." He held Yace's reins out for her to take.

Ruth shook her head. "Mahlon doesn't want me riding," she told him.

A frown crossed his face. "What?! But you love riding," he said. "I'll talk to him."

"No!" Ruth answered abruptly, shocking herself. She swallowed, struggling to recover her composure. "Don't bother him about it," she added with a nervous laugh. "He's obviously worried I'll fall and hurt myself, as I always doing."

Thinking of Chilion formed an ache in her chest. His last moments horrific. There had been so much blood. The pain in his eyes as the hours continued had been too much for Ruth. She couldn't stay and witness his agony. Guilt swamped her as she remembered telling herself she was doing a good thing, searching for Orpah. But she knew she had left to escape, leaving her husband and a distraught Naomi, to face the tormented cries of a grown man on their own.

....

Dark clouds closed in overhead, threatening to unleash their load. Ruth didn't notice. Her secret place was much the same as it had been all those years ago and her heart leapt at the sight of it. If time had visited this place, it hadn't stayed long enough to change much.

The Dead Sea lay exactly where she'd left it and the rocky mountain tops behind her had held their corroded shapes. Happy childhood memories had been stored here, but now she had brought with her the shadows of adulthood; a change nobody had warned her about.

Ruth rubbed her swollen eyes and sat on a large boulder, leaving

Yace to roam the side of the hill. The insides of her thighs hurt, and she wished she'd used a blanket on Yace to soften the ride.

She wondered why happiness in life was short-lived. Those rare and fleeting moments of joy always snatched away.

Without warning, all the pain, hurt and sorrow from the loss of Chilion, flowed through her body again. She glared at the grey heavens above and clenched her teeth. "If you were real, if there was a god up there, Chilion would still be alive!" She pointed an accusing finger at the sky, her body trembling. "But you are *not* real!" she screamed, her throat stinging. "If you existed there wouldn't be … there … wouldn't …" An agonised wail left her lips and echoed down the valley.

She wrapped her arms tightly across her chest and rocked back and forth as tears fell from her eyes.

A drop of water hit her arm. Then another on the top of her head. Two more on her foot. Ruth raised her face to the sky, her cheeks red and salty. The heavens opened and more droplets fell, faster and heavier.

Ruth climbed to her feet and called out to Yace, as heavy rain pushed against her. He had disappeared. Ruth cursed and staggered through the storm, scanning the fog laden hillside for the missing mule.

Small rivers of water materialized, streaming down the hill around her feet.

"Where are you?" she yelled at Yace.

The ground gave way beneath her. She screamed and fell backwards, sliding a short distance down the side of the hill before her clothing caught on an exposed tree root. Small lines of blood appeared on her elbow, and she winced, examining the fresh scrapes as she pulled herself up into a sitting position.

Rain continued to fall. Constant drops connecting with the ground, striking the earth in a persistent pattern. It created a soft hum. The agitation in Ruth's head subsided and a sense of serenity filled her entire body. All sound now dull and distant in her ears.

She drew her sprawling legs closer, watching in confusion as time slowed to a fraction of its natural pace. What was happening she didn't know, but her heart remained unusually calm. Somehow, she knew all was well.

The rain slowed and beams of sunlight pierced through the clouds, warming the drenched clothing on her skin. She wiped the rain-soaked hair from her face, then hesitated. Opening her hand, she held it out to catch a single drop of rain as it descended with the speed of a feather floating through the air. On impact with her skin, the clear bead separated into smaller droplets, rebounding off her hand as if they were tiny gemstones. Each droplet shimmered with colours of the rainbow and sparkled with the power of the sun.

Ruth shivered. Something in her mind shifted. An understanding surfaced, as though a veil had been taken away in her mind. She now saw the rain, the land, and even herself, as one. Could see that the trees were connected to the earth by more than just their roots. That the goats which frolicked below in the rain were bursting with the same spirit which filled the trees. Below, the Dead Sea's surface sparkled with the same intensity of a turquoise sapphire; its life forces no different to that of the fan tailed ravens which flittered above it.

Everything Ruth viewed was as it had been before, and yet, another layer had appeared. Sight that stretched beyond the visible. The world and all things in it were separate parts of a single piece of divine architecture. Multiple, and one.

"Do you see, Ruth?"

It was barely a thought in her mind, just a voice, still and small.

As soon as it had spoken, Ruth's hearing returned to normal, and time resumed its natural rhythm. As she sat in the mud, doubts crept into Ruth's mind. Had she seen what she thought she had?

Hot air blew across the back of her neck, causing her to recoil. She turned to see the missing mule standing above her. "Oh, Yace," she said, wrapping her arms around his nose as he lowered his head over her shoulder. "I think I have been visited by God."

....

The fullness of Ruth's experience faded in her mind as the weeks passed; her thoughts on Orpah who struggled to find the strength and motivation to leave her bed. Ruth helped where she could, bringing food and water to Orpah's bedside, entreating her to take nourishment, but she knew something had changed. There had been bad days in Orpah's childhood, Ruth knew that, but this new darkness that hovered over Orpah was different.

And it wasn't only Orpah. The air in the household had shifted.

As Mahlon's outward displays of grief waned, his previous behaviours returned. Ruth excused them as reasonable. He'd lost his brother, and she wanted him to know she loved him now more than ever, despite how he hurt her.

Her love hadn't stopped Mahlon from disappearing; his absences from the home had grown longer and more frequent as time passed. Through the gossiping of the market visits Ruth discovered he had been seen in the company of numerous women. This new knowledge broke her heart more than all his previous mistreatment. That her husband had reached out to another for comfort in his grief, tore the core of her being.

As the threads of delusions she'd weaved around her marriage unravelled, Ruth found herself on her knees in torment. Grieving in secret the loss of a loving marriage she realised she'd never had. She couldn't tell Naomi, who firmly believed her remaining son was a good man. Couldn't confide in Orpah as her mind wouldn't cope. Even Cajsa wouldn't understand why she hadn't spoken up.

Instead, she sucked back the emotions and did what she had learnt to do over the years. The only thing which made sense. Blame herself for everything that had happened.

....

Ruth glanced across at Orpah as they sat under the great oak in silence. Overhead, the reddish-brown leaves rustled in the gentle wind. Some came loose and fell, becoming lost amongst the hundreds spread across the ground.

Chilion's death had altered Orpah. Although she'd ventured out of the house after months inside, it was clear she had become a prisoner in her own mind.

Naomi shifted her weight, sighing with the exertion.

Ruth turned her attention to her ima-in-law. Naomi had aged a great deal since Chilion's passing. More lines appeared on her face. She wore an ever-present frown. The hunch in her posture had worsened and the pain in her eyes hadn't cleared.

"Who is that?" Orpah asked, her eyes straining to see along the road.

Ruth sat straight and raised her hands to her forehead, blocking the sun from her vision. As the cart grew closer, her heart soared.

"It's my abba," Ruth said, jumping to her feet. She laughed with the glee of a child and ran down the path to meet him. Her stride slowed as she approached. Her abba's usually joyful countenance appeared hard and grim.

"What's wrong?" Ruth asked, placing her hand on the side of the cart, walking beside it as Malak urged the mules to continue towards the house. When she realised he wasn't going to stop, she pulled herself onto the cart beside him.

"Ruth, wait!" Malak shouted, grabbing her hand as she turned to search the back of the cart.

A soft gasp left her lips.

Mahlon lay face up on the hard timber surface, his stiff body rocking with the gentle movement of the cart. Dried blood covered the fabric of his garment from his abdomen to his feet. Three rough cuts, the size of a dagger blade, sat in the fabric in his middle, the telltale signs of a stabbing. The olive-skinned man she used to know was now a blueish purple.

As blood drained from Ruth's face, her body shook, and she turned back to face the front.

Malak pulled the mules to a stop and grabbed his daughter, pulling her into his chest and holding her tight.

"I'm sorry Ruth," he whispered, caressing her hair.

"What happened?" Ruth asked, her voice barely audible.

"He was attacked," Malak replied. "He was found in a ditch outside the village."

The walls of Ruth's chest pressed in on her lungs. "Attacked?"

"I found out who killed him," Malak replied. "We'll gather some men and call the attacker before the village elders." He shifted with discomfort. "I must tell you something before you hear it from elsewhere. Mahlon was accused of sleeping with the attacker's wife." He watched Ruth's face. "But it is a case of mistaken identity, Ruth. This is not the man Mahlon was."

Ruth knew the accusation would prove true. There would be witnesses, and more husbands would come forward with their grievances. The attacker would be judged and sentenced, and the truth of Mahlon's existence would come out for all to hear. Those who believed he was a good man would fervently deny the accusation to anyone who would listen.

Malak cleared his throat as Naomi and Orpah approached.

Ruth remained silent. A cold sensation fell over her, wrapping itself tightly around her body, until she was completely numb.

....

"It won't be the same after you leave, Naomi," Cajsa said, placing her hand on the old woman's shoulder.

Ruth fiddled with Yace's bridle as the women walked towards her. The second mule, Ariel, tossed her head, unhappy to be harnessed to the cart.

Naomi stopped and leant on her staff, smiling. "I guess it won't be the same." She inhaled deeply and scanned the land around her, as if taking in the scenery for one last time. "I knew it was time to return home five years ago. I only stayed on for Mahlon. Now that he's been in the ground with his brother for four months, I think it's time for me to leave." She sighed. "If only we'd left five years ago. I might have returned with sons."

"This is not your fault," Cajsa said, squeezing Naomi's shoulder. She turned to Ruth. "You will miss this old Hebrew, won't you?"

Ruth's heartbeat increased. She hadn't found the courage to tell her parents she was leaving too.

Naomi shot Ruth a look.

Is that judgement? Condemnation? Ruth couldn't decide what was behind Naomi's glare.

"It appears you two have some things to discuss," Naomi said, limping away.

Ruth crumbled under the scrutiny. Tears filled her eyes. "I couldn't bring myself to tell you Ima," she said, falling into Cajsa's arms. "I love you both so much."

Cajsa frowned and wrapped her arms around her daughter. "What are you talking about?"

Ruth caught her breath and pulled back. "I'm leaving with Naomi and Orpah."

Cajsa's face dropped, pain visible in her eyes. "Why?" she asked. "Were you planning on leaving without telling us?" She shook her head. "You have no husband to follow, no children that tie you to the Hebrews. You should come back to live with us until you find another husband."

Ruth sobbed, biting her lip. "I can't," she whispered.

"You are not old," Cajsa said, stroking Ruth's hair. "You will find another man."

"It's not that," Ruth replied.

Cajsa reached out and cupped Ruth's cheek in her hand. "I don't understand," she said, her voice soft. "Explain this to me."

"I don't know how to," Ruth replied. "There is something inside me, telling me to go with Naomi."

Cajsa moved her head closer to Ruth's and lowered her voice. "Is Naomi *forcing* you to go with her?"

Ruth laughed through tears and wiped a hand across her nose. "No, she's not forcing me," she replied. "Naomi is pestering me to stay with you. *This* is my choice."

Cajsa studied her daughter's face. "There's nothing I can do to change your mind?"

Ruth shook her head.

"Then there's something I must tell you," Cajsa said, taking Ruth's hands in her own. "Before you travel to the other side of the world. Walk with me."

The ground crunched beneath their feet as they strolled away from the house. Cajsa tucked her arm into Ruth's as her gaze wandered.

"Before you were born, your abba and I lived further south on the boarder of Moab and Edom," Cajsa said. "We had family there, and many friends." She smiled at the memory. "A good life in a thriving city."

Ruth kept silent. Cajsa had never spoken of her life before.

"I learnt the skills of childbirth there," Cajsa said.

"Before I was born?"

"I had delivered hundreds of babies before *you* were born," Cajsa replied.

"I don't understand what this has to do with me leaving Moab," Ruth said.

"Please, listen," Cajsa said. She rubbed her forehead. "This night, I had been called out to deliver a baby. It was the house of an extremely wealthy family, who were rumoured to continuously impregnate themselves for the purpose of sacrifice. Something inside me snapped."

She cleared her throat and inhaled deeply. "I approached the huge dwelling and passed by the guards who stood by the tall pillars in the entrance. I followed the cries of pain through the lamp lit hallways until I found her. The ima." Casja ran her hand through her hair. "During the contractions I held the ima's hand, offered words of comfort and encouragement. Ordered servants to prepare towels and bowls of hot water. Long after I arrived, she began to push. And then, out of this woman, a baby girl appeared. A tiny blonde-haired babe full of life. I didn't know why, but I *knew* she mustn't be sacrificed."

"What happened to her?"

"Hush Ruth," Cajsa said, holding up a hand. "The ima asked me to leave, ordering I give the baby to the servant waiting outside the room. When I hesitated, she assured me he would take her to a wet nurse. My mind froze. What if the ima *wasn't* lying? What if the babe *was* safe here? As the ima lay back on the bed with exhaustion, I bound the babe up in dirty linen, leaving a gap for air. Then tucked her into my basket, praying she would keep silent. Outside the door a large man waited. He was dressed in the apparel of a high priest of Chemosh, not a normal house servant. It was then at I knew for sure that this babe was destined for sacrifice."

Cajsa adjusted the robe at her shoulder. "I told the priest that the woman wanted time with her baby before she handed it over. His frown told me this was out of the ordinary, but I left the house and didn't stop till I reached home." She closed her eyes. "Your abba was furious, demanding I take the baby back before soldiers arrived at our door. But when I unravelled the linen around her, and her little eyes locked on his, he understood what I had felt. By the early morning, we had packed everything we owned into a cart and left all that we knew and everyone we loved. All for the sake of this child."

"So, I guess ..." Cajsa said, tucking a loose strand of Ruth's hair behind her ear. "... what I'm saying is you never really belonged to us."

A sharp pain pierced Ruth's chest as the realisation of what her ima was saying slammed through her.

Cajsa smiled. "You had blonde hair when you were born Ruth, but it quickly turned red by the time you were two."

Ruth swallowed, attempting to find words for the flurry of emotions that rose up inside her. "Why have you never told me this before?" she whispered.

"To be honest, I never wanted to tell you," Cajsa replied. "But now I realise I have no right to make a fuss about you leaving or hiding the truth of your birth from you. The desire to save you as a baby was strong, almost as if the desire was not my own, but created in me by a higher being. I now understand you were saved for a purpose. Maybe you'll find that purpose is in Israel."

"Oh, Ima. I love you," Ruth said, her voice about to break. "But I'm so confused."

Tears filled Cajsa's eyes. She pulled Ruth into her arms as her body shook with sobs. "I will miss you so much." She reached out to stroke Ruth's hair, then paused. "Didn't you ever wonder where that red hair came from?"

Ruth laughed lightly and pulled back. "I did wonder."

Cajsa wiped her tears and smiled. "Your abba will be here shortly with grain for the journey."

"I'll have to tell him I'm going," Ruth said, anxiety rising in her throat.

"I think he already knew," Cajsa chuckled. "This morning, he bet me a substantial amount of money that you would leave with Naomi. I guess I'll be poor now."

....

Ruth barely noticed her surroundings as they began their journey to Israel. Her mind busy attempting to reorganise all that she understood of her history. There had been many questions she'd desired to ask Cajsa, but confusion had silenced her. What was her real ima like? Had Cajsa known or seen her real abba? Had her birth parents hated her that much, even as an unborn, that sacrificing her was their only solution? There were questions she needed answers to. Emotions ran wild through her body. Deep grief had gripped her, then an intense rage, then confusion and hopelessness. Why hadn't she been told? Who was she?

An elderly man, skin weathered with age, limped towards the cart. He pointed at the three women, pulling his loose patchy robe over his shoulder. "Where are you going?" he asked,

Ruth glanced at Naomi, who slapped the reins in her hands on the mules backs to move them along faster. She wished they'd taken her abba's offer to send male servants with them for the journey, but Naomi had refused, saying El Shaddai would protect them.

"We are travelling to Israel," Naomi answered.

The old man struggled to keep up. "But these women are from Moab," he said. "I know this one." He reached out and grabbed Ruth's robe. "This is Malak's girl."

Ruth flinched, fighting to pull his fingers from her garment. The man let go and stopped in the middle of the road, staring at the cart as it moved away. A scowl spread across his face. "They will eat you alive!"

Ruth turned on the seat of the cart to face him as recognition formed in her mind. She remembered this man. It was Abaddon, the man who had stirred up her neighbourhood, trying to raise an army. His cause; to fight against the Israelites who had invaded the land of

Canaan in the west. He told of the slaughter of men, women, children and livestock. Ruth had been a child. The first time she'd heard of Israel.

"You have no idea how they will treat you over there," Abaddon spat from behind them. He waved his raised arm frantically. "They hate Moabites. They will treat you less than a dog!"

Ruth swivelled on her seat and took Orpah's trembling hand in her own. She watched the trees pass as they continued their way, focussing her thoughts on the squeak in the cart's wheels as they turned.

But what if he is right?

When Abaddon was no longer in sight, Naomi pulled the cart to a standstill at the side of the road. The mules exhaled, blowing dust along the road, before turning their attention to the grass.

"What's wrong?" Orpah asked.

Naomi scratched her grey head and groaned as she stepped down from the cart. "You both should return to your ima's homes. El Shaddai will deal kindly with you both, the same as you have dealt kindly with my family. Your lives with me have not been ones of peace, but I'm sure if you stay here in Moab, El Shaddai will give you rest, both of you, when you remarry."

"No," Ruth said, climbing down. "We are going with you."

Orpah nodded. "We are returning with you to your people."

Naomi sighed. "No, my daughters, you must go back. What would be the point of coming with me? Are there still sons in my womb, who could be your husbands? No, better for you to go back."

Ruth frowned. Marrying again was the last thing on her mind.

"I'm too old for a husband now," Naomi said. She gripped her chest as a dry cough shook her. "And even if I found a husband tonight, and fell pregnant with more baby boys, would you want to wait until they were old enough for you to marry?"

"Why do you talk of marriage," Ruth asked, shaking her head. "Do you think we are travelling back with you in the hopes you will provide us with more husbands?" She glanced at Orpah, who hadn't left the cart.

A strange expression had crossed Orpah's face. She stared back along the road they had travelled, picking at the nails on her fingers.

Ruth shrugged it off. "We are not leaving,"

"No, my daughters, you must go home. It grieves me to send you away, more than it will you. El Shaddai has dealt me another blow."

Orpah covered her face with her hands as sobs rocked her.

Naomi hobbled over to the cart and rubbed Orpah's leg. "It is alright," she said. "Do not take this badly. It is right that you should stay with your own people."

"I'm so sorry," Orpah said as she stepped down. "The truth is you are right Naomi. I am terrified to leave for a land I know nothing about, with people I am afraid of."

"El Shaddai will bless you, daughter," Naomi said, her voice gentle.

Ruth's heart raced as she watched her childhood friend kiss Naomi on both cheeks.

"Forgive me, Ruth!" Orpah cried as she fell into Ruth's arms. "I can't do it. Even with you by my side."

Ruth stroked Orpah's cheek, wiping away her tears. Her lips trembled. "I want to return with you, but I can't leave Naomi," she said in a whisper.

"I know," Orpah replied.

"Something deep inside is telling me I need to go to Israel."

"I know."

"I will miss you so much," Ruth said, hugging Orpah tighter. Her face became serious. "Do not go back to your ima's house. Promise me you will live with my parents until you wed again."

"I promise."

The pain in Ruth's chest soared, as they clung to each other, not wanting to let go.

Orpah pulled back and kissed Ruth's cheek. "Shalom my dearest friend."

Ruth's heart ached as she watched Orpah take her bag from the cart and begin the journey home.

"Why aren't you walking with her?" Naomi asked Ruth, signalling at Orpah. "Quickly bid me farewell and catch her!"

"I'm not going back."

"Your sister-in-law has gone back to her people and her gods. Go with her!"

Ruth's mind fought against the invisible pull on her heart. *Naomi is right, you need to go home. What is there in Israel that could possibly fulfill you that you can't find here? What if Abaddon's predictions come to pass? It is true that Israelites hate Moabites. And you've only now found out the story of your birth. You have much to learn and discover about your ancestry. You could travel to the Edom boarder, find your real parents.*

Ruth squeezed her eyes shut, attempting to shut down the thoughts swirling around inside her head. What was she doing? Her ima needed her, Orpah needed her. And she needed them. But the vision, the still voice, surfaced in her mind. 'Do you see, Ruth?' Something told her she mustn't be separated from Naomi.

Ruth gripped the old woman's hand, holding tight as she fought back tears. "Please stop asking me to leave you. I will do whatever it takes to stay with you. I will go where you go and live where you live. Your people of Israel will be mine, and your god, my god. I'll die in the same place as you. I'll even be buried with you. Only death will separate us!"

She watched Naomi's face, waiting for the next rebuttal and stubborn insistence that Ruth go home. But there was nothing. Naomi's eyes locked on her own for a few fleeting seconds before the old woman turned her attention to climbing back onto the cart.

NAOMI

ISRAEL – 1185 BC

A rosy hue spread across the sky as the crest of the morning sun surfaced on the horizon. The cart rocked back and forth in a gentle swaying motion. Naomi yawned and adjusted a woollen blanket over her legs.

It had been an early start. Determination had woken Naomi; determination to be back in her home by the end of the day. She had torn Ruth from her sleep whilst it was still dark. Naomi closed her eyes and smiled, even though a sense of guilt played on her mind, remembering the wide-eyed panic Ruth had given her when she was jolted awake.

"Are you alright," Ruth asked, loosening the reins in her hands.

"Just old and tired my daughter."

Naomi cracked an eye open and surveyed Ruth. She was a strange damsel. Nothing could have prepared her for Ruth's peculiar entrance into the house after she'd just lost Chilion to his own body's attack against him. As Naomi grieved the loss of her son, Ruth became insistent that she'd seen God, or something along those lines.

Naomi believed nobody could see El Shaddai and live to tell the tale. She was certain Ruth hadn't seen what she thought she had. After struggling many times to explain to Naomi exactly what had happened, Ruth eventually gave up, and spoke no more about the incident.

Naomi told herself it was nothing more than a hallucination, brought on by grief. But a seed of doubt had been planted and now the more Naomi thought about it, the more unfair it seemed. Had El Shaddai, the one she'd faithfully worshipped for a lifetime, shown himself to Ruth, an unbeliever, instead of herself? Why would El Shaddai, during the moment of her greatest pain of losing Chilion, visit a woman who believed that god's were nonsense? Naomi would have given anything in that moment of sorrow to experience the presence of El Shaddai.

The sudden death of Mahlon had shaken her to the core. What was El Shaddai trying to tell her, by taking her husband and sons from her? Was this the price for moving to Moab? And the lies that spread around the countryside about Mahlon ... she couldn't bear it. Did she need to lose all that she held dear, with her family's name dragged through the mud, before El Shaddai would leave her in peace?

But if Ruth hadn't seen El Shaddai, what else could have explained the sudden change in her? She was now decisive and unwavering. Naomi smiled, thinking how proud Mahlon would be of Ruth if he was still alive. After they had wed, it became apparent to Naomi that Ruth continuously looked to Mahlon for direction, seeming so uncertain of her own thoughts and opinions. *Ah Mahlon, you were such a wonderful husband and would have made a good abba.*

"Are you sure you're alright," Ruth asked. "You don't look good."

Naomi chuckled. "Pay attention to the road, it will get steep up ahead." She noticed the furrowed brow on her daughter's forehead.

Ruth had chosen to stick by Naomi, regardless of what she might face in Israel. *"Where you go, I will go."* The words rung in Naomi's ears. Ruth had been adamant that nothing would separate them. She had made that quite clear, and yet Naomi didn't understand why.

It wouldn't be easy for Ruth in Israel; Naomi knew that much. A pagan living amongst people who believed themselves to be a holy nation. That crazed man in Moab had been right – it was most likely Israel would reject Ruth and treat Naomi as a woman who forsook El Shaddai by leaving Israel.

Naomi glanced at the wrinkled skin on her fingers. She turned her hands over. The insides of her palms were dry and cracked from holding the reins.

"You take too much on yourself," Ruth had said the day before, taking the reins from her. "You won't last long if you keep this up."

Naomi had laughed. "Death doesn't scare me," she said. "I'll be happy if I only last to see my beloved Beit-Lechem one more time."

"I would prefer you held onto life for a good while longer," Ruth had laughed. "You have much to teach me about Israel."

The journey from Moab had been uneventful, passing only the occasional traveller. When they had crossed the Jordon and ventured into the land of Israel, Naomi's heart sang for joy at the sight. So much growth and life. The rumours were true. El Shaddai had indeed visited His people. Crops filled the fields, and every watering hole they passed was full. The birds had returned and once again there were sheep on the fields.

"That's it!" Naomi said, pointing to a building on the hill in the distance. "That's my home." She watched Ruth scan the hill. "We'll have to go through the town first to reach it."

Ruth steered the cart carefully through the streets of Beit-Lechem at Naomi's direction. It bustled with activity; alive and thriving. Naomi had forgotten the energy before the famine. All she remembered when leaving with Elimelech, were the grey streets, and the occasional bunch of starved beggars huddled together.

Now, flashes of colour from markets stalls that lined the streets danced before her eyes and the odour of spices and fresh fruit soared through her nostrils, bringing up memories from her childhood. The music. The joy. Venturing into the markets with her ima, demanding to buy something delicious before they left.

It was then Naomi noticed two women following their cart with quizzical stares on their faces. Naomi knew she'd seen one of the women before but couldn't place it. How she wished her memory and eyesight was as good as it had been.

One of the women whispered into the ear of the other beside her. Naomi watched in confusion as the second woman signalled to a man nearby who grinned sheepishly. Within minutes there was a small crowd following behind them, all watching suspiciously.

Naomi glanced at Ruth. Her Moabitess daughter hadn't noticed the gathering behind them. Someone hollered out with excitement. Naomi's eyes shot back and forth across the crowd. Was it the pretty damsel beside her drawing the unwanted attention? Her heart beat hard against the walls of her chest. It had been a long time since she'd been in Beit-Lechem. Were the people no longer friendly to strangers? Would they pull them from the cart?

"Naomi!" A voice cried out from the crowd. "Is this Naomi?"

Naomi squinted in the sunlight and saw a woman further up the paved street, waving her arms above her head.

"Eden!" Naomi called back, her heart soaring. Relief flooded her chest as she watched Eden push through the crowd towards them.

"It *is* you Naomi," Eden said, stopping to catch her breath. She hadn't changed much in their time apart. Still short and round with a beautiful face, although more white hairs laced through the hair on her head. "My Naomi!"

Without waiting for an invitation, Eden climbed onto the cart ledge and threw her thick body down beside Naomi, shifting the cart sideways momentarily. She wrapped her arms around Naomi and pulled her in tight. "I thought you'd never return!"

Another woman caught up and grabbed the side of the cart. "Is it truly you, Naomi?"

"Anna?" The face she recognised before but couldn't put a name to. Naomi reached down and touched Anna's hand as she walked beside the cart.

Anna's long grey hair moved loosely around her fine shoulders. "Naomi, I thought I'd never see you again!"

Eden turned and scanned the crowd behind the cart. "Where are your boys, Naomi?" she asked. "Are they on another cart?"

"Dear friends," Naomi sighed. "Don't call me Naomi."

"Why not," Eden asked.

"Naomi means pleasant," she replied. "And my life has turned out to be anything but pleasant. Call me Mara. For El Shaddai has dealt me a bitter blow."

Eden's eyes widened. "What do you mean?"

"I left here with everything," Naomi said, an ache forming in her chest. "And El Shaddai has brought me home with nothing more than the clothes on my back. He took my family from me. Why would you call me *pleasant*, when El Shaddai doesn't see me that way? El Shaddai has ruined me!"

"We know of the heartache you have suffered," Anna said, still walking beside the slow cart. "We all heard of it and wept for you."

Eden turned to Anna. "Why had I not heard of this?" she asked, heat rising in her face. "I did not know Naomi had lost her family."

"Please do not call yourself Mara," Anna said, ignoring Eden. "You haven't returned completely empty." She signalled in Ruth's direction.

Guilt rose in Naomi's heart. She laid a hand on Ruth's lap, wondering how it must have hurt to hear her speak this way. Ruth had risked everything coming to Israel.

"You are right Anna," Naomi said, massaging the agitation from her brow. "I have not come back empty. El Shaddai may have taken my sons and husband, but He has given me a daughter. This is Ruth."

Ruth sent a quick smile to Naomi's friends before returning her attention to the road and the small children who appeared determined to jump under the hooves of their mules.

"What will you do with no husband or sons to care for you?" Eden asked. "You have no security or protection."

"What are friends for," Anna smiled. "If not to care for each other."

"Not everything is as simple as you think, Anna," Eden muttered.

Naomi nodded. "Eden is right. We have no men to care for us. But I will pray that El Shaddai provides for me before I come begging at your doors."

"Then we will pray too," Eden replied. "That El Shaddai leaves you without want."

Anna nodded in agreement.

"This is my house," Eden said, pointing at the end of the street. "I am so glad you are home again Naomi. We have much to talk about."

Ruth pulled the mules to a stop as Eden leapt from the cart and onto the sandy street beside Anna. Naomi laughed, bewildered at her old friend's agility. Did she not feel pain in her bones?

"Shalom Naomi," Eden said, waving them off. "I will come to visit tomorrow and make sure you have everything you need. Shalom Ruth."

"I'll join you Eden," Anna said. "There's something I've been wanting to show you." She turned back to the cart. "Shalom Naomi and Ruth."

"What is it this time?" Eden asked as they turned to leave. "That last new herb you said would cure headaches had my husband's bowels loose for over a week."

A warmth filled Naomi's heart as she watched them move away.

Ruth urged the mules to walk on.

"*You* were quiet back there," Naomi said to Ruth.

"Why didn't you tell them that I am a Moabite?" Ruth asked. "Surely they will be able to tell once I open my mouth and speak."

Naomi chuckled and squeezed her daughter in laws hand. "Your speech is not so different," she said. "Perhaps it would be wise to let them grow accustomed to you, before you confess your heritage."

"Do you think it'll be that easy?" Ruth asked.

Naomi smiled. "It's easier for people to overlook their differences once they get to know someone."

....

"Over there," Naomi said, pointing at the entrance of her old farm.

Few posts remained standing of the front gate; most littered the ground that surrounded them.

Naomi inhaled deeply. As Ruth led the mules through the entrance and began the narrow track up the side of the hill, Naomi's excitement grew. Within minutes the house came into view, and her heart ached as memories surfaced. She saw Elimelech in the distance, waving his hat above his head in the field, that irresistible grin on his face as Mahlon and Chilion worked beside him. Naomi squeezed her eyes tightly shut against the tears that formed. When she opened them, her boys were gone.

As they approached the house, the years of neglect became evident. Along many parts of the roof there was missing thatch, where supports had caved in. Shutters that blocked the windows had rot and were broken, leaving gaps, allowing the weather to enter freely.

Naomi sighed. Exposed to the elements for over a decade meant the inside was most likely destroyed. Her heart sank, realising the amount of work that would be needed to bring her home back to its former glory. Although she had helped Elimelech in the past to patch up the occasional hole in the roof, this damage was much worse. And this time she didn't have him to help.

The fields added to her depressed state. The rain had livened up the ground but the life that had sprouted were mostly weeds. All Naomi saw was more work than she could handle. And no money to handle it with.

Oh Elimelech!

"It will be ok, Ima," Ruth said, noticing the old woman's eyes watering. "You tell me all the time that El Shaddai will provide."

The cart eventually reached the house and Ruth pulled the mules to a stop. She climbed down and held Naomi as she stepped down to the ground.

Naomi didn't care what Ruth thought of her as she knelt on the moist soil and kissed the earth. Oh, how she had missed it. *My Beit-Lechem.*

She stood up, groaning as her joints screamed at her, then approached the front door. The wood cold against her palm as she ran her hand lovingly over the timber. The wood had held strong, but the hinges were broken, and the door sat loosely in the frame. No doubt busted in by hungry Israelites after they'd left.

Naomi pushed through the door to find the damage inside was much the same as outside. The walls and stairs had erosion. Any furniture they had left in the house had been taken. In the kitchen were the remains of a campfire.

A cool breeze blew through the cracks and holes of the house, creating a sense of despair.

Naomi leant on her staff as she limped through her home, muttering under her breath, refusing to be sucked into the gloom that threatened to overcome her.

Time rolled back to the way she remembered it many years ago.

Beams of light shone through the house, creating a warmth in the air and an orange hue on the walls. She saw little Chilion running through the door from outside, with Mahlon close behind. The humid breeze filled her nostrils with the scent of harvesting. A young Elimelech poked his head through the window and smiled, his hat sitting lopsided on his head. The handsome smile that melted Naomi's heart every time.

"Are you ok, Ima?" Ruth asked.

Naomi blinked and her family were gone. The warm and bright world of opportunity had been replaced with the grey dullness of her new life.

"Yes, my daughter." Naomi replied. "I'm going to sit for a moment. This journey has taken its toll on me."

The muscles in her arms throbbed as she lowered herself onto the bottom step of the stairs. She watched Ruth disappear out the front door.

They couldn't stay here. At the first rain they would be washed out. Tomorrow, Naomi decided, she would find someone willing to give them lodging in the city.

"There's only enough grain for tonight," Ruth said, reappearing through the door. She held up the loose bag of grain.

Naomi groaned, and placed her head in her hands, wishing El Shaddai would take her life. This wasn't how she'd imagined their return would be. Maybe they should have stayed in Moab. She sat up and scratched her chin as an idea formed in her mind. "Did you see the fields of crops on our way in?"

"The weeds?" Ruth asked.

Naomi snorted. "No, not our crops. The other farms we passed. Some of the harvesting has already begun which means it's the beginning of barley harvest."

Ruth's eyes narrowed. "We have nothing to buy barley with?"

"We don't need to buy it."

"You want me to steal it?"

"My daughter," Naomi said, signalling Ruth to sit beside her. "El Shaddai is the God of provision. He has designed a way for those without food to be cared for."

Ruth sat on the cold step beside Naomi.

"El Shaddai ordered my ancestors to leave any pieces of barley that the harvester missed on the ground. El Shaddai said this was to be for the poor and the stranger."

"We are poor, and I am a stranger," Ruth replied. "But what if the Israelites no longer follow this command?"

"Would he have sent bread to Israel if the people had disobeyed him?"

Ruth took Naomi's hands in her own. "Let me go to the fields now. I will find a harvester who is kind, and follow them, to pick up what they miss."

"But it is getting late, my daughter," Naomi said, glancing towards the window.

"It is only the middle of the day," Ruth replied. "There is time."

Naomi gazed into Ruth's bright optimistic eyes. "It is hard work."

Ruth nodded.

"Go ahead, my daughter. May El Shaddai guide you."

RUTH

ISRAEL – 1185 BC

By the time Ruth left Naomi, the sun hung in its afternoon position. She cursed the clouds gathering on the horizon; a sure sign rain would be coming. After reassuring herself that there would be plenty of time to glean before the rain reached them, she pulled a scarf tightly over her head to cover her hair. Then she went to find Yace.

As they reached the broken gate at the edge of Naomi's farm, Ruth pulled Yace to a stop, glancing up and down the road. That morning, they had entered from the left.

"What do you think, Yace?" She bit the inside of her mouth. Naomi had said to try the farms they had passed earlier, which would mean taking Yace left, but something inside her desired to go right.

She laughed nervously and rubbed her face in her hands. "I'm going crazy."

Yace pawed the ground and tossed his head.

"I agree," Ruth said. "We're wasting time."

She squeezed her legs around Yace's round stomach and shortened the right rein in her hand. She let him set the pace as he stepped out onto the worn dirt road and rode up the gentle slope.

Ruth hated leaving Naomi on her own and had spent a good amount of time making sure she would have everything she needed in arm's reach.

"Stop fussing," Naomi had scolded her. "You'll run out of daylight."

When Ruth had attempted to bring in furniture from the cart, Naomi stopped her.

"Why are you still here?" Naomi asked. "Don't worry about unpacking, we can't stay here for long."

"What do you mean?" Ruth asked, placing a chair on the ground.

Naomi raised her eyebrows, opening her hands out to the room around them.

Ruth remembered the unease that had crept into her heart at that moment. It had stayed with her, even now, as she rode Yace further from the farm.

She was unprepared for what had awaited them on their arrival into Israel. From Mahlon's talk, his family was rich beyond measure, had a house that supplied every need and was apparently the envy of the country. He'd been right about the large house, but Ruth hadn't expected the sight of mould that covered the walls, or the leaky open roof, or the lack of clean water. She hadn't come for riches. Mahlon's tales of wealth hadn't brought her here, but she *had* expected there would be a liveable and watertight home.

Once again, the thought entered her mind. *What have I done? Why did I leave Moab?*

The landscape changed the further she rode. Despite the famine breaking in Israel, and the rains soaking through into the depths of the earth, the terrain appeared to cling to its rugged exterior. Wild shrubs beside the road became denser, littered amongst rocks, their roots twisted with the effort to pierce the rigid ground.

As Ruth pushed Yace on further, a dull ache in her spine formed.

"You're not the smoothest beast to ride Yace," Ruth said, squirming on his back.

He flicked his ears, ignoring her.

Sweat trickled down her neck as they came across a row of tall cypress trees planted along the boundary of a farm. Ruth calculated there must be at least a hundred. As they passed by the tall trees, riding out of one tall shadow into the next, she spied reapers behind the foliage, busily harvesting the field.

She pulled Yace to a stop and watched from the road. Hunched over in the heat, they worked in pairs, moving forward harmoniously.

The first man or woman would seize a handful of barley stalks. Then slice it off with a sickle near the base; a quick movement with the flick of the wrist. The stalks would fall from their hands as they stepped forward and reached for the next handful.

Behind them, another worker gathered up the fallen stalks in their arms, stopping every now and then to bundle the sheaves, using cut stems as ties.

A donkey and cart worked its way through the field, led by a man who gathered bundled sheaves onto the cart. Once full, he led the donkey out of the field. Ruth knew where he would be going. She'd worked all the jobs needed on her abba's farm; had experienced the process of cutting to separating the grain. All this was familiar to her, but there were other people working in the field, doing something Ruth hadn't seen in Moab.

She squeezed her legs and moved Yace closer to the farm boundary, watching as these unsynchronised people followed behind the reapers.

These people weren't part of the human machine that harvested, but an unorganised group of young and old, searching the ground at random. There was no method. Ruth watched as now and then they would pick up a stalk of barley. Some would put it in a bag they were carrying, whilst others used the folds of their robe to carry their load.

Yace tossed his head.

Ruth hushed him. "Calm down, old grump." She rubbed his furry neck. "How will I know how to glean the fields if I don't watch first?"

Yace leant down and rubbed his nose against the inside of his leg.

Ruth bit her lip as she watched the men and women glean the field, questions filling her mind. *Did she walk into the field, or did she need to ask the owner for permission? Where should she leave Yace so he wasn't stolen? How long was she allowed to stay? Was there a limit to the number of people who could glean at any one time?* She inhaled deeply. *Calm down.*

Yace pulled at the reins and shifted his weight beneath her.

"You're right," Ruth said, swinging her legs to one side as she slid down his abdomen to the ground with a gentle thud. "How quickly I have forgotten you pulled a cart today."

Yace snorted. He stepped away from her and lowered his lips to the ground in search of edible foliage amongst the small rocks.

Ruth's attention returned to the field. The scent of freshly sliced barley reached her as the breeze switched directions. A familiar aroma, bringing memories of her parent's farm to her awareness.

As she stood, watching the Hebrews work, the hairs rose on the back of her neck. Within seconds, a hand gripped her firmly on the shoulder. Ruth spun around to see a man peering down at her. She opened her mouth in protest but remembered what Naomi had said. If she spoke, they would know she was a foreigner.

The man's leathery skin and unkept beard were barely visible under the sweat and dirt. He belched, causing Ruth to recoil as the stench of old wine oppressed her. Repulsed by his lack of personal space and body odour, Ruth stepped back into Yace, landing on his front hoof.

Yace sidestepped in fright and kicked out, connecting his hind leg with the man's thigh.

A scream erupted from the man's mouth as he fell sprawling to the ground beside Ruth. His face twisted in agony as he clutched his thigh with both hands and hissed through his teeth. He pulled back his long robe to reveal an unnatural bend between his knee and hip.

"You've broken it!" he squealed.

"What's going on!?" a voice called out.

Ruth's heart raced as she glanced up to see two other men approaching. She reached out and seized Yace's rein, pulling him closer as she stepped away from the first man.

The new men stumbled on their feet; balance inhibited by alcohol. Ruth's eyes shot over to the Hebrews in the field. Too far away to hear if she screamed.

"I asked what's going on?" one of the advancing men questioned again.

Ruth stood paralysed, unsure which of the men to focus on.

The first man's face had turned a lighter shade, almost as pale as the gritty soil of the road. Beads of sweat formed on his nose and forehead as he gritted his teeth. "Her mule broke my leg." He squirmed, groaning in distress.

The second man's head rocked about on his shoulders as he stopped. With great effort he glanced at Ruth, then at his friend on the ground, then back at Ruth. "We only want to say hello, pretty damsel," he slurred. "No need to set your mule upon us."

"Ignore the witch!" the first man choked. "I need help!"

Ruth clutched Yace's rein tighter, as her heart pound hard against her chest. Her body trembled. She glanced back at the field. The workers were still oblivious, too focused on their work.

The men are drunk and injured. Mount Yace and leave.

Without Ruth noticing, the third man had come around behind her, grabbing Yace's rein.

"Stay back!" Ruth shouted, holding her hand out, attempting to pull the rein from his hand.

An unsettling grin formed on the third man's face, and his eyes widened. "Ah." He nodded slowly with enthusiasm. "You're not a Hebrew damsel. What are you? Edomite? Philistine?" He crossed his arms and surveyed her, his eyes travelling from the sandals on her feet to the scarf wrapped over her hair, his expression full of hungry appreciation. "I thought there was something different about you, and your voice confirmed it."

The second man chuckled. "Does it matter what country this pagan comes from?" he asked. "Whatever one it is, she'll be starved for a man."

"That is truth," the third man said, his eyes still on Ruth. "Pagan women love to entice men into their bedrooms, for one night or many nights. As the harlots they are." He reached out to touch Ruth's cheek with the back of his hand. "That's what you want, isn't it, beautiful pagan?"

Ruth flinched and swatted his hand away. "I beg you to leave me alone," she said. "Don't do something you will regret in the eyes of your god."

The second and third men exchanged expressions of mock confusion, then burst out laughing.

Ruth's chest tightened; each breath becoming more difficult than the last.

"You are correct, harlot," the second man said. "We *are* the sons of El Shaddai. And *you* don't belong in this land. This is our inheritance. El Shaddai told us to rid this land of your people."

"Would someone help me!?" the first man bellowed. He cried out as the muscles around his broken bone contracted in spasms. The second man stumbled towards his friend on the ground, laughing. "It's probably not as bad as you think it is."

"Look at it!" the first man screamed.

The third man sneered at Ruth. "You heard my friend," he said. "We are El Shaddai's precious people." He raised his face and stared down his nose. "We have El Shaddai's approval to do what we want, especially to people like you." His arm shot out with the speed of a snake and grabbed her wrist. "We won't kill you, but you at least owe us a small treat as repayment for your mule's bad behaviour towards our friend here."

Ruth winced in pain as she struggled against his grip. He smiled, holding on tight, unfazed by Ruth's effort to free herself.

"Don't do that," the man whined. "We only want to be friends."

"She's only pretending to fight you," the second man laughed, egging him on. "I've heard they do that."

The third man pulled Ruth into his chest as she pushed against him. As he wrapped his arms around her, his finger caught the end of her scarf. It slipped off and floated through the air as weightless as a feather, before landing on the road behind her.

The third man's eyes lit up. "A red beauty!" he said.

Ruth shuddered as he ran his hand over her hair. The vile stench rising from his unwashed body and the fear that stormed inside her caused her stomach to spasm forcefully.

The man watched in shock as the contents of Ruth's stomach exploded from her mouth and over his garments. He released Ruth from his arms and jumped back in revulsion, tripping over and falling backwards.

Ruth wiped her lips with the back of her hand. She heard the second man gagging but refused to take her eyes off the third.

The third man glanced down at himself, his face twisting in anger. "You filthy pagan!" He climbed to his feet and lunged towards her, his hands aiming for her throat.

Ruth closed her eyes, her brows furrowed, willing her mind to leave her body for the duration of what was about to happen. *Please God, spare me!*

A thundering echoed in her ears, the sound of a thousand galloping horses, before a rush of wind pushed against her. Then silence. She opened her eyes precariously. A darkness had overshadowed her, wrapping her up in its safety.

In front of her, the third man had stopped in his tracks. He stared at something above her head. His body shivered; all signs of masculinity replaced with childlike fear.

Ruth refused to move a muscle. She sensed protection from whatever hovered above her, but she knew about spirits, and heard they could turn on those they offered protection to. If this was a spirit, she didn't want to upset it.

The third man reclaimed his composure and swallowed, before stumbling backwards, towards the second man and out of the shadow. His eyes stayed fixed above Ruth's head.

"We weren't doing anything," he said, raising his hands in surrender.

The first man wailed as the other men took him, lifting him from the ground and wrapping his arms across their shoulders. As the first man's leg dragged across the road, he screamed out one last time before fainting, slumping in their arms.

Ruth watched, frozen, as the men trudged away, dragging their friend's limp body in silence, one staggering step at a time. Soon they were out of sight, but Ruth refused to move. Yes, the men had gone, but now the prospect of another danger loomed above her. The shadow hadn't moved off. Surely, she would be wise to fear the thing that had sent her attackers crawling back into their hole.

She counted to ten in her mind, then turned with caution.

It was a human. A non-spirit, flesh and blood man, sitting astride a muscular brown stallion.

An odd sensation tingled through her nerves, and she laughed with relief before slapping her hand across her mouth to control herself.

The sun sat behind the man's back, creating a black silhouette, blocking his appearance from her view.

The stallion shifted its weight between its back legs and reached its fine nose out to sniff at Ruth's robe, before pulling back and snorting.

She'd forgotten about her sick. With her free hand, she self-consciously wiped the remaining residue from the front of her robe.

"It isn't wise for you to be on this road alone," the rider said, in a tone that reminded Ruth of Mahlon.

Had she been stupid to walk this road on her own? Naomi hadn't said anything about dangers on the road. Cold, liquid self-doubt spread through her chest. Before she could reply, the rider wriggled in the saddle and pulled his horse's mouth away, urging the stallion to move on.

Ruth watched his back as the horse accelerated to a trot, then slowed canter as it continued up the road. She noticed the man's hair was mostly grey-white but peppered with brown strands. She could tell by the colour that he'd seen at least sixty summers, but he held himself and rode as someone much younger.

The unknown rider turned right, disappearing into the row of cypress trees that lined the farm. He reemerged on a laneway which led down to a large house. Much larger than Naomi's. Enveloping the house was a high stone wall, surrounded by the same cypress trees as the farm boundary.

The built-up tension left Ruth's body as she picked up her scarf from the ground and wrapped it back around her hair.

The rider intrigued her. Not many people could afford a horse, and this horse was unlike any she'd seen before. Her abba had spoken of the horses from Egypt, of their beauty, with their broad foreheads, large eyes and small muzzles. How they floated as they moved; how they raised their tails high in the air and arched their necks.

Ruth wiped sweat from her brow with the loose end of her scarf. One thing puzzled her. He might be wealthy, but his presence had the other men cowering to get away. What was that all about?

Yace tugged at the reins.

Ruth let him loose and glanced back to the field workers. Still harvesting; unaware of her ordeal. She had promised Naomi she'd come back with food, but the longer she stood on the side of the road, the more her confidence diminished. Questions whispered in her mind, threatening to derail her determination.

What if the workers treat me as the men on the road had? Do Hebrews truly hate all people from the surrounding nations?

Yace snorted loudly.

Ruth glanced to her left and noticed a reaper and his helper approaching the boundary. She swallowed and adjusted the folds of her scarf.

The man stopped close by and stood tall, placing his hands on his hips. His garment wrapped around his waist, leaving the white hairs and skin of his chest exposed to the elements. Wrinkles lined the seasoned skin. He arched his back, cracking it into place, before wiping his sweaty brow with the back of his furry arm. He leant on the timber rail that separated them and rubbed his sizable nose, sniffing. "Are you here to glean?"

Ruth examined his face, questioning if he was trustworthy. He was mostly bald, but white hair sprung from almost everywhere else.

In the most Israeli accent she could create, she replied with the line Naomi had instructed her with. "Please let me glean and gather after the reapers among the sheaves."

"There's plenty to share in here," the reaper replied, waving his hand over the field. "Come and help yourself."

The boy behind the reaper smiled and waved. "Shalom," he called out.

The older man pointed at a nearby tree. "Tie your mount to that branch over there and come follow behind us," he said. "One of the servants will see your mule out here and take him into the stables."

Ruth hesitated.

"Trust me," the older man said, waving Ruth to join him. "It'll be fine. You've found the best farm to glean in." He turned to walk away. "My name is Tobias, and this lad here is Chalil."

Chalil dipped his head at Ruth.

Tobias coughed and spun a sickle skilfully in his hand. "Is this the first time you have gleaned?" he asked.

Ruth nodded, rubbing the back of her neck. The sun was lowering fast, but its heat still cut through the air.

"Don't worry," Tobias said. "There's no skill involved. At all. I'll cut the barley. Chalil will pick up the pieces and bunch them together. All you need to do is follow Chalil, and you can take whatever you find on the ground that he's missed."

Ruth glanced from Tobias to Chalil as the temperature in her cheeks rose. She would be working lower than the lowliest of the servants on the field, a far cry from the life on her abba's farm.

"There's no shame in gleaning," Tobias said, stretching his arms out in front of him. "What is your name?"

"Ruth."

....

A droplet of sweat glistened as it ran down the bridge of Ruth's nose. She wiped it off and opened the bag that hung loosely from her shoulder. Inside was a handful of barley. Her heart sank, knowing she'd have to come back tomorrow for more. Perhaps search for another reaper. One who wasn't as good at their job.

Ruth glared at the sky, her eyes squinting. Around her, insects clicked and buzzed low to the ground. There was no shade in the field, no reprieve from the merciless sun. The clouds which had hung on the horizon earlier had disappeared. She hadn't wished for rain before, but now Ruth would give anything to get out of the heat.

She pulled her scarf loose and draped it further over her forehead to give more shade, then continued to follow behind Chalil.

As they neared the farmhouse, a strange sensation washed over Ruth. She surveyed her surroundings, keeping her face mostly hidden under the scarf.

Her eyes stopped on the rider as he stood by the gate. His eyes were on her.

Ruth turned her face away, pretending to reach for a stalk of barley on the ground. By the time she peered up again, the rider had his back to her and moving towards the house.

"That's Boaz," Tobias said, scratching at a sweaty itch in his beard.

Ruth stood tall, pushing loose strands of hair away from her forehead as she frowned at him.

"That man you're staring at," Tobias said. "That is Boaz, son of Salmon."

Ruth's cheeks flushed. "I-I wasn't …"

"He's the most respected landowner in Beit-Lechem," Tobias said, with a nod. "One bad word from him and you'd never find work on any farm in Beit-Lechem again."

Ruth swallowed. "Does he own *this* farm?"

Tobias chuckled and spat on the ground. "Does he own this farm? What a question." He picked at his thumbnail with the sharp edge of his sickle. "You're not from around here, are you?"

Ruth rubbed the sting of the sun from her arm. "No," she said. "I'm from Moab."

"That's a long distance away," Chalil chipped in. "What are you doing all the way over here?"

Tobais raised his large eyebrows in Ruth's direction.

Ruth glanced at her feet, fiddling with the fabric of her bag. How much should she tell of her past? "I married a Hebrew who had moved to Moab," she said, after a pause. "When he died, my ima-in-law wanted to come back to her home. I came back with her."

Tobias' brow creased as he tilted his head to the side. "Wait," he said. "Your ima-in-law isn't Naomi, is it? The one who married Elimelech?"

Ruth nodded.

"I heard about what happened to her," he said. He took the soft hat from his head and wiped it across the back of his neck. His bald head shone with the reflection of the sun. "How much bad luck can one person have?"

"She wanted to change her name to Mara," Ruth said. "That's how bad she believes El Shaddai treated her."

Tobias laughed. "I can see Naomi doing that." He flipped the hat back over his head. "She's always been so dramatic."

"You know her well?" Ruth asked.

"Know her?" Tobias roared. "I tried to marry her! Asked her many times, but she was always chasing after the big lad, Elimelech." He sighed, but a smile soon crossed his face. "Come. Let's go into the house and rest."

BOAZ

ISRAEL – 1185 BC

Boaz placed his hands over the bottom sill of his bedroom window and leant outside as the first rays of sunlight peeked over the mountain range. Crisp, morning air caused goosebumps to rise over his body. He barely noticed, his thoughts busy reliving the events of the previous day. The recollection clear in his mind as if it happened only a moment ago.

He had been returning from the city when he'd noticed her. A woman in distress, some distance up the road, about to be set upon by men. As far as he knew, she could've been someone's old ima, about to be beaten and robbed. Spurring his brown stallion forward, he reached them within a minute, prepared to use any measure to stop the attack.

When the men pulled back, nausea rose in Boaz's stomach. He recognised them. Old farm hands, criminals as it turned out, who had worked on his land previously. The last time he'd seen them was when he'd dragged them before the elders for judgement, after discovering they'd violently forced themselves on a young woman in his fields. Boaz believed they'd been stoned or banished. He never thought he'd see them near his farm again.

The men cowered in his presence, reluctantly picking up their friend from the ground and dragging him away from the woman. But nothing could have prepared Boaz for what happened next.

The woman had turned to face him, and he'd frozen in the saddle. It was as if she could see right through him. Deep, blue-green eyes peered into his face, her brows creasing, searching for something she couldn't see. He had never witnessed such beauty, and it paralysed him.

The bangles on her slender brown wrists clinked against themselves as she wiped something from the front of her robe. The golden ring in her nose glistened as it caught the light of the sun. She stared at him as though she had seen a god, which unsettled him further.

Finally, after regaining his senses, he had shifted uncomfortably in the saddle and told the woman she shouldn't be on the road alone. As the words left his mouth in a voice he hardly recognised, he signalled Aziel, his stallion, to head for home.

He'd seen her again later that day, in his field, working behind Tobias, but hadn't the courage to speak to her.

The memory of yesterday was only brief, but for some reason it persisted in lingering at the forefront of his mind.

He pushed away from the window and threw his hands into the bowl of icy water beside his bed, splashing it against his face. After wiping his face dry with a clean cloth, he rubbed his sore knee, wishing the pain would leave.

The woman returned to his thoughts.

Maybe she would return today.

....

The sun hung directly overhead, in the middle of the sky, when he noticed the woman back in the field. She wasn't working behind Tobias and Chalil today, but another, less experienced, harvester team that Boaz had yet to meet. He pulled at his beard. Out of the corner of his eye, he recognised a familiar walk.

"Enosh!" he called out. "A word?"

The older man strode over to his master.

"Yes?" Enosh replied, his eyes flickering with suspicion.

Boaz nodded towards the field and held out his hand. "Who is the new harvester team there?"

Enosh squinted in the direction Boaz was pointing. "That's Reuben and his wife Bilha."

"And the woman behind them?" Boaz asked.

"She does not work for us," Enosh replied. "She is a Moabite woman who came back with Naomi from the country of Moab." He scratched the back of his head as a scowl formed on his face. "Who knows why Naomi brought her back here? I can't think of any self-respecting Hebrew woman who would do that."

"Moab?" Boaz asked, eyebrows rising. "Is this the Naomi who married my cousin Elimelech?"

"Yes, that's the one." Enosh replied. "Tobias told me yesterday. Apparently, they all died. Well, the men that is. I'm surprised you hadn't been told, given Elimelech is your cousin."

Boaz frowned, wondering if he'd heard Enosh correctly. How was it possible that they were no longer alive? What had happened in Moab? Sadness formed in his chest. They hadn't been close, and their encounters usually ended in disagreements, but the thought that he would never again speak to Elimelech seemed incomprehensible.

"And the woman out there," Enosh continued. "She married one of Naomi's sons before he died. When Naomi came home, Ruth insisted on coming back to Israel with her. She asked Tobias if she could glean behind the harvesters."

"Who's Ruth?" Boaz asked.

Enosh frowned. "The Moabite."

"Ah," Boaz said, his eyes on Ruth. "And she turned up here to glean yesterday?"

Enosh nodded. "She came back today and has continued to work from this morning until now, although she has rested briefly in the shade by the gate."

Boaz stared into the field, his mind racing. He'd heard rumours that his cousin Elimelech had embraced the worship and traditions of the Moabites. He hadn't believed the stories. But this was the first time he'd heard anything about a daughter-in-law named Ruth.

"Did you need anything else?" Enosh asked.

Boaz shook his head. "You have told me everything I need. But make sure the harvesters know Ruth is to be left alone, even as *our* women are left to work in peace. She may be from Moab, but that doesn't mean she's easy pickings. Tell the men to keep their hands to themselves."

Enosh bowed himself, then passed through the gate, back to his work.

Boaz returned his attention to the fields. Ruth continued to glean, oblivious to his gaze. There was business which needed his attention, but this young woman, who had cared for his old relative, intrigued him. It was time to meet her.

....

As Boaz walked across the field towards her, Ruth stood tall, watching his movements with apprehension. His heart sank, hating the idea that she perceived him as a threat.

"Shalom," he said, greeting her with a wave.

Ruth hesitated, surveying him. "Shalom," she said finally.

"I need to speak with you," Boaz said. "... about your presence here."

Ruth glanced at Rueben as he continued to work on, moving further away from them.

"Don't be afraid," Boaz said. "From now on, don't glean in the fields of another farm, but stay here, and close by the young Hebrew women who work for me."

Ruth's brows narrowed under her scarf.

Boaz cleared his throat. "What I'm saying is keep your eyes on the fields that the women harvest and follow after them."

Ruth remained silent, wiping sweat from her forehead.

Growing uncomfortable in her continued silence, Boaz's thoughts scrambled together. "I've ordered the young men who work here not to assault you."

He watched the colour drain from her cheeks.

"Not that they *would* attack you," Boaz said, holding his hands up in reassurance. He rubbed his eyes in frustration, groaning inwardly.

Ruth swallowed and glanced around them.

Boaz sighed, as a weak smile crossed his lips. "Listen," he said. "If you are thirsty, go and drink from the vessels of water the young men have drawn."

Ruth's lip trembled as she choked back a sob.

Boaz cursed under his breath, convinced he'd offended her in some way.

Without warning, Ruth fell to her knees and bowed herself to the ground at his feet.

"What are you doing?" he asked, suddenly uncomfortable. He glanced up at the harvesters in his field, some who had stopped working to watch. He took a step back.

"Why are you paying attention to me?" Ruth asked, her voice muffled under layers of her scarf. "I am a foreigner! I thought you came over to throw me out of your field, but you have shown me kindness."

Boaz lowered himself to kneel on the freshly harvested ground beside her. "I've heard all about you," he said, wiping away the chaff that stuck to his palms. "Heard what you did for your Ima-in-law after your husband's death. How you left your own parents, and the land of your birth, to come here, to a strange people."

"I *had* to come back with her," Ruth replied. "There's a reason I *need* to be here."

Boaz's eyes narrowed. "What do you mean?"

"I can't explain it," Ruth replied. "It's like a knowing."

"Like a divine or higher power has set a desire in your heart?" Boaz asked.

Ruth nodded. "Yes."

"I knew it," Boaz laughed. "I knew Israelites weren't the only favoured people." He stopped, noticing the confusion on Ruth's face. "Sorry," he said. "I've had many a discussion with others about whether El Shaddai has interest in other peoples besides Israel."

A quizzical smile formed on Ruth's face. She glanced back to the workers in the field.

"May El Shaddai reward you for your actions," Boaz said. He watched her eyes wander, wondering if she'd heard him. "May you receive a rich reward from El Shaddai, who you've come to confide in."

Ruth fiddled with the ends of her scarf and smiled. "So much grace I have found in your eyes," she said. "You've comforted me, and spoken kindly to me, as if I was one of your own maidservants, and not the immigrant I am. You have no idea how much this means to me."

Boaz returned her smile and climbed to his feet, groaning as his left knee reminded him of his age. "You keep working then, Ruth of Moab."

He winked at her before he turned to walk off, then cursed at himself. Why had he winked? Or more disturbingly, why had he let his heart be touched by a woman who appeared half his age?

....

"They're all coming in now, master," Enosh shouted, helping the servants lay out bread and grain along the long wooden tables in the cool shade of the house.

The sun was at its hottest, and the fields were ablaze with heat, appearing to shiver against the horizon.

Boaz scanned the harvesters as they passed through the gate, their conversation becoming louder as they filled the courtyard, making their way to the tables.

There was no sign of Ruth.

After searching, he found her outside the gate, sitting on the ground in a sliver of shade provided by the wall.

"What are you doing?" he asked, placing his hands on his hips.

Ruth's eyes widened. "I thought – it's just the harvesters had stopped, and I thought I would rest awhile until they came back. I can keep working if that's what gleaners would normally do."

"That's not what I'm asking," Boaz said. He held his hand out to her. "Come with me."

Ruth followed him through the gate and towards his workers who were all seated in the courtyard. He pointed to the long tables. "Come over here and eat some bread. Make sure you dip some of it in the wine. You'll never have tasted anything so good."

He watched Ruth as she settled beside one of the women, then he took his seat at the head of one of the tables. After a few moments, he realised the harvesters were watching him in silence, patiently waiting.

"Right," Boaz said, getting to his feet again. His mind had been unreliable since the small hours of the morning and was showing no signs of improvement.

He held his hands out, palms to the sky above. "Blessed are you, El Shaddai, ruler of the universe, who brings forth bread from the earth."

"Amen," the harvesters said in union.

The conversation immediately continued as each man and woman helped themselves to the food provided.

Boaz spoke with those beside him but kept an eye on Ruth. She hadn't taken any nourishment yet. He picked up a basket of roasted grain and asked the harvester to his left to pass it along the table to her. As it reached her, she turned to Boaz, and mouthed the words 'Thank you.'

Enosh moved his stool closer to Boaz. "There are bad murmurings going on in Beit-Lechem."

"What murmurings?"

Enosh dipped bread in the wine bowl and thrust it into his mouth. "About you buying all that land before the famine broke," he replied, chewing with his mouth open. "Word is getting around that you planned to buy the land at dirt cheap prices, then set yourself up as ruler over Beit-Lechem."

Boaz scoffed. "That's not what I'm doing." He reached for a clay mug of water. "I bought the land off people who couldn't keep their farms running. They'd have starved to death if I hadn't bought them out, paying twice the amount the dry land was worth."

"*I* know that," Enosh replied. "But you know what conclusions people draw. You need to say something publicly in the city to stop the rumours before there is an attack launched against us."

"Do they forget the laws?" Boaz replied. "I will be returning the land to the rightful owners at the year of Jubilee, at a loss no less." He ran his hand through his hair as frustration built.

"It's those same owners who are complaining and stirring the people up," Enosh replied. "They believe they were cheated, that you knew the famine was about to break before you bought up their lands."

Boaz rolled his eyes. "So, I'm a god now, who can predict the weather." He stared into the distance, chewing on the bread in his mouth. "We'll give all the land back then," he shrugged. "Find every disgruntled farmer and have their land returned to them by the end of the fortnight."

"What?" Enosh spat.

"You heard me."

"But master, shouldn't we at least wait till the end of the harvest?" Enosh asked. "Take what profit we can, from the land, before handing it back."

"No," Boaz shook his head. "If they can believe they have been wronged by my generosity before, they'll cry maltreatment at the gift of land without a full crop. Let's not give them an excuse to complain further."

"But —"

"— Enosh, El Shaddai will provide." Boaz interrupted. "I've never been without, and I doubt this loss will ruin me."

Content with that explanation, Enosh returned to his food.

Boaz watched Ruth as the harvesters finished their meals and one by one left the table to return to the fields. The bowl of roasted grain still sat in front of Ruth, mostly eaten, but she struggled to finish it.

Boaz rose from his seat and walked down to sit across the table from her. "You don't have to eat it all."

Ruth smiled, her mouth full. She swallowed with a grimace, then washed it down with water. "I haven't had this much to eat in days," she replied. "I think my stomach has shrunk."

"Take it," Boaz said. "Throw the rest in your bag."

"Thank you again for your kindness," Ruth said as she brushed her lips with the back of her hand and stood. "I will return to the fields now."

As Boaz watched her walk away, Chalil passed by him.

"Chalil."

"Yes master?"

"See that woman there," Boaz said, pointing at Ruth's back.

"I see her," Chalil replied. "The woman from Moab."

Boaz nodded. "Let everyone know she's allowed to glean between the sheaves, as well as behind the harvesters. However, don't make it obvious; I don't want her humiliated." He stared into Chalil's honest young face. "Also, I know you take pride in your meticulous work, you barely miss one stalk of barley behind any harvester. But if Ruth is behind you, I want you to pull out some of the grains from the bundles and leave them on the ground on purpose. If you see any of the workers reprimanding her, tell them this is my wish."

Chalil bowed, then ran off to tell the other young men the master's plan.

Relieved that Ruth would be cared for, Boaz's thoughts returned to the troublesome farmers. The sooner he sorted this bad business the better. He had tried to do everything right, but there was always something biting at his heels.

He pondered on that thought for a moment and wondered if maybe, on a deeper level, there *had* been greed at the core of his land grab.

Perhaps he'd been unwilling to admit that at the time, with pride convincing him what a saviour he was, for helping farmers in their time of need.

And now, because of it, he was facing a potential uprising, and could lose everything.

RUTH

ISRAEL – 1185 BC

Ruth groaned in discomfort as she placed her hands on her hips and stretched out her back. The muscles refused to loosen. Hours of walking the fields in a hunched position had taken its toll.

Above her, the harsh bite of the sun softened, and the skies had turned an orange-pink. Ruth would have to leave the fields soon, if she was to be home with Naomi before dark.

Yesterday she'd returned late, long after the sun had set. She'd found Naomi asleep on a makeshift bed in the kitchen. After watching the rise and fall of Naomi's chest, Ruth breathed easily, satisfied the old woman was still alive. She then organised some linen into a rough bed on the floor next to her.

They'd woken before dawn, their bodies aching from the unpleasant sleep, and left early to ride to the city in search of somewhere else to lodge.

Naomi's friend, Eden, set them up in an adjoining chamber to her house, with room in the stable for their mules. She had implored Naomi to join their family for meals, but Naomi, ever stubborn, insisted they would provide for themselves.

After sorting their living arrangements, Ruth left Naomi in the city and rode to the fields.

Following lunch with the field workers, little Chalil insisted she work behind him. Dread had filled her heart, but she'd agreed, not wanting to offend. As they'd made their way into the fields, Ruth glanced at Rueben and Bilha, behind whom she'd managed to find a significant number of missed stalks before lunch. This was unlike Chalil's tidy work, where almost no stalk was left behind and gleaning was difficult.

But the unexpected had happened. Chalil's usual attention to detail fell by the wayside. He wasn't scouring the earth for every stalk Tobias had harvested. Ruth suspected he was ill.

And now, as the sun painted the sky in late afternoon colours, Ruth couldn't hold it in any longer. "Are you alright Chalil," she asked, frowning. "You aren't working as well as you were yesterday."

Chalil laughed. "I know," he replied. "And it is killing me to do my job this badly, but the master commanded it."

"What do you mean?"

"He told me to leave more barley out for you to glean," Chalil replied.

Ruth's mind filled with confusion. This continued display of compassion from a stranger unsettled her. What did he want in return? "Thank you for telling me, Chalil."

A few meters away, Tobias called them to a stop. "Time to finish up." He signalled to Ruth. "I'll show you where the gleaners thresh their pickings, then you won't have to carry the whole lot home again. Follow me."

As Ruth walked behind them towards the house, she realised there were no other gleaners left on the fields, just a handful of harvesting teams. They passed through the gate into the large courtyard and towards the stables. Ruth glanced towards the house. A sense of relief filled her. Boaz was nowhere to be seen. They continued past the stables to the threshing floor. Inside, two donkeys and a handful of sweaty men continued to work the grain.

Tobias tugged at Ruth's sleeve. "See that rock there," he said, pointing to a large flat-topped boulder that lay at the entrance of the threshing room. "That's for the gleaners. All you do is lay your bag of barley on top and thump it like crazy with the stick beside it. We call it the Thumping Stick. Once you think it's had enough – and it'll take a while so give it a good whack – tip your bag out over the rock and the breeze will do the rest, blowing the chaff off the grains for you."

Tobias turned and left to chase after Chalil before Ruth had time to tell him she'd known how to de-chaff a barley stalk since she was three.

Apart from the movement in the threshing floor, there was no one around. Just the quiet of the late afternoon. The walls of the gate and buildings cast long shadows across the courtyard, and a cool breeze settled in.

Ruth placed her bag on the large stone and picked up the Thumping Stick. She brought it down easily on the bag, again and again, releasing grains from their little pockets. Her muscles stung, but she pushed on. The current pain would be worth the relief of riding home with only the grain in her bag.

She continued to hit the mound, working her way into a rhythm of raising the stick and bringing it down, repeatedly. Thud. Thud.

Without warning, panic surged through her body as memories of Mahlon resurfaced. The thud as his fist hit her face, the second her stomach, the third her back. Over and over. Recollections in her mind screaming at her, telling her to run, even though she never could, paralysed in shock.

The Thumping Stick slipped from Ruth's fingers as her knees collapsed beneath her. She slid down the boulder to the ground. Her bag of grain tipped and spilt open over the side of the boulder, releasing its contents onto the hard stone pavers which lined the courtyard.

Ruth pulled her legs close and tucked her head down, wrapping her arms around her knees, oblivious to the spilt grain. She refused to cry as panic in her chest grew.

Mahlon was gone, he couldn't harm her any longer. And yet he hadn't left. At least not in her mind.

How is this possible?

A soft touch on her shoulder caused her to jump.

Ruth glanced up into the brown eyes of a woman standing beside her. A woman she'd hadn't seen on the farm before. Brown frizzy curls bounced out from the delicate scarf over her head. The fine jewels on her wrists and ankles clunked against each other as she sat on the pavers beside Ruth.

"Are you alright?" the woman asked, running a reassuring hand over Ruth's arm. She smelt of fresh cedar and frankincense.

"I'm alright," Ruth said, wiping her moist eyes with the back of her scarf.

"Are you sure? You don't appear alright to me."

Ruth let out a nervous laugh. "I guess not." She sighed and viewed the woman beside her. Such beautiful fine fabrics were used to create her garments. The type of fabric that should hang in the halls of a king, yet this woman sat adorned in them, on the rough ground.

"An unpleasant memory visited me from my past," Ruth said. There was a sense of calm and safety around this mysterious woman. "It held such power, even now."

"Ah yes," the woman replied, nodding. "I have my own share of memories I'd rather avoid."

Ruth swallowed. It was a memory, nothing more. Mahlon held no power over her.

"My name is Devorah," the woman said. "And I'm guessing from your accent that you're *the* Ruth from Moab who has the whole farm talking."

"Talking?"

Devorah chuckled. "Don't worry, nothing bad," she said. "We don't get many exciting visitors here. And there's all the stories about your sacrifice, leaving your parents to come here with Naomi, plus all the other juicy reasons for why you wanted to come to Israel." She bounced her eyebrows at Ruth suggestively.

"I don't know what you've heard," Ruth said, smiling self-consciously. "But my story isn't juicy at all. It's a wonder people are talking about it."

Devorah shrugged. "You have to admit, it's not the *normal* thing to do," she said. "It's different, and *you're* different. That's enough to give people a reason to chatter. You'll find those of us in this area enjoy gossip as much as a tasty snack."

Ruth frowned. She didn't want to be different. She wanted to slip into the Hebrew life unnoticed. Find out why she was supposed to come here; why she'd been prompted to follow Naomi.

"Why are you two sitting in the dust?"

It was Boaz.

Ruth shrunk in his presence.

He scowled at Devorah. "You're sitting in that delicate fabric which arrived not one moon ago!"

Devorah rolled her eyes and scoffed. "It will wash out, *dear* cousin."

Ruth watched Boaz. His voice signalled frustration, but there was nothing on his face that indicated he was mad. Ruth sensed a complicated bond between them.

Boaz turned his head and locked eyes with Ruth briefly before he disappeared into the threshing floor.

"He's *your* cousin?" Ruth asked.

"Unfortunately," Devorah said, climbing to her feet. She dusted off the fabric of her apparel. "I'm his cousin from the *bad* side of the family." She laughed at herself. "But it's not all bad though. He can pretty much afford anything I want."

"Being rich doesn't sound too hard," Ruth laughed, using the boulder to pull herself up. Her face became serious as she wiped down the front of her robe with her hands. "Is there anything I need to be warned about?"

"What do you mean?" Devorah asked, adjusting the bangles on her wrist. "Are you referring to Boaz?"

"I only met him yesterday," Ruth replied. "And have only spoken with him a handful of times. Yet he has shown me favour. More than other gleaners in the field."

"What are you worried about," Devorah asked. "If you can get more from a man than you think you deserve, don't question it!"

Heat rose in Ruth's cheeks. "I'm worried he wants something in return." Her gaze fell to the pavers under her feet.

Deborah covered her mouth, struggling not to laugh. "Oh my goodness, he will *not* want anything in return from you as a woman, if that's what you've been worrying about. My ima has been trying to match him up with Hebrew damsels since the day he was born and has failed in all her efforts. He's too picky. And I mean no offence, but you're not even Hebrew. You'll be fine."

A surge of relief flushed through Ruth's veins, as she watched the hysterics on Devorah's face.

"No, you do *not* need to worry about that one," Devorah smirked. "You're totally safe there."

Inside the threshing floor, a donkey brayed loudly.

"I think," Devorah said, pulling her scarf off to re-tie it around her brown curls. "I think Boaz is genuinely moved by the kindness you have shown an old woman of our people." She tilted her head to the side. "That's one thing he's a sucker for. People in need." She picked up the Thumping Stick from the ground where Ruth had dropped it. "I'll help you finish threshing your gleanings. I haven't played with the Thumping Stick since I was a child so this could be interesting."

....

"My daughter, you are back," Naomi said, greeting Ruth at the door. Her old eyes lit up at the sight of the full bag Ruth held in front of her.

"It's about an ephah of barley, Ima."

"Come in and let me wash your feet," Naomi replied, hobbling out of the doorway. "You must be tired. I did not expect you'd be working this long. There's only you and I to feed; you don't need to work so hard."

"I will wash my own feet today," Ruth said. "You can barely get down on the ground, Ima." She threw the bag of grain onto a small table in the centre of the room. "I have leftover bread from lunch too." She pulled out the wrapped bread Boaz's servants had given her. "It's for you."

Naomi reached out with the insistency of an infant receiving a new toy. She sat on a nearby stool and unwrapped the package, before breaking off a portion of bread. Her eyes closed and she let out a moan of appreciation. "This is good. Very good."

Ruth sat and watched her ima-in-law devour the bread. All the aches and pains of the day had been worth it.

Naomi opened her eyes. "Where did you glean today? Whose field?" She slapped her hand against the bag of grain on the table. "Blessed be the one who took such good care of you."

Ruth glanced at Naomi, concern rising in her heart. "We had this conversation this morning, remember?"

Naomi shook her head, staring into an empty space beneath the ceiling. "I don't remember that conversation. I may not have been listening, too stressed about finding lodgings."

"I did tell you about it this morning on our way here," Ruth continued. "The farm I worked yesterday, and today, is very large, and the owner is extremely wealthy. He is Boaz, son of Salmon."

Ruth jumped in alarm as Naomi let out a holler and threw her cane in the air.

"El Shaddai bless that man!" Naomi said. A broad smile crossed her wrinkled face. "El Shaddai doesn't hold back kindness from the living or the dead!" She rose to her feet and paced the room with a newfound energy. She shook her finger at Ruth. "If this man is the Boaz I think he is, then he is a relation of ours. A *close* relative!"

"What does this mean for us?"

"You *don't* know what this means?" Naomi asked. "Ruth, El Shaddai led you to this field!" Her eyes darted back and forth as she rubbed her hands together and nodded slowly. "You must stay there."

Ruth massaged the bone between her brows. Had she been led there?

"Did Boaz say anything to you?" Naomi asked, her eyes eager.

Ruth glanced upwards. *What* had *they talked about?* "He told me to stick with his workers until the harvesting season is over."

Naomi took Ruth's hand and cupped it in her own. "That is good, my daughter. Do that and you'll be safe. Follow the women workers. I have been so worried about you, but now that I know you're in the field of Boaz I can rest, knowing you won't be assaulted!"

....

A full month passed before Ruth saw Boaz again. The initial suspicion she held against him had faded. Her conversation with Devorah put her at ease, and since then, Boaz had been away on business, giving Ruth space to get on with the work she needed to do.

She spied him out of the corner of her eye, one sweltering afternoon, as she drew water from large vessels.

"Shalom Ruth," Boaz said, pulling himself up on the bench. He sat beside the water pots.

Ruth acknowledged his presence with a nod. "Shalom." She held a clay jar of water to her lips, watching Boaz over the rim as she drank. Despite his mostly grey-white hair, he didn't appear as old as she'd been told. Someone had guessed around seventy summers, but at this proximity Ruth guessed around sixty. His skin had aged well and his strength and stamina in the field matched that of a young man.

Ruth wondered how long his hair was. She'd never seen it out; always pulled back in a loose bun behind his head.

Boaz turned his face away, rubbing the back of his neck. "I hope your weeks of gleaning have proved profitable."

A wry smile crossed Ruth's lips. "Thanks to *you* they have," she replied, placing the clay jar on the bench beside his hand. "But I think you'll notice a significant drop in your earnings this season due to Chalil's declining ability to bundle barley stalks."

Boaz shot her a feigned expression of surprise.

Ruth laughed. "Perhaps Chalil wasn't the greatest choice to leave secret orders with," she said. "Maybe Tobias would have been the better man to entrust your plan with." She wiped beads of sweat from her brow with the back of her hand. "But thank you," she continued. "Naomi and I have needed this help."

Boaz slid down from the bench. As his feet hit the ground a sharp gasp left his lips.

Ruth's eyes narrowed. "What's wrong?" she asked.

"Nothing is wrong," he replied.

Ruth motioned to the palm tree that grew in the courtyard not far from where they stood. "Walk over there and back."

Boaz took a few steps towards the tree.

"There it is," Ruth pointed. "You're limping."

Boaz laughed. "It's not that bad."

Ruth's lips tightened. She dropped her bag to the ground. "Sit down here and pull up your robe. I'll check your leg."

She glanced up and smirked at the shock displayed on his face. "I'm a healer," she assured him. "Or was training to be."

"That doesn't mean I'm going to pull up my garments," Boaz replied.

Ruth let out an exacerbated sigh. "I'll be unable to concentrate on my work in the fields until I've figured out what's wrong with you."

Boaz hesitated.

"Blame my ima," Ruth said, holding her hands up in surrender. "She filled my head with this nonsense. Please sit!"

"Fine I'll do what you ask.," Boaz said, as he found a chair.

After he'd positioned himself in front of Ruth, still refusing to pull his garments up, she moved her hands to his ankles and squeezed around his bones with gentle fingers. "Any pain?"

Boaz shook his head.

Ruth watched his face for signs of discomfort as her hands moved up to the skin of his calf muscles on both sides. He stared back with intense curiosity. Heat rose in her cheeks, and she turned away.

She moved her hands further up, continuing to gently prod the muscles. At the knees she noticed he flinched. Watching his face, she squeezed again on the right. There was no reaction. Then on the left; the same small, almost unnoticeable flinch.

"Your left knee," Ruth said, pulling her hands out from under his garments and sitting back on her heels. "You can stop pretending now. Do you want to move your apparel out of the way so I can examine it properly?"

Boaz paused, then pulled his garments up, tucking the loose folds of fabric between his knees. "It's not bad all the time," he said as Ruth shuffled closer. "Some days the pain is non-existent and other days I can't even walk on it."

Ruth moved her hands around his sore knee with soft fingers. "It's not good, but not too serious." She held his knees together, examining both from different angles. "It's extremely swollen."

After letting go of his limbs, Ruth stood, and snatched her bag from the ground. "You can put your legs away now." Her watchful eyes surveyed Boaz as he let the hem of his garment fall to his ankles. Anyone else would have jumped out of their skin if she'd touched a swelling in that way.

"What's the verdict?" Boaz asked, with no hint of concern. "What's wrong with me?"

"It's swelling around the joint bone," Ruth replied. "It sometimes happens to people as they age." She regretted her choice of words the instant they left her mouth. She glanced at Boaz, anticipating the scowl she was sure would appear on his face. "Not that you're old, it's just —"

"Yes, Ruth, I *am* old," Boaz chuckled. "You're allowed to say it."

His laugh put her heart at ease. Their interactions had been minimal, but each time he had left her wondering why he was so pleasant. If she'd said that to Mahlon, had unintentionally inferred that he was lacking in some way … She couldn't bear to think of it.

Boaz rubbed his hands along the tops of his thighs. "How do I fix it, healer?"

Ruth scrunched her mouth to the side, biting her lip. "We can't get rid of it altogether, but a mandrake ointment for the pain and willow bark for the swelling will help a lot." She adjusted the strap of her bag on her shoulder. "Another option, which is expensive, is an opium-based mixture from Egypt. It will help with the pain." She helped him to his feet. "But most importantly, have a joyful heart."

"Why is that?" Boaz asked.

"It's something my ima always told me," Ruth laughed. "*'A joyful heart is good medicine, but a broken spirit dries up the bones.'* Remember to pass that onto anyone who wants a long life."

"I like that saying," Boaz said, nodding slowly in approval. "I'll have to write it down."

Ruth shrugged. "I never learnt how to write." She glanced up at him, as her stomach sank. *Why did you share that piece of information? You know nothing of this man, yet you reveal something this personal. Now he knows you're illiterate. And sharing things your ima said?*

Ruth hushed the thoughts that raced through her mind. Somewhere, deep within her, she sensed a great kindness in Boaz. A safe place where she was able to express whatever came into her heart. A person who saw her, heard her.

"I can teach you."

"Sorry?" Ruth asked.

Boaz grinned, scratching his beard. "I can teach you to write. And read. If you want to learn these things."

Although Boaz created a calm within her, Ruth wasn't sure if what he was offering was appropriate. "I don't have time," Ruth said, running her hand over her scarf. "I should head back to the fields, to glean some more before the sun goes down."

"I'm serious," Boaz said, crossing his arms. "If you knew how to read and write, it would change your life. You could do anything."

Ruth shrugged. "How much can a Moabite do in the land of Israel?"

"What do you mean?"

"The people in the city have discovered I'm not a Hebrew woman," Ruth replied, swatting a fly away. "The religious leaders have been informed and now I'm no longer allowed to enter with the women of Israel to worship. All because my forefathers didn't give water and bread to Israel when they came out of Egypt. As if it was I who had done this." She waved her hand in front of her face as the fly circled back. "The word getting around is that Mahlon broke the Law of Moses when he married me."

Boaz's brows furrowed. "I'm not sure about marriage, but the law does prohibit Moabites from entering the assembly. Not even I am permitted to enter."

"What do you mean?" Ruth asked. "You're a Hebrew, and a male. You can do anything you want."

Boaz chuckled, re-tying the messy bun on his head. "There's a lot about me you don't know. My ima was an Ammonite from Jericho. According to the law, not even the tenth generation of our family will be allowed to enter the assembly."

"It makes no sense," Ruth said, raising her head. "The divine creator has revealed things to me, a Moabite, so I know without a doubt that there is no favouritism to Hebrews alone. Anyone from any nation can be called, as is decided by the creator alone."

Boaz's eyes narrowed. "What have you been shown?"

Ruth glanced at her feet. "I've tried to explain it to Naomi, but it's hard to put into words," she replied. A smile crossed her face. "For a brief moment, my mind was opened to see things I couldn't see before." She moved a red curl from out of her eyes and tucked it back under her scarf. She paused, watching for his reaction. "You don't believe me."

"Of course, I do," Boaz replied, his eyes intent on her own. "I just don't know what to make of it yet."

BOAZ

ISRAEL – 1184 BC

A bead of sweat tickled as it ran down the back of Boaz's neck. He ignored it, unable to believe what he was hearing.

The woman who stood before him appeared convinced she had been given divine insight. Boaz wondered if Ruth had mentioned her experience to anyone else besides Naomi. His countrymen would not take to the idea that a woman, and one from Moab of all places, had been given this blessing. He could see the men of his town spluttering with indignation, professing that there were numerous cleansing rituals to follow before any person could come into the presence of El Shaddai.

"I need to head back to the fields," Ruth said, lowering her hand to her raised foot, adjusting the strap of her sandal. "Naomi hasn't been well these last few days. I'll need to get home early." She turned to leave, then paused, facing him again. "Make sure you get that ointment. Any good physician knows how to make it."

Boaz watched Ruth as she turned and walked towards the fields. He scratched his head, unsure what was going on inside him. Something had changed. This woman showed more interest in the spiritual than any person he'd ever met. He realised a bond was forming. A stronger connection than he'd had with any other woman.

At first, Boaz thought it may have been her beauty that brought up this conclusion. That would be enough to draw any man. But he knew this wasn't it; something else was happening.

Why had she left Moab? Why did she care for an old woman with no apparent benefits from doing so? Why did she care about entering the assembly, when she'd clearly experienced some sort of heavenly exposure outside of the holy places?

Enosh appeared beside him.

"How did it go in the city today?" Boaz asked, struggling to focus his mind on business.

"A waste of time if you ask me," Enosh grunted. "Why does it take a month of discussions to sort something that could be fixed in a day? The elders of the city finally agreed that you were allowed to give the farmers their land back without compensation."

"It's politics," Boaz replied. "People hear someone giving land away for free and they want to determine if they can find a plausible way to line their pockets in the process."

"Well, the farmers were grateful to receive the deeds to their land *before* the year of release," Enosh said. "All they could talk about was what a great man you were, a true Abba in Israel, and how unnecessary your generous actions were."

Boaz laughed. "Oh, how fickle is man." He patted Enosh on the back. "You've done well."

....

"What is my cousin thinking?" Devorah asked, as she walked into Boaz's bed chamber. "It wouldn't be anything to do with the new gleaner, would it?"

Boaz scowled, placing his reed pen on the table before him. "Would it hurt you to show a small amount of respect? Knock before you barged in?"

"Ah," she replied. "Deflecting my question with another question. And yes, it would hurt me. I'm your cousin and I shouldn't have to knock." She peered over his shoulder, reading the papyrus before him. "I like that bit," she said, pointing to the middle of the page. "*'A joyful heart is good medicine, but a broken spirit dries up the bones.'*" She nodded with approval. "I must admit Boaz, your skill with words is improving."

"Move back please," Boaz replied, pushing her away with his head. "Your breathing is loud. And the words you read aren't from *my* mind."

"Oh? You copied them?"

"These are the wise words of Ruth's ima."

Devorah chuckled. "Of course they are."

"What's that supposed to mean?"

"Dear cousin," Devorah answered, as she moved to the open window. "I'm not the only one who has noticed you spending every free minute you have with the young damsel. I am the most surprised though. I never thought you'd be interested in anyone."

"It's nothing."

"Nothing?" Devorah asked. "*Nothing* would be a random chat on the shallow things of life that mere acquaintances exchange as they pass by. You have been sitting with her every afternoon for the last two months. I smell a romance blossoming. And scandal."

Boaz shook his head in disbelief.

"I'm assuming there will be a section of poetry on your parchments about her," Devorah teased, clasping her hands together and dramatically holding them against her cheek. "The tension of failing to grasp something valuable, held just out of reach?"

Boaz flung his pen at her. "Leave cousin, before I send you back to your parents to live."

Devorah laughed. "How I love your empty threats." She picked up the reed and placed it back on the desk, before heading to the door. "Did I tell you my parents are coming to stay in a few days? I received a letter last week."

"No, you didn't," Boaz replied. "But since you've given me no notice, I'll leave it in your capable hands to make sure the servants set up the guest rooms tomorrow."

Devorah shut the door as she left, leaving Boaz to puzzle over his emotions. He knew she was right; he'd spent much time with Ruth lately. He should have known people would notice.

The pull towards Ruth was strong, and although he was young at heart, he knew his years were far more advanced than her own. She was beautiful, inside and out. Maybe he would risk telling her how he felt.

He let the thought circle in his mind, weighing up the pros and cons. She deserved a younger man who could live out his days with her. Yet as Boaz grew closer to Ruth, imagining life without her friendship would be a slow death.

He picked up his reed and placed it in the ink jar.

He would tell her tomorrow.

....

Ruth's laugh rang in his ears. "Where are we going?"

"You need to wait," Boaz chuckled. "I never realised you were impatient."

They walked past the big house and around the bend to a section of his farm that couldn't be seen from the main road. As they rounded the corner, a large orchard came into view below them.

Ruth gasped. "How have you hidden this from me?" A grin spread across her face as she surveyed the entirety of the orchard from the date palms to the pomegranate, fig, olive trees and grape vines. Amongst the greenery, farm hands worked, harvesting, fertilising and watering.

Boaz's heart swelled at the delight on Ruth's face. He longed to pull her into his arms. Instead, he held out his hand. "This track can be slippery."

Ruth placed her hand in his. A mischievous smile danced on her lips. "Am I holding your hand, in case *you* fall?" she asked.

"I may be old," Boaz laughed. "But I'm not *that* old."

With her hand in his, he led Ruth down the track to a bench carved from stone, under the shade of a palm tree.

He withdrew his hand as they sat and pointed towards the orchard. "We began planting this before the famine arrived. Although it was only a quarter of the size back then. Now it's grown to this. I plan to expand it in the coming years."

Ruth sighed. "It's wonderful." Her shoulder brushed against his. "I never thought I would love it here in Israel, but it is growing on me."

"Do you think you'll stay in Israel for the rest of your life then?"

Boaz asked, as the beat of his heart increased.

Ruth smiled. "Would you hate it terribly if I didn't?"

Boaz turned to face her, taking her hands in his own. Her skin soft, and warm, unaffected by the gleaning. He stared into her green eyes; deep and clear as the mountain rivers.

A familiar voice shouted out above them. "Sorry to interrupt, but my parents have arrived early and somehow ran their cart into the side of the front gate. Now they're stuck."

Boaz dropped Ruth's hands and turned to see Devorah stumbling down the path to meet them. Mountains of delicate orange fabrics and purple jewels hung off her body; dressed for a banquet with the city's elite.

"Devorah, I have a hundred servants up there," Boaz yelled back. "Ask them to help."

Devorah roller her eyes. "Do you think I wouldn't have tried that before trudging all the way out here? The wheel has caught on the latch of the gate, or something of that fashion, and all the servants are too afraid to touch it. They fear breaking your gate or my parent's cart. Ima is in such a state."

Boaz groaned. "All right, I'll be up in a minute." He paused. "Why didn't you send a servant to tell me?"

"They're all busy, so I came to see what you're up to."

Boaz turned to Ruth. "Sorry but I must get back. I will see you tomorrow?"

Ruth smiled with a nod. "Of course," she replied.

As he passed Devorah, she leant towards his ear. "What are you two up to?" she whispered with a smirk.

"I'm sending you back with your parents," Boaz muttered under his breath.

....

As his family gathered around the table for their evening meal, Ruth refused to leave Boaz's mind. As soon as the day finished, and she returned home, a sadness filled his heart. He stared at the meat on the plate before him, his appetite gone.

"I can't believe we managed to dislodge the cart without any harm coming to the servants," Devorah said, breaking a piece of bread from the main loaf. "I admit, I was waiting for you to lose it Boaz, but you never did." She glanced at her cousin as a wicked smile played on her lips. "Why *were* you as relaxed as you were, despite the catastrophe? Was something on your mind Boaz?"

"What is this?" Dalia asked, sitting tall. "Is there a woman? Tell me who it is. No don't tell me, I want to guess."

Gad held his wine in the air. "Leave the man alone. He's had enough trouble already from your meddling and match making."

"Keep your big nose out of this Gad," Dalia said, waving her hand at him. "My meddling has finally paid off."

Boaz glanced from one of them to the other. This was not a conversation he wanted to have in front of everyone.

"I don't think you can take any credit for this one, Ima," Devorah said. "This one is a foreigner."

Dalia choked. "Not a Hebrew? No, Boaz, she *must* be a Hebrew."

"Ima!" Devorah scoffed. "Why is that a problem? *You're* not even a Hebrew."

"Nobody where I live knows that," Dalia said quietly. "Besides, this is different. Gad wasn't a man of high standing. I was able to slip into Hebrew life unnoticed. Boaz is different, he has a reputation to uphold."

Gad faked a smile. "Thanks," he muttered. "A man of low standing, am I? My self-confidence will never recover."

Devorah pouted her lips at Gad. "I love you, Abba."

"Let's not get carried away," Boaz said. "Ruth is a friend only. There is no talk of marriage."

"But you're thinking about it aren't you," Devorah said, giggling.

"What I'm thinking about is retiring to my bed chamber," Boaz said, standing. "Shalom to you all."

"But you've barely eaten," Dalia said. "Tell me more of this Ruth."

Boaz wiped his mouth and took one last sip of his wine. "My head hurts, Aunt. I'll see you all in the morning."

....

There was a soft knock at the door.

"Yes?" Boaz called out.

Dalia entered and closed the door gently behind her.

Boaz turned back to his writing. "You're much more polite than that daughter of yours. Barging in whenever she pleases."

"I know," Dalia said, as she walked towards him. "Devorah is headstrong. I blame Gad." She laughed.

Boaz turned his chair to face her, sensing the words that were about to spill from her mouth. "Tell me what you've come to say," he said. "Because we both know you won't sleep until you fulfil your job as a caring aunt."

Dalia sighed. "You're a good man, Boaz." She sat on the edge of his bed. "There are a lot of reasons why pursuing this damsel is a bad idea."

Boaz leant forward in his chair. "I'm listening."

Dalia swallowed. "First, Devorah has informed me she's from Moab, of all places, and that she's told you she believes in El Shaddai. She may have bewitched you into believing she has a newfound love for El Shaddai, but once she has you trapped in marriage, it'll all disappear."

"You don't know that," Boaz replied, scratching his eyebrow. "She left her own country and family, everything she knew, to return with Naomi. All that based purely on what she believes was a directive from the heavens."

Dalia dismissed his argument with the wave of her hand. "It wouldn't be a stretch to surmise that Naomi told her about the property they owned in Beit-Lechem. This Ruth sounds like she came from a poor family in Moab. It's not hard to join the dots."

"Her parents were wealthy,' Boaz replied. "Besides, what if El Shaddai *did* lead her here?"

Dalia frowned. "That's reading into it, don't you think? Lots of people say El Shaddai has given them a message when they don't want someone peering too deeply into their story."

"But why would she *choose* to come to Israel?" Boaz asked, running his hands through his hair. "I know how you and Ima were treated by the Hebrew women. As undesirable insects stuck on the underside of their sandals. Why would Ruth come into a country of such prejudice, and face that level of persecution, unless directed here?"

"Let's leave El Shaddai out of it for a moment and move on with my second concern," Dalia said. "Have you thought of the potential destruction to your wealth and all you've built?"

"What do you mean?"

"Should you choose to pursue and marry Ruth," Dalia continued. "There is a high chance your traders will refuse to continue doing business with you, based on the perceived lack of judgement on your part."

"It's an incredibly small chance, Aunt," Boaz replied. "Besides, I'd be happy to part with all my wealth if it meant my heart was content."

Dalia smiled. "Devorah would come running back to us in tears, no doubt."

Boaz laughed. "She'd recover."

"But my last concern is this," Dalia said, lowering her voice. "It's your age. You are a lot older than her, Boaz. If I was to guess, I would say she wasn't older than thirty summers. Do you understand what this will mean for her?"

Boaz glanced at his feet. All of Dalia's previous arguments could be worked around, managed, ignored even, but this last one hit a nerve. A thought he'd also been struggling with and so far, had managed not to acknowledge.

"If you can't think of yourself Boaz, think of Ruth," Dalia said as she stood. She placed a hand on his shoulder. "Be her protector. Care for her. Find her a young husband that will be around long enough to have children and grandchildren with her."

A dull ache formed in Boaz's chest. All the images he had allowed himself to imagine, of his future with Ruth, transformed in his mind. Hot tears pricked his eyes as he saw Ruth grieving his death, struggling without him as his lands were ripped out from under her. He saw her childless, broken by sorrow, thrown onto the street as a beggar, growing old and on her own.

Boaz dropped his head into his hands, groaning loudly. "You're right," he said, rubbing his fingers against his closed eyelids. "This is not the way."

Dalia put her arms around him, hugging his head to her chest. "Oh Boaz," she said with a gentle voice. "Life is full of hurt. But you will mend, and maybe not now, but in the years ahead, you will watch her marry and blossom into a beautiful ima. You will find your own Hebrew wife and know that this was the right decision."

Boaz tapped his aunt's arm with affection, wishing his ima was still alive. She'd know what to do. He'd convinced himself that El Shaddai had led Ruth into his life, but maybe he'd read the signs wrong. El Shaddai had now sent Dalia, to remind him of his true path.

RUTH

ISRAEL – 1184 BC

Excitement intensified in Ruth's chest as the fields came into view. Their visit to the orchard yesterday had set her mind into a confused and delirious mess. She had relived the moment over and over in her mind as night fell and sleep eluded her. His hands cradling her own, his gentle eyes viewing her as a treasured gift.

With Mahlon, she had been young, and he had been clever, lulling her into a false sense of security and an intense love that proved unreliable.

Boaz was different. His nature calm and consistent. No highs and lows. Completely steady.

Then yesterday, as he'd held her hands at the orchard, a realisation had dawned on her. It was no coincidence that she had followed Naomi home; that Naomi had sent her to the fields; that the field she arrived at belonged to Boaz. This had been planned for her.

Elated, she urged Yace to pick up his pace towards the stables, his hooves clipping the pavers of the courtyard.

There was no sign of Boaz, but Ruth knew he'd be along soon.

....

As each hour dissolved into the next, and the sun moved across the sky, Boaz's absence became more noticeable.

At lunch, Ruth searched amongst the workers as they filed through towards the tables, but Boaz wasn't with them. His seat at the head of the table remained empty for the duration of the meal. After waiting until the last few harvesters slowly stood to return to work, she sat on her own, wondering if something had happened to him. None of the chatter around the table indicated anything was wrong. But he never missed the meal if he was home. Perhaps business had called him away again.

After lunch she put off going to the fields, instead taking the path Boaz had led her to yesterday, by the orchard. As she rounded the corner, she saw him sitting below her, in the shade of the palm trees, his face serious.

"Boaz!" She called as her steps quickened.

At her voice, he sat up, and watched her step and slide down the steep track. As she reached the bottom step, he stood and walked towards her.

"Boaz," Ruth said, gasping for breath.

"Shalom Ruth," he said, standing before her. "I hope you've had a profitable day in the fields." He bowed, then brushed past her to ascend the steps.

Stunned, Ruth turned and watched his back as he climbed up to the road.

"What?" She held her hands together above her head and ran her tongue over her dry lips. A sensation hit her chest, as if someone had punched her, as emotions of uncertainty welled up inside her. "What is going on?"

As Boaz disappeared, Ruth sat on the stone bench in the shade of the palm trees. She watched the workers in the orchard, her mind reviewing her memory from the previous day. Had she not responded to his affection in the way he desired? No, that couldn't be it as she hadn't had the chance to respond. Devorah interrupted before Ruth had time to accept *or* deny his advances.

Is he avoiding me?

In all her time on this farm, even as a stranger, he'd shown more attention to her than this day. And after what had happened yesterday, it made no sense. He always sought her out.

A deep knot formed in her stomach as she realised Boaz was deliberately avoiding her. Maybe he was not so different to Mahlon after all.

....

Her bones ached. Ruth never paid much attention to them, but today, with turmoil in her heart, the aches were louder than ever.

She led Yace into the stables of their Beit-Lechem home and sat on the stool beside him, watching loose grain in the feed vessel disappear into his soft lips.

"I am confused Yace," Ruth said, rubbing her face in agitation. "I don't know what happened today."

Yace snorted.

"Ruth!"

It was Naomi. "Ruth." This time louder, as urgency flowed through her voice.

Ruth leapt from the stool and ran inside, fear flowing through her body.

"Ruth, oh there you are." Naomi stood at the top of the stairs, leaning on her staff.

Ruth placed a hand on her chest. "Please don't yell out like that again," she said as the thudding of her heart slowed. "I thought you'd hurt yourself."

"Never!" Naomi replied, limping towards their room. "I've had an idea. Come in here."

Ruth cursed in a low voice, wiping sweat from her palms as she followed Naomi.

"The idea I have," Naomi said. "Will fix all our problems in one move."

The pain in Ruth's limbs returned as the flush of panicked adrenaline drained from her body. "I'm keen to hear that idea."

"I won't be here forever," Naomi said, as her brow puckered. "And I want to know you'll be alright after I die."

Ruth nodded but her mind wandered; unable to focus on an event that far into the future when she had other, more present problems pressing her.

"Pay attention, my daughter," Naomi said, leaning forward to take Ruth's hand in her own. "Isn't that what I should do, seek after your security so everything will be well with you?"

Ruth smiled. "I know you want the best for me, Ima."

"Then listen," Naomi said, her voice stern. "Boaz, son of Salmon, is a close relative of mine."

At the mention of his name, Ruth's heart sank. She closed her eyes.

"Surely you remember Boaz," Naomi stated. "The man whose women you've been working the fields with?"

Ruth opened her eyes, unable to bring herself to tell Naomi that of course she remembered who Boaz was. She had spent more time with him than she had with any of the young women who worked for him.

"This is what we need to do to secure your future," Naomi said, oblivious to Ruth's distress. "Tonight, Boaz will be winnowing barley at the threshing floor. It's the end of the barley harvest and farmers always celebrate the end of the crop."

The last day? Ruth hadn't even noticed, assuming she would head back again tomorrow to glean.

"You need to have a bath, put on some perfume. Then dress in your best robe and head back to the farm, to the threshing floor."

Ruth frowned. "Why?"

"It's a Hebrew thing," Naomi said, waving Ruth's questions away as if they were irritating insects. "Pay attention and I'll explain."

Naomi had told Ruth about a lot of strange Hebrew traditions in their time together, but this one was new.

"Once you reach the threshing floor, you can't let Boaz know you're there," Naomi said. "Find somewhere to hide until he has finished eating and drinking. When you see him leaving, follow him. Watch where he lies down to sleep and go in. When you find him sleeping, lay at his feet."

"Won't he wonder what I'm doing?" Ruth asked.

Naomi shook her head. "No, he will know exactly what it means. When you find him, go in and uncover his feet. Then lie down and wait."

"I just wait?"

"Yes, that's all you need to do," Naomi replied. "Wait and see what he says. He will tell you what to do."

Ruth wondered if Naomi's mind had finally left her. She watched the old woman as the instructions marinated in her mind. None of it made any sense. It was clear to her that Boaz didn't want anything to do with her. This strange request of Naomi's only added to the distress that sat in her chest.

But if Naomi was suggesting something this odd, maybe it was part of a divinely orchestrated plan. If she followed through with it, it would also give her a way to find out what was going on with Boaz. If it turned out that Naomi *had* lost her mind, and this *wasn't* a Hebrew tradition, she would endure the intense shame and embarrassment that was sure to follow. Then find another farm to work on.

"Wait," Naomi said, squinting. She wagged her finger at Ruth. "I remembered something else. When he wakes, you must tell him to spread the corner of his garment over you, to let him know he's a redeemer for this family."

"What does that mean?"

Naomi sighed. "It means he can marry you to carry on Elimelech's family name."

Ruth stood up and kissed Naomi on her wrinkled forehead, sensing a shadow of foreboding wrap around her. Everything in her body told her to say no. She pushed the felling aside and nodded. "I will do everything you've asked, Ima."

Ruth peered out from the wooden stable doors. Her heart sank. Heavy clouds hung in the night sky, blocking the moons light, covering the street in darkness. She pulled Yace through the opening; his hooves crunching against the road as he resisted moving forward.

Naomi had warned Ruth about the undesirables who roamed the streets at night, but assured Ruth that El Shaddai would give her safe passage. Ruth swallowed and climbed onto Yace's back.

As they made their way through the city, Yace appeared to sense danger even where it wasn't. Acting skittish around every corner and jumping each time a mouse scurried past or a window rattled in the wind.

By the time Ruth reached the farm, her nerves were frazzled.

A loud commotion from inside the courtyard hit her as she reached the gate. She glanced around and almost laughed. Numerous plans had formulated in her mind of how to break in once she reached the farm, but the time spent devising had been pointless. The gate stood open, and no one appeared to be keeping watch.

Ruth slipped off Yace with ease. "You need to be quiet now," she said, stroking his long nose. "No calling out to the other mules."

Lamps flickered and echoes of laughter bounced off the walls as they entered. Yace's hooves clip-clopped against the stones of the courtyard as Ruth hurried him across to the stables, keeping in the shadows.

She froze as cheerful voices approached. Yace continued forward, unaware she'd stopped and stepped on her foot with his sharp hoof. Ruth pulled him to a stop and bit her lip, trying to suck back the pain as a low groan escaped her throat.

The voices stopped.

Ruth held her breath and prayed Yace could sense the need to keep silent.

There was a laugh, and the conversation continued, moving past Ruth and into the main house.

Once Yace had been tied up inside the stables, Ruth crept to the entrance and peered out, her eyes focused on the threshing floor. All the noise appeared to be coming from that direction. She needed to find Boaz and keep an eye on his movements. As the merriment continued, Ruth scuttled closer, keeping low to the ground, until she reached the outside wall of the threshing floor.

Naomi's instructions rang in her ears. Ruth rolled her eyes and cursed. *I am officially insane. Trespassing. Stalking. Why did I listen to you, Naomi?*

Through a gap in the bricks, where mortar had fallen away, Ruth spied a few of the men as she pressed her face close. As far as she could tell, there were no women present.

"And here's to Enosh," Boaz slurred, walking into Ruth's view. He raised a large clay mug. "The finest overseer we've ever had."

"The finest?" a voice called out. "He sacked most of us before you sent him crawling to get us back! Twice!" Laughter filled the room.

"No," Enosh said, wavering on his feet. "The real honour goes to one man,"

Ruth watched Enosh as he lost his footing and fell to the floor with a thud, sending his wine into a pile of neatly swept chaff. Another roar of laughter erupted.

Enosh giggled, attempting to climb to his feet. "No, the one man who deserves the honour is Boaz."

The chuckling men thumped their feet on the ground in unison. It continued to grow louder as they turned Boaz's name into a chant.

Something stirred inside Ruth. Something she thought she'd long forgotten.

As the thumping of feet continued, she found herself back in the village of Moab, surrounded by dancers drenched in sweat, thrashing around to the beat of the drums. A baby cried in the distance and the stench that she thought she'd never face again, filled her nostrils.

Ruth fell into a tight ball and pushed her hands over her ears. "No, no, no …"

"Are you alright?" a voice asked.

As the loud commotion from the threshing floor continued, Ruth peered up into Devorah's face.

"What's going on?" Devorah asked as she crouched beside Ruth, wiping the tears from her cheeks. "You're trembling like a leaf." She pulled Ruth into her arms. "What are you doing here?"

Ruth paused. She hadn't planned on getting caught. Any ideas for reasonable excuses to explain her presence on the farm at this time of night eluded her. She glanced at Devorah, knowing this woman wouldn't stop asking until Ruth told her the truth. But she couldn't tell her what Naomi had instructed her. It was all too crazy. "I could ask you the same thing," Ruth finally replied.

Devorah let Ruth out of her arms and smirked. "My reasons are obvious. One, I live here. Two, I'm spying on the men enjoying themselves at a celebration that us women aren't invited to."

"Seems unfair," Ruth said, glancing back towards the merriment.

"Oh, it is," Devorah scoffed, watching the men through the gap. "As if this farm isn't carried on the shoulders of us women as much as the men."

Ruth watched as Devorah sighed, wondering how much Devorah had done to help around the farm.

"You still haven't told me why you're here," Devorah said with a grin on her face. "I do, however, appreciate the effort you put in to distract me. That's something I'd do. But now, you must tell me."

Ruth swallowed. If she told the truth, there was no way of knowing how Devorah would react. Even Ruth believed Naomi's plan was absurd.

"I left my bag here today, and I came back to collect it," Ruth said hesitantly. "I was about to leave when I tripped and hurt my foot." She held up her injured limb, a purple bruise forming in the shape of Yace's hoof. "That's when you found me."

Devorah leant forward, squinting in the dark. She pulled back, disgust on her face. "No wonder you were upset," she said, climbing to her feet. "Make sure you head fast through the city when you return, as not to run into any troublemakers."

"I will."

Ruth left Devorah and returned to the stables, waiting a moment before glancing back to the threshing floor. Devorah, barely visible, ran across the courtyard, a flurry of purple, to the main house. She disappeared under one of the arches.

....

Ruth waited in the shadows. Eventually, after hours of drinking, the band of men from the threshing floor dispersed, heading in all directions. Most took the direction of the workers quarters.

When the courtyard had cleared, Ruth slipped out from the stables and moved silently across the pavers, staying away from the lamps. As she approached the threshing floor, she spied Boaz steadying himself with his hand against a pillar.

"I'm too old," he slurred. "Too old." He moved forward with slow deliberate steps and extinguished several oil lamps as he passed them. "What am I doing?" he asked himself, in the now darkened room. "This is the servants job."

Ruth watched as he stumbled towards the back of the threshing floor and followed him in with soundless steps.

"Where's my ..." Boaz searched the ground on his hands and knees. "Where is my bed? And my table? Devorah! What have you done with my furniture?"

Ruth froze with her back against the wall.

"She changes everything, that woman," Boaz muttered. "She has no respect for anyone. Send her home with her parents." He sat awkwardly on the ground and lay his head against the edge of a pile of grain. A contented groan left his lips as he closed his weary eyes. Within minutes he was snoring.

Ruth moved forward, light on her feet as she stepped towards him. She lowered herself onto her knees at his feet, glancing around in the darkness. They were completely alone.

Naomi's words echoed in her mind. Uncover his feet. *What does that even mean? Remove his sandals?* Ruth wished she'd taken the time to ask for clarification.

Her fingers trembled as she reached down to grasp the strap of his sandal. A shaky breath passed her lips as she picked the knot loose, slowly unwinding it.

A snore caught in the back of Boaz's throat, and he became silent. His breathing stopped.

Ruth froze, too scared to move. She glanced up at Boaz. *What am I doing? This is crazy. Crazy people behave in this way.*

After a few seconds Boaz exhaled, and he fell back into a steady and gentle rhythm.

Ruth bit her lip in concentration as she slipped the sandal from his foot and lay it on the ground beside him. *One down.*

Boaz muttered something and rolled onto his side, wriggling against the grain to get comfortable.

Ruth waited till he settled again then moved with caution, removing the second sandal.

The next step, according to Naomi, was to lay at his feet and wait. Still doubting Naomi's sanity, Ruth lay as comfortably as she could beside Boaz.

Outside thunder rumbled as a storm approached.

I am officially insane.

BOAZ

ISRAEL – 1184 BC

A mass of yellows and blues swirled around him, then blacks and greys.

Boaz blinked, straining his eyes against the bright and nauseating kaleidoscope of colours.

Dalia floated into his vision, lopsided and colourless. "I've taken your farm and given it to the city elders, because you said olives didn't grow in Israel."

"I've never said that!" Boaz protested, but she'd already disappeared.

Devorah swirled into view. Large golden hoops, which reached her hips, hung from her ears. In her hands she held piles of Boaz's writing parchment. "I'll show you where you should put these." She held her hands over a small fire which appeared beside her and opened her arms wide, letting the pile of parchment slip from her fingers.

"Nooooo!" Boaz ran forward and tripped into a void of darkness which opened beneath him.

Devorah's voice echoed above him as he fell. "Where are you going? We need to burn all of it." Devorah vanished and Ruth appeared, hovering opposite him in the darkness as he continued to fall.

"Help me!" he begged, his arms flailing around.

Ruth shook her head. "How can I help you when you can't even help yourself?"

Boaz watched as grassy earth appeared below him, increasing in size as he fell towards it. He braced himself for impact and smashed into the dirt with a thud. Pain shot through his back.

"Why didn't you stop your cousin?" Ruth demanded as her bare feet settled on the grass with ease.

Boaz groaned as he sat up, holding his side. A sharp stab sliced through his chest. He'd broken a rib; he was sure of it.

Ruth continued to advance. The scarf which usually graced her head was nowhere to be seen. Red flame-like curls swirled around her face, as bright as a crown of fire, glowing in the darkness around them.

"Why?" She pointed at him, and a strange stinging filled his chest. "Don't you know what you want?"

Boaz gasped as Ruth's body transformed into grains of sand and blew away in the wind.

A soft blue light appeared, breaking through the thick blanket of darkness. Columns of ice pushed through the grass around his feet, continuing to rise higher and thicker till they reached the ceiling above him.

Boaz shivered. A new pain surfaced, moving its way through his flesh and deep into his bones as his body temperature dropped. Breath morphed into condensation, leaving his mouth in puffs of white.

Above him, large blocks of ice broke and fell, colliding with the ground in thunderous roars. Flashes of light blinded him as he crouched, throwing his arms above his head to protect himself.

"Aaaah!" he screamed and woke with a start. His eyes adjusted to the darkness around him. He pushed himself onto his elbows, his breathing fast and shallow. He rubbed his arms, shivering against the cold air. It had been a dream. No broken bones.

But this wasn't his sleeping quarters. The sensation of grain, squeaking under his back as he moved, brought him to his senses. The festivities; the drinking.

Boaz rubbed his forehead, attempting to relieve the thudding ache that had surfaced. He could have sworn he'd made it back to his room.

Torrential rain slammed against the roof above him, and the threshing floor lit up as lightening whipped across the sky. Boaz blinked. A mound appeared at his feet. He kept his eyes on the mound until the next flash.

It was a person.

"Who are you?" Boaz demanded, his voice breaking as he pulled a dagger from his belt. Beads of sweat formed on his brow and his heart raced.

The mound doubled in size and sat up. Boaz waived his dagger at it. *I may be drunk, but I will not die this night!* "Make yourself known!"

"It's Ruth," the mound replied.

Boaz squinted in the darkness as Ruth adjusted a shawl around her shoulders.

"Spread your garment over me," she said.

"What?" Boaz gasped, placing his hand on his chest as it rose and fell rapidly.

"You're my close relative," Ruth replied. "A redeemer."

"I can't hear you," Boaz yelled. He could barely see her in this light, and he couldn't hear her over the rain.

Another bolt of lightning danced across the sky and Boaz saw her face. Soft and beautiful. The crack of thunder bounced off the walls around them.

"Naomi told me of this Hebrew tradition," Ruth shouted back. "Where a relative can marry a widow with no children to continue the dead man's name." She rubbed her arm and turned her face from him. "If this isn't true, let me know and I will leave."

Boaz lay back on the grain and let the dagger slip from his fingers, laughing with relief as the rain lessened in intensity. He rubbed his face with both hands. A loud sigh left his lips. "Oh Ruth." He chuckled as he sat back up. "El Shaddai bless you."

He watched her shuffle uncomfortably in the dark. "Come and sit beside me." As Ruth moved towards him, he held out his hand. "I think I know you, and then you show me more of yourself and I'm bewildered. To ask this aging man to redeem you? To marry you? You could have the pick of any young man around here, rich or poor." He inhaled and laughed again.

"Is this what *you* want?" Ruth asked, wrapping her arms around her knees.

"Don't be afraid of that," he told Ruth. "I would do anything for you, and of course I'll perform this request for you."

"People will assume I'm after your wealth," Ruth said.

"Are you?" Boaz asked.

Ruth glanced at him suspiciously.

He laughed. "I'm joking!" he said. "Everyone in the city knows about you and your kindness. They won't think it's about money."

"That's an exaggeration."

Boaz smiled. "It's not," he said. His face dropped. "There *is* one problem."

"A problem?" Ruth asked.

"Since you've come to me under the tradition of redemption," Boaz replied. "We must follow it to the letter. It's true that I'm a close relative, but there's a man who is closer than I am."

"What does that mean?"

"It means that now you've commenced the redeeming process, we have to follow the law and ask this man if he wishes to redeem you first."

Ruth tensed beside him. "But I don't know this man," she said. "Would I have no choice but to marry him if he chooses to redeem me?"

Boaz stared at her. "I'm not sure," he said. "I don't know this custom well. But I do know the process of redemption must go through the closest relatives first."

Ruth fell silent.

Boaz watched her eyes dart back and forth, seeing panic rise. "We can forget you asked me," he said, his voice soft. "If you don't want to follow this through. I won't speak of it. No one will know."

A surge of anger formed in the pit of Boaz's stomach, as he thought of Naomi, who had set Ruth up to ask him without checking for closer relatives first. His mind searched for ways around it. He could ignore the relative, marry Ruth and none would be the wiser. But if this relative found out, and realised he'd missed out on securing the farmlands belonging to Naomi, as well as a beautiful bride, there would be trouble.

"Naomi doesn't want her husband's name to perish from the face of the earth," Ruth replied. "We will follow it through and pray the relative is not interested."

Boaz's heart sank. A man would be stupid to turn down this offer. There was no way he'd say no. "Don't ride home now," Boaz told her. "Stay on my farm for the rest of the night. And in the morning, I'll find this man. If he decides to take on his customary rights and responsibilities as the closest redeemer, he'll have his chance to say yes. But if he isn't interested, as sure as El Shaddai lives, I will redeem you."

Outside, the rain slowed to a sprinkle. A loud symphony of croaking burst forth in the courtyard as the thunder receded to mere echoes in the distance.

"Why did you ignore me today," Ruth said abruptly.

"I don't know," Boaz said, shaking his head. "Bad judgement on my part. I knew we were becoming close, and I didn't think you should marry an older man, only to bury him a few years later." He sighed. "Now I wish I'd just asked you to marry me, before Naomi got this idea in her head."

....

Boaz sat astride his stallion; nerves threatening to unravel.

Aziel tossed his head and snorted as he pranced along the muddy road to Beit-Lechem, flicking streaks of dirty water up the back of his muscular hind legs.

The sun sat low in the sky, hovering above the horizon. It was early, and the road quiet.

Boaz's mind replayed the events of the night before in a never-ending spiral.

Ruth had slept at his feet until morning, awaking when he roused her before the time of the rising sun. Although the sky had lightened to a navy blue, darkness still covered the land. It was enough to prevent the recognition of another person.

Ruth had yawned and stretched like a mountain cat.

"You need to leave now," Boaz insisted, pulling Ruth to her feet.

Ruth massaged the tiredness from her eyes and picked up her shawl to leave.

"Wait," Boaz said, rubbing his hands together. "Bring your shawl here and hold it out for me." He leant over a mountain of grain and scooped handfuls into Ruth's scarf, before tying it around her shoulders. "I don't want you going home to your ima empty handed."

After she left, Boaz had lain back down, trying to catch more sleep in the few hours before the sun rose. His mind had other plans. An hour later he gave up and emerged from the threshing floor.

In the corner of his eye, he saw Enosh approaching.

"El Shaddai be with you Enosh," Boaz said as they passed.

Enosh groaned and pressed his fingers against his temples. "El Shaddai bless you," he replied.

Boaz stopped. "Are you alright?"

"Are you?" Enosh laughed. "That new wine of Gad's gave me strange visions all night and has left me with a thumping headache. Did you sleep?"

Boaz frowned, remembering his own peculiar dreams. "Not much."

"I'm off to dunk my head in cold water," Enosh moaned as he

trudged away. "That's if I can find the old well in these shadows."

Boaz watched Enosh for a moment before making his way to the stables. As he threw a blanket over Aziel's back, a servant rushed over.

"Leave it master," the servant said. "I will attend to Aziel for you."

"You are up early Aaron," Boaz said, stroking his beard as he stepped back to let Aaron take over.

"I've been up for over an hour already, master," Aaron replied, pride clear in his voice.

Panic had surged through Boaz's body. *Did you see Ruth in the threshing floor with me?* He pushed the thought from his mind. "Thank you, Aaron," he said, watching the young man work. "I'm going to change my garments, then return for Aziel."

Now, as he approached the gates of Beit-Lechem, under the early rays of the rising sun, the uneasiness in his stomach returned. *What if my relative wants Ruth?*

Boaz cursed loudly, knowing he would have to stand by and watch it happen. He tried to calm himself, remembering that everything that happens has a reason, and if Ruth was to wed this man, then it must be meant to be.

He slowed Aziel to a walk as he scanned the gate. The bench seats sat bare. Too early in the morning for the elders to gather.

After reaching the entrance, he slid off Aziel and tied his bridle to a nearby pole. Then he sat. And waited.

....

His belt irritated him, digging into his abdomen. He'd spent the last hour rising, sitting and pacing; unable to settle his nerves.

One by one, the elders of the city arrived and took their seats. There didn't appear to be any rhyme or reason to their arrival, each one staggering out through the gates in their own self-authorised time.

"Shalom Boaz!" one of the friendly faced, white-haired men called out. "Is today the day we convince you to join our group of elders."

"I'm not old enough yet," Boaz frowned, feigning offence.

The elder chuckled then turned to face his fellow seniors. The mutterings between them continued.

Boaz laughed to himself, imagining potential city dramas they would have to fix today.

What would they do about that man, who had been spotted working on Shabbat, but insisted he was only taking a stroll?

Were the accusations against an unmarried woman flaunting a tunic made of wool and linen true, or a false story brought to life by a jealous man whose advances had been shunned.

Would they really have to find all the people and places an unclean man touched before anyone realised he'd been sitting in a pile of dead animals earlier that morning?

One of the elders glanced at Boaz and a scowl formed on his face. His eyes remained on Boaz as he turned and muttered something to the man beside him.

Boaz recognised that glance and knew the words that would have left the man's mouth. Although there were elders amongst the Hebrews that wished him to join their ranks, there were others who would rather die than see a half blood in their elite circle.

Choosing to ignore the ignorance of his countrymen, Boaz strained his eyes over the crowd that grew larger, as people entered and exited the city gates. Searching for the relative he needed, even though there was no guarantee he would be coming into the city on this day.

Boaz had only seen this relative a handful of times. The last being a wedding festival before the famine. His name was Ira. A man, not much older than Boaz. Their interactions had been short, but Boaz knew him well enough to recognise he was the greedy type. Always on the search for a quick coin, with no concern for anyone who was hurt in the process. For this reason, Boaz had kept clear of Ira.

As he continued to search the road, Boaz spied his relative approaching.

He wore a large hat on his head. It matched the long robes he wore, which swept along the ground. Jewelled gold rings hugged his fingers. He walked towards the city gates with the aid of a walking stick.

Boaz leapt forward, pushing through the crowd. "Ira!" he called.

"Shalom Boaz," Ira laughed, when he reached him. "What an excitable man you are today."

"Where is your cart?" Boaz asked. "I've never seen you walk this road before?"

Ira rolled his eyes. "Stupid beast fell down a way back," he said with disgust. "Acting as if it had never felt the whip before. I've never liked mules. Unreliable creatures."

"Never mind that now, Ira," Boaz said, taking hold of Ira's elbow. "Come and sit with me."

A sly smile crossed Ira's lips as they walked towards the gates. "Are you reconsidering that proposition I put to you years ago?" He licked his lips in excitement. "You won't be sorry, I promise you."

Boaz chuckled, watching his relative doing maths in his head. "Not today," he replied. "I have another matter to discuss."

"Well, I am intrigued," Ira laughed as they came to a standstill by the gate.

"Come, elders," Boaz said. "And sit down here with us. We have a matter to decide."

Excited chatter spread through the elders as they took their seats.

"As you've probably heard," Boaz said as they sat together. "Naomi, who returned from the land of Moab, can't afford to run the farm which belonged to our brother Elimelech."

Ira smirked. "And you want to see if I desire to buy it off her?" he asked. "Is that what this is about?"

"Naomi wants to be redeemed," Boaz said slowly, as beads of sweat ran down his back. He cleared his throat. "I thought you should know about it," he said. "You're the first in line with redeemer rights. You can make it official in the presence of those who are listening here, and before the city elders. If you don't want it, tell me, as I'm the next in line to redeem it."

His heart thumped hard against the walls of his chest.

"I never thought the day would come," Ira laughed, slapping his leg. "When I would have one up on you Boaz." He couldn't contain his glee. "Of course, I'll *redeem* it! You never see land coming up for sale these days!"

"Very well Ira," Boaz said, keeping his voice calm. "There is another part of the deal. As nearest relative, when you redeem the land from

Naomi, you will also have to redeem the widow of her dead son."

"Who doesn't want an extra woman," Ira laughed. He glanced around at the crowd which had gathered, enjoying the attention he was receiving. "My other two wives might not be happy, but they'll learn to shut up."

"The woman was born and raised in Moab," Boaz added.

Colour drained from Ira's cheeks. "A Moabite?" he repeated, shifting uncomfortably.

"Any children you have by her, will take the name of her dead husband," Boaz continued. "Not your name. And the land you redeem would also stay in the dead man's name for her children to inherit when old enough."

Ira glanced at Boaz and scoffed. "I can't do that," he said, shaking his head. "I'd put my own estate at risk. You go ahead and redeem it Boaz. As per our customs, I will give you my sandal to seal the agreement." He bent over and untied the straps of his sandal and pulled it from his foot, holding it out to Boaz. As Boaz reached out, Ira pulled it back. "This is not a good deal. Why on earth did you think I'd be interested?"

"You had the first right as closest relative," Boaz replied.

Ira shrugged and gave the sandal to Boaz. "I hand over to you my right to redeem. Acquire it for yourself."

The heavy weight crushing Boaz's chest, suddenly lifted. He held up Ira's sandal for the crowd to see. "You are all witnesses this day. I have pledged to acquire all that was Elimelech's, and all that was his sons, Chilion and Mahlon's, from Naomi, including the foreigner Ruth, the widow of Mahlon." Hot tears filled his eyes. "I'll take Ruth to be my wife and keep the name of those who have died alive, along with their inheritance. Their name will not disappear out of their family or their hometown. You all are witnesses."

"We are witnesses," one of the elders murmured. He leant forward and placed a hand on Boaz's shoulder. "I know she isn't the Hebrew woman you desired, but I pray El Shaddai will make this Moabite like Rachel and Leah, who together, built the nation of Israel."

"May El Shaddai make you a pillar in Ephrathah and famous in Beit-Lechem," another elder added.

"He is already famous in Beit-Lechem," a woman called out from the watching crowd.

"With the children El Shaddai gives you from this woman," the elder continued, ignoring the laughter rippling through the crowd. "May your family be as large as the family of Perez, the son Tamar bore to Judah."

As the business dealings wrapped up, the crowd dispersed, and the to and fro of life returned to normal.

Ira snatched his sandal from Boaz's hand. "Did you put me through all that, humiliating me in front of everyone, knowing I'd turn it down, anyway?" He slipped the sandal back on his foot and tied the straps around his ankles.

Boaz smiled. "I had no intention of humiliating you Ira," he said. "But I *was* hoping you'd reject the offer."

....

The dusty breeze was hot against his skin as he strolled through the streets of Beit-Lechem, but he didn't care. He was a man who couldn't remove the smile from his face, followed by a large brown stallion with the temperament of a quiet lamb.

Boaz had asked a few shop owners in the marketplace if anyone knew where Naomi and Ruth lodged. Most people knew who they were, the old Ima of Israel with the foreigner, but nobody knew where they lived.

After wandering around till midday, Boaz came to a stop beside an old well in the middle of the city. He drew a bucket for Aziel, who shoved his muzzle into the water before Boaz placed it on the ground. He sat on the edge of the well and watched locals passing by.

Overhead the sun shone brightly. The breeze shifted directions and soon a cool breeze pushed away the heat, signalling the changing of seasons. With the harvest of grains finished, the grapes would be ripening soon.

Without warning a shadow fell over him. He lifted his eyes and faced a woman with red curls, brown skin and green eyes. He stood and took her hands in his.

Ruth tilted her head to the side. Her eyes narrowed. "What is it?"

Boaz pointed at her. "Redeemed," he said with a wide grin, unable to keep his face serious. He then turned his finger to point at himself. "Redeemer."

EPILOGUE

ISRAEL – 1183 BC

Naomi raised a hand to her forehead, shielding the sun from her eyes, watching a brown hawk hover above her. It held such grace, and endurance.

The old woman groaned inwardly, wishing she hadn't lost her youth. The freedom to soar. Those days, too long ago. Infirmities brought on by age advanced faster as time went on. Naomi could barely walk unaided now.

The warmth of the air moved through her lose grey hair. Heavy laden with moisture, it made breathing difficult and created beads of sweat over her skin. An irritable layer of stickiness.

She yawned, her thoughts lingering on the changes she'd witnessed in the last year.

Boaz had thrown a generous sum of money into her old home, restoring it to its former beauty, and together with Ruth, they'd all moved in. The stairs were no longer an issue for her old knees as Boaz had built an additional room on the lower floor, her own private sanctuary.

She sighed and closed her eyes, relaxing her aching back into the chair Boaz designed and built. It had wheels and could be moved along with her still sitting in it. She had sat in it during Ruth's wedding, asking the servants to roll her over to other conversations when she tired of her current one.

The wedding festivities had been joyful and lasted for weeks. Benefits of wealth, Naomi supposed. She rubbed her chin with fingers now bent with age. Crooked and stiff bones. They throbbed with pain most days.

Naomi knew El Shaddai would announce her time soon, but there was someone she desperately wanted to meet before she was taken from the earth. *El Shaddai will have to wait.*

A yellow butterfly flapped around her face before landing on her frail, sun spotted arm. At least, she *thought* it was a butterfly. Her eyes, which had become dull, made it difficult to tell. *Perhaps a yellow moth?* The wings opened and closed slowly, as the insect relaxed, fresh from its cocoon.

It reminded Naomi of Ruth. An impulsive young girl who had transformed into a mature woman, full of beauty and grace.

"Yes, you are beautiful," Naomi told the resting insect. "And I'm waiting, just as you were, to see new life."

She watched the insect take to the air and disappear from the scope of her blurred vision.

A hazy outline approached.

Naomi smiled. "I know that shape," she said. "Bring that swelling stomach closer to me."

Ruth's laughter filled Naomi's ears as she stepped towards the chair.

As the large bulge approached, Naomi reached out with both hands and leant forward, laying her ear against it. It moved against her face. "Hello my little boy," she said. "Hurry up now. I want to meet you before I die."

"Why are you certain it is a boy?" Ruth asked, resting her hand on Naomi's shoulder.

Naomi shushed her. "This one *will* be," she said. "If El Shaddai directed you here to marry Boaz and continue the family of Elimelech, then this baby in your stomach is a boy." She stretched out her trembling hand and took hold of Ruth's. "Have you sent word to your ima?"

"Yes," Ruth replied, running her hands over her stomach. "Ima and Abba will be arriving any day now."

Naomi patted Ruth's arm. "This is a good thing," she said. "I think he is close."

....

A bright star, in the night sky, caught Ruth's attention.

She knew it was miles away, but from where she lay, it appeared close enough for her to reach out and pluck from the open window. Her eyes, moist from sweat, squinted against the star, stretching its light beams into the dimly lit room.

"Are you alright?" Cajsa asked as she kneeled closer to Ruth's exposed belly.

Ruth turned to face her ima, her breathing laboured. She nodded. Within seconds, her abdomen tightened as another contraction took hold. "Ima!" she screamed, writhing around, clutching handfuls of linen in her closed fists.

Cajsa wiped sweat from her daughter's forehead. "I'm here, I'm not leaving."

Ruth moaned through clenched teeth and grabbed out for Cajsa's hand.

After a minute the pain subsided and Ruth lay flat on her back, her breathing steady once again. She glanced at Cajsa, and her face crumpled. "Don't let me die," she whimpered.

Cajsa hushed her, wiping Ruth's tears away. "You're not going to die Ruth; everything is happening exactly as it should." She picked up the sweat-soaked towel from Ruth's body and threw it towards the door, before taking another from a clean pile to wipe down her daughter's body.

"You don't know that," Ruth moaned as tears ran down her cheeks. "Rivka died."

"Rivka's baby hadn't lined up," Cajsa replied, fanning Ruth's face with a round palm leaf. "Your baby is lined up perfectly, ready to enter the world with no problems."

Ruth's gaze landed on the lamp across the room. Its flickering light bounced off the walls and shone against her exposed skin.

"Where is Boaz?" Ruth asked, attempting to pull herself into a sitting position.

"He doesn't need to be here," Cajsa replied. "Men only interfere."

Ruth whimpered and shook her head. "I want him here." A moan passed her lips as the contractions returned, increasing in strength until Ruth screamed out, gripping her stomach.

"There's no time to send for Boaz," Cajsa said, patting Ruth's hand. "This baby is almost here."

HILLS OF MOAB

....

Boaz paced outside as the wailing of his wife echoed across the moon lit fields. Tears of hopelessness stung his eyes. In everyday life, he had all the resources and power to protect her, yet in this moment, there was nothing he could do to remove her from this agony.

His knowledge of birthing was limited to the livestock on his farm and the animals usually kept silent during delivery. They would stand, then lay, then stand, but never showed indications of pain or distress, unless something was wrong.

Boaz glanced up as Malak approached.

"Ruth will be fine," Malak said. "She has an extremely experienced midwife by her side."

Boaz smiled weakly, wiping tears from his beard, shifting his weight between his feet as he watched the older man.

Hours earlier, when Ruth's parent's cart had come into view on the path leading up to the house, Boaz observed the lack of resemblance Ruth held with them. He'd shared his thoughts with Ruth as they watched the cart approach, saying their baby might skip a generation and take after Ruth's parents instead of her.

Ruth had cleared her throat, as she tucked her arm into his. "They're not my birth parents," she explained, laying her head against his shoulder. "They told me as I left Moab," she added. "I'm still struggling with it. Maybe why I've never mentioned it to you." She stood tall as her eyes narrowed, straining to focus on the back of the cart.

"Wha ... ? Is that –" A small giggle left her lips, as she bounced on her feet. "Orpah has come with them, Boaz!"

Boaz had let the subject of her birth slide, sensing her discomfort. He knew when she was ready, she would trust him with this part of her life.

Above him another scream erupted through the window, bringing him back to the present.

"She's in agony," Boaz said, his voice breaking.

Malak put his arm around him. "Let's go for a walk."

Boaz nodded. His throat stung as he swallowed.

....

Naomi sat on the edge of her bed, as tormented moans filtered down through the flooring above her. Eden and Anna sat either side of her, both holding her hands. Waiting. New life was coming.

She watched Orpah pace the floor in front of them, remembering the grief she had endured, sending Orpah home.

"I told you today was a good day to visit," Eden told Anna. "If we'd come yesterday, as *you* wanted, we would have missed this."

"It has been going for a while now though," Anna said, concern in her voice.

Naomi's heart ached for Ruth. It had been years, but she hadn't forgotten the suffering of childbirth.

Cajsa's muffled voice echoed through the ceiling. "You need to push now Ruth. Push and it will be over before you know it."

A sensation of anticipation filled Naomi's chest. *Not long now.*

Anna tapped Naomi's hand. "It won't be long now."

"I think we can all agree that is pretty obvious," Eden scowled. "You don't need to comment on everything Anna. If you hadn't noticed, we're in the room here too."

"I'm sorry I'm excited," Anna replied. "You could at least pretend to be, for Naomi's sake."

Naomi rolled her eyes. The best of friends, yet always at each other's throats.

Above them, Ruth cried out, an agonised groan.

"Keep pushing," Cajsa's faded voice instructed. "Keep pushing. Almost there."

After several more exacerbated groans, the room above them fell silent. Cajsa's muffled curses seeped down through the ceiling.

Naomi gripped her friend's hands tightly; certain her heart would stop. *No, El Shaddai, do not act bitterly against me again. I cannot lose Ruth or the baby.*

Then she heard it. The fresh howl of a newborn. Tears of relief and gratitude filled her old eyes as she lifted her face to the heavens in thankfulness.

Eden let out a relieved sigh and laughed. "Congratulations, Grandima," she said. "May many more children come to this house."

Orpah stopped her pacing and turned to face Naomi. A smile crossed her lips. "Your family name continues."

....

Ruth reached out for the wriggling newborn as Casja lay it on her bare chest.

"It's a boy," Cajsa whispered, as a large grin spread across her face.

Ruth tucked her chin down, to get a better view of the small babe. She glanced up and caught Cajsa's moist eyes full of pride.

"You did well," Cajsa said, stroking Ruth's forehead. "I'm utterly proud of you."

Ruth closed her eyelids and relaxed her head back on the pillow behind her, keeping the little babe secure in her arms. His body was warm against her own, but he shivered against her.

"I think he's cold," Ruth said, scanning the room for a cloth to place over him.

Cajsa nodded. She found a nearby blanket and lay it across them.

Ruth watched her son squirm and kissed his petite nose. He moved his head from side to side, then raised a closed fist to his toothless mouth and sucked his knuckles.

"He's ready to feed," Cajsa laughed.

"Can we take him down to Naomi," Ruth asked. "She'll be desperate to meet him."

"Naomi can wait, Ruth," Cajsa frowned. "He is hungry, and you need to rest."

Ruth shook her head. "You don't understand. To Naomi, this child is hers."

Confusion crossed Cajsa's face. "You're right, I *don't* understand," she replied, sitting back on her heels. "This is *your* child Ruth, not Naomi's."

"It's a Hebrew thing," Ruth replied, kissing her son's head, keeping her eyes on her ima's.

....

As Cajsa stepped down the stairs, a small bundle wedged carefully in her arms, Boaz's heart skipped a beat. "How is Ruth," he asked. He placed his hands behind his back to hide the tremors.

Cajsa nodded, as she stepped off the last stair and approached Boaz, pulling the linen wrap away from the newborn's face.

"Ruth is doing perfectly fine," Cajsa said, peering up into Boaz's red eyes. "As is your son, *Abba*."

Boaz let out a shaky breath. "I am overwhelmed." He couldn't remove his attention from the tiny creature in her arms. "He is smaller than I imagined he would be." He glanced at Cajsa. "Can I hold him?"

Cajsa grinned. "Ruth asked me to take him to Naomi," she said. "But here, hold him. He is *your* son after all."

As he took the bundle from Cajsa's arms, Boaz was surprised to discover how light his son was. He wriggled in Boaz's arms, amongst the layers of linen; his little lips and tongue searching in the fabric.

Boaz glanced at Cajsa, confusion in his eyes.

Cajsa laughed. "He's a hungry lad, Boaz. We had best get him to Naomi and back to Ruth."

Boaz nodded and followed Cajsa to Naomi's room and waited in the open door. The sound of old women's excited giggling exploded around him.

"Praise El Shaddai!" Anna cried out, as she bounded over to Boaz. She glanced back at Naomi. "El Shaddai didn't leave you without a family after all."

"He is the tiniest creature," Boaz said, completely besotted. He reached out and gently stroked his son's cheek with the back of his finger.

"Birth size doesn't matter," Orpah said, pulling fabric aside for a better view of the infant. "Maybe this boy will grow up to become famous in Israel."

"One thing is certain, Naomi," Anna said. "This boy will make you young again."

"And he'll be able to care for you as you age," Eden added.

"As I age?" Naomi smirked. "I think it's too late for that. Now bring the child to me. I can't see him from here."

"Let's not forget Ruth upstairs," Cajsa said, crossing her arms. "She bore this child; made all of this possible."

Eden nodded in agreement. "Ruth obviously loves you Naomi," she said. "And that, in itself, is worth more than *seven* sons."

As the chatter continued around Boaz, his focus became centred on his son. The large eyes that struggled to focus and the small fingers that opened and closed. Boaz recalled the names he and Ruth had spoken of. Chaya for a girl and Obed for a boy. "I guess you're our Obed then," Boaz said, placing a finger in Obed's tiny hand.

"What was that?" Naomi asked. "Did you say something Boaz?"

A broad smile crossed Boaz's face. "His name is Obed." He walked towards Naomi, and carefully placed his son in her frail arms.

Anna sighed. "I never thought I'd say this again," she said. "But I'll be telling people that Naomi has a son."

Eden laughed. "Then they'll think you're crazier than they already do."

Boaz ignored the women and watched Naomi coo over his son. He knew the years of darkness this old woman had travelled through over the last few decades. Now the light returned to her, giving her new purpose. She would be in their lives and the lives of their child.

Naomi glanced at Boaz and pulled him down by the shoulder until he was crouched close beside her.

"I have a feeling about your son, Boaz," she said quietly, her eyes lingering on Obed.

"You have a *feeling*?" Boaz asked, placing a hand on the bed to balance himself.

Turmoil crossed Naomi's face. "I thought this was all about me and Elimelech, and continuing our family name," she said. "But the arrival of this child has changed something. Something bigger than all of us combined." She paused, her face growing serious as her eyes rushed back and forth. "What you and Ruth have done has set Israel on a path that cannot be changed."

"What do you mean?" Boaz asked, his eyes narrowing. "How can one child change the course of an entire nation?"

Naomi shushed him with her hand.

"There is no turning back now. The age of kings is upon us."

Printed in Great Britain
by Amazon